IN THE
LOOKING
GLASS

IN THE LOOKING GLASS

TWENTY-ONE MODERN
SHORT STORIES
BY WOMEN

EDITED BY *NANCY DEAN*
AND *MYRA STARK*

G. P. PUTNAM'S SONS, NEW YORK
Capricorn Books, New York '

SBN: 399-1183713 (Hardcover)
SBN: 399-50363-3 (Softcover)
Library of Congress Catalog
Card Number: 76—48851

Printed in the United States of America

ACKNOWLEDGMENTS

"Reclamation" copyright © 1976 by Glenda Adams. (First appeared in her collection *Lies and Stories*, published by Inwood Press, 128 Post Avenue, New York, N.Y. 10034.)

"Raymond's Run" copyright © 1970 by Toni Cade Bambara. Reprinted from her collection *Gorilla, My Love* by permission of Random House, Inc.

"Pleasure" copyright © 1976 by Barbara Baracks.

"Downhill" copyright © 1975 by The New Yorker Magazine, Inc., from *Distortions* by Ann Beattie. Used by permission of Doubleday and Company, Inc. (First appeared in *The New Yorker*, August 18, 1975.)

"The Fifth Great Day of God" copyright © 1975 by Sandy Boucher. Reprinted by permission of McIntosh and Otis, Inc., and the author.

"In the Forests of Riga the Beasts Are Very Wild Indeed" copyright © 1970 by Margery Finn Brown. Reprinted by permission of Russell and Volkening, Inc., as agents for the author. (First appeared in *McCall's Magazine*, July 1970.) From *Prize Stories: The O. Henry Awards, 1972.*

"A Letter to Ismael in the Grave" by Rosellen Brown, copyright ©
1971 by Simon and Schuster, Inc., used by permission of Doubleday
and Company, Inc. (First appeared in *New American Review*,
Number 12, August 1971.) From *Prize Stories: The O. Henry Awards,
1972*.

"A Day in the Life of a Smiling Woman" copyright © 1973 by
Margaret Drabble. Reprinted by permission of the Harold Matson
Company, Inc.

"The Yellow Wallpaper" by Charlotte Perkins Gilman, reprinted by
The Feminist Press, Old Westbury, N.Y. 1973.

"A Sorrowful Woman" copyright © 1971 by Gail Godwin. Reprinted
from her collection *Dream Children* by permission of Alfred A.
Knopf, Inc.

"An Apple, an Orange" copyright © 1970 by Diane Johnson.
Reprinted by permission of the Helen Brann Agency. (First published in *Epoch*, Fall 1971.) From *Prize Stories: The O. Henry Awards,
1973*.

"The De Wets Come to Kloof Grange" copyright © 1951, 1953,
1954, 1957, 1958, 1962, 1963, 1964, 1965 by Doris Lessing, from
her *African Stories*. Reprinted by permission of Simon and Schuster,
Inc., and John Cushman Associates, Inc.

"A Cup of Tea" copyright © 1923 and renewed 1951 by John
Middleton Murry. Reprinted from *The Short Stories of Katherine
Mansfield* by permission of Alfred A. Knopf, Inc.

"Red Dress—1946" copyright © 1968 by Alice Munro. Reprinted
from her collection *Dance of the Happy Shades* by permission of
McGraw-Hill Book Company, New York, and McGraw-Hill Ryer-
son, Limited, Canada.

"Asylum" by Joan Murray, used by permission of the author.

"Where Are You Going, Where Have You Been?" copyright 1965, 1966, 1967, 1968, 1969, 1970 by Joyce Carol Oates. Reprinted from her collection *The Wheel of Love* by permission of the publisher, Vanguard Press, Inc.

"Dynastic Encounter" copyright © 1970 by Marge Piercy. Reprinted by permission of Wallace, Aitken and Sheil, Inc. (First published in *Aphra*, Volume 1, Number 3.)

"The Fifteen-Dollar Eagle" by Sylvia Plath, copyright © 1960 by the University of the South. Reprinted by permission of the editor. (First appeared in the *Sewanee Review*, 68, 1960.)

"In the Basement of the House" copyright © 1975 by Jane Rule. From her collection *Theme for Diverse Instruments*, published in Canada by Talonbooks.

"A Piece of News" copyright © 1937, 1965 by Eudora Welty. Reprinted from her volume *A Curtain of Green and Other Stories* by permission of Harcourt Brace Jovanovich, Inc.

"The Lady in the Looking Glass," from *A Haunted House and Other Stories* by Virginia Woolf, copyright © 1944, renewed 1972 by Harcourt Brace Jovanovich, Inc., reprinted with their permission and with the permission of the author's literary estate and The Hogarth Press.

Poetry selections that precede sections are taken from *No More Masks: An Anthology of Poems by Women*, edited by Florence Howe and Ellen Bass (New York: Anchor Press, 1973).

CONTENTS

THE GIRL

This tossing off of garments
Which cloud the soul is none too easy doing
With us today.

—Amy Lowell, "The Sisters" (1925)

IN THE LOOKING GLASS

Of the sixteen short stories in the *O. Henry Prize Stories* of 1956, only two were written by women; in 1973, of the collection's eighteen stories, nine were by women—testimony to the steadily increasing number of women writing today and the excellence of much of their work.

In the Looking Glass is a product of that development. It presents stories written out of what can best be described as a feminist consciousness: a core of concerns, problems, conflicts, and preoccupations common to women in a male-dominated society. Simone de Beauvoir wrote in *The Second Sex*, "One is not born but rather becomes a woman." The outpouring of novels and stories by women in the last fifteen years proves that the process of becoming a woman in our culture is a central and urgent theme of contemporary fiction.

However, not all stories written by women may be described as written out of a feminist consciousness, and so there are fine twentieth-century short-story writers who are not represented here.

Women may be heard to say to other women, "But reading about women is so embarrassing—like looking into the mirror." Though men have been studying men for generations without embarrassment—as heroes, questers, poets, villains, commanders, and kings—women think themselves narcissistic, childish, and vain when they are self-concerned. Men have found the history of men to be the history of *people*; women need to see the study of women as the study of that half of the world usually omitted in men's history. One studies women because they have been invisible and silent for so long.

THE INVISIBLE WOMAN

Snow White's stepmother asks of the mirror, "Tell me, who is the fairest one of all?" For women, the looking glass has long been a reflection of their identity. Valued as a love object, woman came to believe that the image she saw in the mirror was her identity. "Smile a lot," says the mother in "Reclamation"—"without those teeth you would be nothing." But for modern woman the image in the looking glass has become wavering and insubstantial. Like the looking glass that reflects two contradictory images in Virginia Woolf's disturbing and ambiguous story "The Lady in the Looking Glass," the mirror holds no certainties for modern woman.

Yet the mirror may be asked to reveal the truth, by reflecting what is "out there," by aiding objectivity. We can look into the mirror not out of vanity but for Woolf's reason: to know a person's life. Mirrors are looking glasses, means for looking at the truth about oneself or another person. The ending of the Woolf story—"People should not leave looking glasses hanging in their rooms"—suggests the powers of truth to be found in those reflectors of reality.

We may find the image in a mirror ambiguous and puzzling. Does a woman's mirror reflect the self or an artificial construction—Woman fashioned, indeed created, by culture and society? In Doris Lessing's novel *The Summer Before the Dark*, Kate Brown explodes with anger at the "years of her life—it would certainly add up to years!—spent in front of a looking glass. Just like all women. Years spent asleep or tranced. . . ." Trying on different faces before the glass—"there were hundreds she had never thought of using besides those which were creditable to her, and pleasing, or nonabrasive to others"—she realizes how the mirror has confined and limited her, imposing upon her a false and constraining image.

Kate Brown discovers to her horror that when she does not conform to the groomed and smiling image in the glass, she is invisible to others. Kate Manning, the narrator of "In the Forests of Riga the Beasts Are Very Wild Indeed," feels herself disintegrating. "There is," she discovers, "no face in the mirror." Kate, a strong, intelligent, and cultured woman who once cooked a Thanksgiving dinner for thirty people with her hand in a splint, who has made homes for her family "in twenty houses around the earth," who has taken to heart her grandmother's advice to "Stay fierce . . . stay lean," nevertheless believes she is becoming "Dear nobody."

The imagery of many stories written by women in our time expresses a frightening sense of nothingness, a bewildering loss of identity, fear of annihilation of the self. In Ann Beattie's "Downhill," Maria, wandering alone in the house, fears she may "disappear forever—just vanish while rounding a corner, or by slipping down, down into the bathwater, or up into the draft the fire creates." This feeling of being without identity, this encounter with the blankness in the looking glass, is a central theme in contemporary women's fiction. The quest for self-definition, the journey within and without to self-discovery, is a traditional theme of literature. Traditionally it has been man who ventured forth, but in our time woman as well undertakes this journey, recording her struggle to move from agonist to protagonist, to seek and to discover, not merely to wait and endure.

But before woman can embark on such a quest, she must free herself from the myths and stereotypes that have determined her nature and role in our culture. The traditional division between the public male world of work and power and the private female world of nurturing and feeling has led to a society in which women have gained their identity through their relationship to men. "True womanhood" and "feminity" have been viewed as narcissism, dependence, submission, passivity—the subordination of all other abilities to life-support and service functions. The belief that a woman discovers herself through love, marriage, and motherhood is implicit in the stereotypes of women that exist in our culture and are reflected in our literature. Women have been the submissive or shrewish wife; the Earth Mother, the Angel Mother, or Portnoy's Mother; the Pure Young Maiden, the Bitch Goddess, or the Witch Woman. These have been the images the mirror of literature has held up to view.

One cannot read the contemporary fiction written by women without becoming aware of a sense of enclosure existing along with a desire to escape from crippling stereotypes. The voice is an isolated voice, raised in lonely monologue, speaking of what is often perceived as the double prison of home and self. "The Yellow Wallpaper" describes a woman, confined to a sick room and kept from writing, who projects her feelings onto an imagined woman locked up behind the pattern of the wallpaper. Often these stories develop images of woman's confinement within the family. "I Stand Here Ironing," by Tillie Olsen, ends with a hope that her daughter's life will not bear the impress of the iron as helplessly as does the dress on the ironing board. Alice Munro's best-known story, "The Office," begins: "The solution to my life occurred to me one evening while I was ironing a shirt." The solution, as Virginia Woolf realized long ago, is A Room of One's Own.

Traditional stories by men often treat the attempt to "find the self" through a test against an adversary leading to "recognition," a moment of illumination. The insights depicted in this collection often turn upon a woman's recognition of her situation as woman within society, as in the Munro and Rosellen Brown stories, or in relation to a man, as in the Welty, Drabble, and Adams stories. But in most stories a contrasting method is used by which, instead of gaining self-knowledge, the characters remain ignorant or accepting of their misery, and the moment of recognition comes to the reader alone.

Here, too, are powerful stories of protective, apparently compassionate husbands who drive their wives mad by understanding everything except their need to be complete people defined by their own energies and talents, not by conventional roles. (The fascinating theme of the compassionate husband and the mad wife occurs, interestingly, in both the earliest story of the collection and one of the most recent—"The Yellow Wallpaper," first published in *New*

England Magazine, in 1891 and Ann Beattie's *New Yorker* story, published in 1975.)

Gail Godwin has imagined the perfectly helpful husband, compassionate enough to "help" his wife do her tasks but not intelligent enough to ask why they are "hers." Since he expects her to resume the housekeeping and child care when she is well, she chooses death. Godwin presents an anti-fairy tale which *ends* with a Sleeping Beauty. In the traditional fairy tale Sleeping Beauty is awakened by the Handsome Prince; from Godwin's tale we learn that the traditional Sleeping Beauty remained a dead woman, even after the awakening kiss.

Lack of imagination and understanding are perhaps inoffensive in themselves, but they are dangerous when combined with power over another. The physician husband in "The Yellow Wallpaper" laughs at his wife's obsession about the wallpaper, which would not matter if it were not in his power to keep his wife sequestered from the world in an old nursery with barred windows and a gate at the top of the stairs.

However, men are not singled out in these stories as wholly to blame for woman's plight. Many female characters see themselves ultimately as actors and responsible for their own actions, not primarily as passive. The passive ones are shown as victims of their own ideas. Joyce Carol Oates gives us Connie, who "knew she was pretty and that was everything." In a perverse fashion, Arnold and Connie are "made for each other," drinking in the same poison of teenage songs, magazines, and movies. That careful mother, mouth full of pins, fitting dresses on her daughter, coaching her to fulfill Mother's own fantasies, perpetuates the rigid role. The initiation rite, in men's stories a battle or a fight, becomes winning a man or passing society's popularity test at a dance. It takes anxiety and effort to fulfill conventional roles and learn to be women in our society, but it is women's own compliance with the rules, with the expectations of mothers, husbands, doctors, teachers, and lovers, that permits oppression.

These stories give us no solution, although they do show us women resisting male fantasies, like Laura in Sylvia Plath's story and

Jenny Jamieson in Margaret Drabble's. The beautiful, capable, efficient Jenny Jamieson smiles and speaks confidently of tomorrow, having just realized that the system which her sensible ways supported, "the actual situations, unillumined by her own good will and her own desire to make the best of things, was beyond hope."

The complexity that Drabble conveys transcends any easy remarks about women's setting aside passivity or "adjusting to their biological limitations." Heroism in men has meant some triumph over the body and the spirit; it will mean, and has meant, the same in women—with a difference. Men have constructed artificial battlegrounds to prove their bravery in withstanding pain, their courage in facing death; women's testing in childbirth, involving both risk of her life and expectation of pain, has come by nature and to almost all women. To survive biologically as a woman involves a testing of courage and the acceptance of death, as women have always known. Drabble's Jenny Jamieson may be an early example of the literary treatment of female heroism—one that will involve women as women, not women being heroic in the way men are. Shakespeare's Cleopatra is heroic as a man is heroic; Jenny Jamieson is heroic as a woman is.

BREAKING THE SILENCE

It is clear, then, that we can identify fiction born out of the feminist consciousness. It is acutely aware of women striving to liberate themselves from society's view of them, and to understand their own feelings as they do so. It is concerned with identity, with the conflict between a woman's free self and her defined and given status in the world. It explores the thwarting of women's potentialities and the full development and realization of those potentialities—intellectual, emotional, and professional.

Indeed, many stories were feminist by this definition before the term became used in literary circles, stories like Doris Lessing's "The De Wets Come to Kloof Grange," Eudora Welty's "A Piece of News,"

Katherine Mansfield's "The Daughter of the Late Colonel," Susan Glaspell's "A Jury of Her Peers." The new feminist criticism, in rediscovering and reexamining American women writers of the nineteenth and early twentieth centuries once largely ignored or dismissed as provincial, has revealed how central to women's experience are the works of writers such as Kate Chopin, Mary Wilkins Freeman, Mary Hunter Austin, Jessie Redmon Fausset. If reexamined, Woolf's and Mansfield's short stories often reveal a similar feminist awareness, and so do stories written during the thirties, forties, and fifties.

In the early sixties a new force began to affect women writing— the resurgence of feminism that has come to be known as the Women's Liberation Movement. Simone de Beauvoir published *The Second Sex* in France in 1947. Translated and read in England and America during the fifties, its radical examination of woman and her life in Western culture profoundly influenced succeeding generations of women. The sixties saw a flood of books that called into question every aspect of woman's life: a new discipline—Women's Studies—came into being; a new criticism rose—Feminist Criticism—that reconsidered traditional subjects and worked to recover women's lost history. New presses such as The Feminist Press and Daughters, Inc., were formed as alternatives to major publishing houses; they republished forgotten works by women and provided outlets for new writers. Little magazines such as *Aphra* and *The Ladder* were established to publish women's writing. Women were, as Tillie Olsen noted, breaking the silence of centuries.

It is not possible to read the fiction written by women in our time without realizing its close connection with the ideas of this strong social movement. Just as the Romantic revolution in English poetry was intimately connected with the ideas expressed by the revolutionary movements of Europe during the early nineteenth century, so this literature is born out of the energies of rebellion and discovery, of the struggle and ferment of the Women's Movement. As such, it is open to the charge of being doctrinaire, polemical, and strident when the ideas that fuel it have not been fused with deeply felt experiences. But however remote writers may be from any organized political activity, their lives and work have been significantly touched by it.

The ferment of ideas generated by the Movement has opened up new areas of subject matter and of manner. Black writers such as Toni Morrison, Alice Walker, and Toni Cade Bambara are writing firm, tough-minded stories that shatter the old stereotypes. Small presses are permitting women to publish stories about lesbianism, a subject usually rejected by establishment presses. Another class of "Invisibles" is the older woman, usually ignored in our society. For this reason we have begun our collection with a section called "The Older Woman," stories that reveal her as strong-minded, passionate, and thoughtful instead of doddering, insipid, and simpering as television commercials and most stories portray her.

Indeed, there is a new voice in these stories. Frank O'Connor, in an illuminating discussion of the short story, suggests that "the short story has never had a hero":

> What it has instead is a submerged population group—a bad phrase which I have had to use for want of a better. That submerged population changes its character from writer to writer, from generation to generation. It may be Gogol's officials, Turgenev's serfs, Maupassant's prostitutes, Chekhov's doctors and teachers, Sherwood Anderson's provincials, always dreaming of escape.

Contemporary fiction has added a new group to this catalogue—women. One hears submerged voices speaking from underground. The "basement of the house" where Jane Rule's heroine lives is a metaphor for her membership in a submerged population. She speaks a repetitive, obsessive language that expresses her depressed condition. But at times the voice is strong, rebellious, assertive, growing out of a new-found sense of power, of openness toward experience, like the little girls in "Raymond's Run."

Many of the authors in this collection are interested in new ways of seeing, rather than in new ways of organizing what they see. Their stories are essentially traditional in structure. Occasionally, a very old form is a means of revealing new perceptions. Gail Godwin begins, "Once upon a time there was a wife and mother one too many times." Drabble begins, "There was once this woman. She was in her thirties. She was quite famous, in a way." Both of these modern fairy tales work against type.

The drive of some of the most successful stories is toward shaping a language to express individual perception. In "The Fifteen-Dollar Eagle" Sylvia Plath's striking use of verbs—squinch, blow, droop, seep, wobble, waver, press, lower, skip, backtalk, flood, anoint, drift, nudge, scallop, smear, flush, swerve, crack, mimic—catches the intensity of the narrator's repulsion and fascination with the tattooing she is watching.

Furthermore, an ancient doctrine of style has entered a new phase. In contemporary architecture it has become dogma that form follows function; in literature, this creed is far older; language should be appropriate to content. But for women writers who were published in the past, that doctrine was violated. Everything had to be expressed in beautiful words. The truth might be ugly but it had to be phrased with elegance.

Now, however, women no longer have to write decoratively in order to be published. In *The Prisoner of Sex*, Norman Mailer, after a bout of reading women's writing of the liberation period, noted this new style: "Impossible to avoid the conclusion. A few of the women were writing in no way women had ever written before." He is surprised by the strength of women's prose:

> The base of male conceit was that men could live with truths too unsentimental for women to support. . . . now women were writing about men and about themselves as Henry Miller had once written about women. . . . What a shock!

The radical change in prose style these stories reveal suggests that the sentimental mind-set that kept women writing prettily has broken down. The world looks different to us; we can no longer write charmingly about ugliness. The new style expresses unwillingness to hide among the old amenities:

My left hand. How can I describe my left hand? It has gnawed cuticles, a wedding ring grown too large, grave freckles, wormy blue veins, a medic-alert bracelet on the wrist, a scar on the forefinger where I broke a dish of pickled beets twenty years ago.

Now we begin to hear the submerged voices. And in the newest voices, the prose is more than unsentimental and mature; it is tough and antisentimental; it utterly rejects convention. In "Pleasure," a grotesque and violent life is forced upon the reader by quick juxtaposition of vulgarities perceived by the eleven-year-old narrator.

There is no doubt a rapid development and expansion in women's writing has gathered force. New subjects, nothing forbidden, new manners coexisting with more traditional styles and methods—and the new change in consciousness: impossible now to get the old picture of the world back into focus so that people and tasks appear acceptable when they are no longer—all these are reflected in these stories. This literature is our new mirror: in it, we discover ourselves.

Nancy Dean and Myra Stark
Hunter College,
City University of New York
New York City, 1976

THE OLDER WOMAN

HER EAGLE OF EXPERIENCE

And still the clipped wing leans against
Her eagle of experience.

—Naomi Replansky, "Two Women" (1952)

VIRGINIA WOOLF

THE LADY IN THE LOOKING GLASS

A Reflection

People should not leave looking glasses hanging in their rooms any more than they should leave open checkbooks or letters confessing some hideous crime. One could not help looking, that summer afternoon, in the long glass that hung outside in the hall. Chance had so arranged it. From the depths of the sofa in the drawing room one could see reflected in the Italian glass not only the marble-topped table opposite, but a stretch of the garden beyond. One could see a long grass path leading between banks of tall flowers until, slicing off an angle, the gold rim cut it off.

The house was empty, and one felt, since one was the only person in the drawing room, like one of those naturalists who, covered with grass and leaves, lie watching the shyest animals—badgers, otters, kingfishers—moving about freely, themselves unseen. The room that afternoon was full of such shy creatures, lights and shadows, curtains blowing, petals falling—things that never happen, so it seems, if someone is looking. The quiet old country room with its rugs and stone chimney pieces, its sunken bookcases and red and gold lacquer cabinets, was full of such nocturnal creatures. They came pirouetting across the floor, stepping delicately with high-lifted feet and spread tails and pecking allusive beaks as if they had been cranes or flocks of elegant flamingoes whose pink was faded, or peacocks whose trains were veiled with silver. And there were obscure flushes and darkenings too, as if a cuttlefish had suddenly suffused the air with purple; and the room had its passions and rages and envies and sorrows coming over it and clouding it, like a human being. Nothing stayed the same for two seconds together.

But, outside, the looking glass reflected the hall table, the sunflowers, the garden path so accurately and so fixedly that they seemed held there in their reality unescapably. It was a strange contrast—all changing here, all stillness there. One could not help looking from one to the other. Meanwhile, since all the doors and windows were open in the heat, there was a perpetual sighing and ceasing sound, the voice of the transient and the perishing, it seemed, coming and going like human breath, while in the looking glass things had ceased to breathe and lay still in the trance of immortality.

Half an hour ago the mistress of the house, Isabella Tyson, had gone down the grass path in her thin summer dress, carrying a basket, and had vanished, sliced off by the gilt rim of the looking glass. She had gone presumably into the lower garden to pick flowers; or as it seemed more natural to suppose, to pick something light and fantastic and leafy and trailing, traveler's-joy, or one of those elegant sprays of convolvulus that twine round ugly walls and burst here and there into white and violet blossoms. She suggested the fantastic and the tremulous convolvulus rather than the upright aster, the starched zinnia, or her own burning roses alight like lamps on the straight posts of their rose trees. The comparison showed how very little, after all these years, one knew about her; for it is impossible that any woman of flesh and blood of fifty-five or sixty should be really a wreath or a tendril. Such comparisons are worse than idle and superficial—they are cruel even, for they come like the convolvulus itself trembling between one's eyes and the truth. There must be truth; there must be a wall. Yet it was strange that after knowing her all these years one could not say what the truth about Isabella was; one still made up phrases like this about convolvulus and traveler's-joy. As for facts, it was a fact that she was a spinster; that she was rich; that she had bought this house and collected with her own hands—often in the most obscure corners of the world and at great risk from poisonous stings and Oriental diseases—the rugs, the chairs, the cabinets which now lived their nocturnal life before one's eyes. Sometimes it seemed as if they knew more about her than we, who sat on them, wrote at them, and trod on them so carefully, were allowed to know. In each of these cabinets were many little drawers, and each almost certainly held letters, tied with bows of ribbon, sprinkled with sticks of lavender or rose leaves. For it was another fact—if facts were what one wanted—that Isabella had known many people, had had many friends; and thus if one had the audacity to open a drawer and read her letters, one would find the traces of many agitations, of appointments to meet, of upbraidings for not having met, long letters of intimacy and affection, violent letters of jealousy and reproach, terrible final words of parting—for all those interviews and assignations had led to nothing—that is, she had never married, and yet, judging from the masklike indifference of her face, she had gone through twenty times more of passion and experience than those whose loves are trumpeted forth for all the world to hear. Under the stress of thinking about Isabella, her room became more shadowy and symbolic; the corners seemed darker, the legs of chairs and tables more spindly and hieroglyphic.

Suddenly these reflections were ended violently and yet without a sound. A large black form loomed into the looking glass; blotted out everything, strewed the table with a packet of marble tablets veined with pink and grey, and was gone. But the picture was entirely altered. For the moment it was unrecognizable and irrational and entirely out of focus. One could not relate these tablets to any human purpose. And then by degrees some logical process set to work on them and began ordering and arranging them and bringing them into the fold of common experience. One realized at last that they were merely letters. The man had brought the post.

There they lay on the marble-topped table, all dripping with light and color at first and crude and unabsorbed. And then it was strange to see how they were drawn in and arranged and composed and made part of the picture and granted that stillness and immortality which the looking glass conferred. They lay there invested with a new reality and significance and with a greater heaviness, too, as if it would have needed a chisel to dislodge them from the table. And, whether it was fancy or not, they seemed to have become not merely a handful of casual letters but to be tablets graven with eternal truth—if one could read them, one would know everything there was to be known about Isabella, yes, and about life, too. The pages inside those marble-looking envelopes must be cut deep and scored thick with meaning. Isabella would come in, and take them, one by one, very slowly, and open them, and read them carefully word by word, and then with a profound sigh of comprehension, as if she had seen to the bottom of everything, she would tear the envelopes to little bits and tie the letters together and lock the cabinet drawer in her determination to conceal what she did not wish to be known.

The thought served as a challenge. Isabella did not wish to be known—but she should no longer escape. It was absurd, it was monstrous. If she concealed so much and knew so much one must prize her open with the first tool that came to hand—the imagination. One must fix one's mind upon her at that very moment. One must fasten her down there. One must refuse to be put off any longer with sayings and doings such as the moment brought forth— with dinners and visits and polite conversations. One must put oneself in her shoes. If one took the phrase literally, it was easy to see the shoes in which she stood, down in the lower garden, at this moment. They were very narrow and long and fashionable—they were made of the softest and most flexible leather. Like everything she wore, they were exquisite. And she would be standing under the high hedge in the lower part of the garden, raising the scissors that were tied to her waist to cut some dead flower, some overgrown branch. The sun would beat down on her face, into her eyes; but no, at the critical moment a veil of cloud covered the sun, making the expression of her eyes doubtful—was it mocking or tender, brilliant or dull? One could only see the indeterminate outline of her rather faded, fine face looking at the sky. She was thinking, perhaps, that she must order a new net for the strawberries; that she must send flowers to Johnson's widow; that it was time she drove over to see the Hippesleys in their new house. Those were the things she talked about at dinner certainly. But one was tired of the things that she talked about at dinner. It was her profounder state of being that one wanted to catch and turn to words, the state that is to the mind what breathing is to the body, what one calls happiness or unhappiness. At the mention of those words it became obvious, surely, that she must be happy. She was rich; she was distinguished; she had many friends; she traveled—she bought rugs in Turkey and blue pots in Persia. Avenues of pleasure radiated this way and that from where she stood with her scissors raised to cut the trembling branches while the lacy clouds veiled her face.

Here with a quick movement of her scissors she snipped the spray of traveler's-joy and it fell to the ground. As it fell, surely some light came in too, surely one could penetrate a little farther into her being. Her mind then was filled with tenderness and regret. . . . To cut an overgrown branch saddened her because it had once lived, and life was dear to her. Yes, and at the same time the fall of the branch would suggest to her how she must die herself and all the futility and evanescence of things. And then again quickly catching this thought up, with her instant good sense, she thought life had treated her well; even if fall she must, it was to lie on the earth and molder sweetly into the roots of violets. So she stood thinking. Without making any thought precise—for she was one of those reticent people whose minds hold their thoughts enmeshed in clouds of silence—she was filled with thoughts. Her mind was like her room, in which lights advanced and retreated, came pirouetting and stepping delicately, spread their tails, pecked their way; and then her whole being was suffused, like the room again, with a cloud of some profound knowledge, some unspoken regret, and then she was full of locked drawers, stuffed with letters, like her cabinets. To talk of "prizing her open" as if she were an oyster, to use any but the finest and subtlest and most pliable tools upon her was impious and absurd. One must imagine—here was she in the looking glass. It made one start.

She was so far off at first that one could not see her clearly. She came lingering and pausing, here straightening a rose, there lifting a pink to smell it, but she never stopped, and all the time she became larger and larger in the looking glass, more and more completely the person into whose mind one had been trying to penetrate. One verified her by degrees—fitted the qualities one had discovered into this visible body. There were her grey-green dress, and her long shoes, her basket, and something sparkling at her throat. She came so gradually that she did not seem to derange the pattern in the glass, but only to bring in some new element which gently moved and altered the other objects as if asking them, courteously, to make room for her. And the letters and the table and the grass walk and the sunflowers which had been waiting in the looking glass separated and opened out so that she might be received among them. At last there she was, in the hall. She stopped dead. She stood by the table. She stood perfectly still. At once the looking glass began to pour over her a light that seemed to fix her; that seemed like some acid to bite off the unessential and superficial and to leave only the truth. It was an enthralling spectacle. Everything dropped from her—clouds, dress, basket, diamond—all that one had called the creeper and convolvulus. Here was the hard wall beneath. Here was the woman herself. She stood naked in that pitiless light. And there was nothing. Isabella was perfectly empty. She had no thoughts. She had no friends. She cared for nobody. As for her letters, they were all bills. Look, as she stood there, old and angular, veined and lined, with her high nose and her wrinkled neck, she did not even trouble to open them.

People should not leave looking glasses hanging in their rooms.

MARGERY FINN BROWN

IN THE FORESTS OF RIGA THE BEASTS ARE VERY WILD INDEED

Take it on faith, make it a handclasp between friends: I am an ordinary woman, unmemorable in looks and endeavors. No one ever followed me home. I never won a prize in a raffle. Once, when I was riding by an open window on a bus, an apple core flew in and gave me a black eye. Later I married, had four children, lived in twenty houses around the earth, gave parties, seamed curtains, dreamed, encountered God, respected beauty, and one Thanksgiving, with my left hand in a splint, cooked dinner for thirty people.

My life has been "usual, simple, and therefore most terrible." Tolstoi? Dostoevski? No matter. What does matter is that since a

9

massive cardiac eight months ago, I am obliged to take quarazine. You say it bluntly: the zine rhymes with *"cousine,"* a word that comes to mind because *Rosenkavalier* is spinning on the record player down the hall, and Ochs is importuning *"ma cousine."* Every note, every hemidemisemiquaver is etched on crystal. None of it matters.

Until eight months ago, music was an integral part of my life. So were books, as necessary to me as breathing in and breathing out. Now when I look at the rows and rows lining the hall—great books, mediocre books, poets, spellbinders, historians, windbags, *flâneurs,* friends—I feel a terrible sadness. This morning I tried again to read Yeats. "What shall I do for beauty, now my old bawd is dead?" The words march valiantly across the page. The meaning sputters through my head like a damp firecracker.

So, you may say. So you cannot enjoy music or read Yeats. So you walk with an obscene white cane and your dreams are stained with the echoes of cigarette smoke. So what? Bear with me, please. We have just left the runway, seat belts are still fastened. To get back to quarazine, its basic ingredient is warfarin. (Warfarin, oddly enough, is the basic ingredient in rat killers.) Quarazine is an anticoagulant. The thinner the mixture, the easier it is for blood to pump up and down the arteries, in and out of the main firehouse, thus lessening the possibility of a "recurring incident," to quote Doctor Chiclets.

How much quarazine do I take? It varies. Every Wednesday I go to Chiclets's office on Sutter Street and have a blood test, to determine the coagulating rate. Every Thursday between one and three, Miss—an old miss—Franklin telephones and says, "Mrs. George Manning? Katherine Manning? Your new dosage until next Wednesday is eleven. Repeat after me, Mrs. Manning, eleven milligrams." Eleven, I say. Eleven, incise it on your heart. Eleven, scrawl it on the Cinderella wallpaper in the bathroom.

I keep quarazine in two phials inside the mirrored medicine chest. The lavender pills are two milligrams. The peach are five milligrams. Eleven is two peach and one half lavender. After I take the quarazine, I close the medicine chest, regard the face in the mirror, and speak to it. I say, "You in there, old tomodachi, you with the sags and the bags and the puffy saucers under the eyes, you have taken your quarazine today. Do not repeat. Repeat, do not repeat today."

Why the ritual?

Thin blood can drown you. It drowns rats.

Stretched out on the mauve-taffeta bed in my room, I am waiting now for Miss Franklin to call. The headboard is a tortured rococo from Venice. The Boulle chest I paid too much for at Butterfield's auction. On top of it are a lamp made from a Waterford candlestick, a princess telephone, and a book bandaged in blue, Yeats.

Yesterday, Wednesday, I went to the doctor's. I am not obliged to remember what happened yesterday. I am not a stone, a lizard. I have free will. I will think how beautiful the light was last night at dusk, the light made Hiroshige blue stripes on the water. I said. "Have you ever seen a more beautiful sunset? My head feels strange."

Before I closed my eyes, I saw my husband and my son exchange a look of utter boredom. (They are not mean, mind you, they don't know how to be mean.) I'm bored with me, too. There is not a damn thing I can do about it while I'm taking quarazine. It has dissolved the inside of my head. There's a forest in there now. It's thick and black. Nothing stirs in the forest. The sun never shines. The growth still grows, chokes. You know the painting by Rousseau, the one where the lion is eating the leopard headfirst? Rousseau's trees and leaves and branches are shiny-green enamel. Ungloss them. Smudge them black, the lion has finished eating the leopard, the stillness is eternal . . . that is my head.

I am ashamed to tell anyone about the forest. It *is*. I am positive of it. The knowledge comes straight from the "zero bone." Emily Dickinson? Whitman? The zero bone tells you when you have had an encounter. A glance can be an encounter, or a word, a body's spontaneous gesture, the shape of a cloud, autumn leaves burning. You never forget encounters, nor do you search for them; they leap at you, unannounced. An encounter can be like a sunburn. Off peels a layer of skin, exposing a tender red hurting surface that toughens gradually. An encounter can mystify, enlighten, or terrorize. What it can never be is superficial.

Is it true for you? Has your life, like mine, bulged with people? Yet I have had few encounters, fewer still related to joy. A blistering night in Santiago, so long ago air conditioning had not been invented. My back burned with prickly heat. The woman in the next labor room screamed with every breath, *"Madre de Dios, Madre de Dios."* My doctor did not believe in anesthesia, so my first child was born *au naturel*. It took two days.

When I first saw Jamey, he was upside down, a tiny fish, shimmering under a waxy overcoat. The doctor said, "Mrs. Manning, you have been an excellent patient. I am going to give you a whiff of something before I sew you up." I told him to keep it. I didn't want to miss one second of this encounter—an upside-down baby with a pirate's grin and with an impudent gleam in his eye.

Another hot night, years later in Rome, an Embassy reception for R., a famous soprano. I had heard her sing, but never met her before. She wore a chrome-yellow Balenciaga, hoops of perspiration under her arms. Unlike her arrogantly assured stage stance, she looked shy, a please-like-me little girl at her first party. Everyone in Rome had turned out to meet her. Directly ahead of us in line was the British commercial attaché. I remember his guardsman's mustache and rabbity teeth. "In the foddist of Rrrrriga," he said, apropos of something, "the beasts are very wild indeed."

When I was introduced to R., I said good evening. She looked me right in the eye. "Pray for me," she said. Startled, I said lightly, "Any special time?" There was no answering smile. "All the time," she said, "starting now."

Warrenton, Virginia. A shabby farmhouse with splintery floors and tribes of field mice. I lived there with the children for a year until we could join my husband in Djakarta.

A year is twelve months. He did not write for nine weeks. I found I could function without sleep for two days. Third night, my room would swarm with people, and the people would speak, and my own voice answered, shrilling through the empty dark. One night, I encountered God. He said four words. Did I imagine him? Did He imagine me? The words still live.

So fly a pennant for Warrenton, mute the strings in Djakarta. A mammoth blood-red moon, a hunter's moon, my husband said. The bamboo swayed, swivel-hipped under the window. I cannot even remember the girl's name. All that comes back is the smell of DDT. (Do you know about the parrot Paderewski trained to perch on the piano and say, "You're the greatest, you're the greatest, the greatest"?)

After that night in Djakarta with the hunter's moon, George would never again imitate Paderewski's parrot, and I would never again be his hatchet woman, chopping down his adversaries, making his life free of rent or wrinkle. Which makes neither of us superior. It merely removed one of the hundred reasons we took each other in marriage and bedhood. Vigor, in any event, is a marginal virtue in a woman. If I could create a new façade, I would be lazy and lovely and amiable as the trumpet vine lacing the house where I was born.

Durham, New Hampshire, a brown, shingled house rimmed in Gothic green. Emmett, my stepbrother—his father married my mother—gets violent every ten years or so. He would never hurt me. We were close as twins. I taught him to ride a bicycle. He paid for my first permanent, caddying. When Father died, the house went to Emmett. I came home to Durham to help him dispose of the incunabula of eighty-some years.

The two of us alone, the night after the funeral, walking down the cellar steps.

"You know how Father hated taxes," Emmett said. "One night last winter he hauled me out of bed and made me bury a wad of treasury notes in the wine cellar. Then I had to cement over it. You're coming with me while I dig it up. I need a witness."

The back of my neck was ice. I kept walking down the steps, too frightened to turn back. "We will have to find Father's ax, won't we, Kate? You wouldn't know where he kept it, would you? I stayed in Durham. I took his crap year in, year out while you roamed, here, there, everywhere. . . . We're going to find that ax if it takes all night, aren't we, Kate?"

Encounters remembered. Deeds done. Words said. Tracer bullets lobbing over the forest. I was named Kate for my Irish grandmother. She dyed her hair with tea leaves and thumped the floor with her blackthorn if the service was poor or people didn't do as she liked. Stay fierce, she used to say, stay lean, Kate, take no man's guff.

Lardy, defanged, I exist in a mauve bedroom, waiting for the phone to ring. If only I didn't have to take quarazine. "If only" is a greased pole to nowhere. All there is is what is. Me. This minute. My left hand. How can I describe my left hand? It has gnawed cuticles, a wedding ring grown too large, grave freckles, wormy blue veins, a medic-alert bracelet on the wrist, a scar on the forefinger where I broke a dish of pickled beets twenty years ago. The framework consists of five fan-shape bones covered with skin the color of cheese. The bones are cut into five uneven strips, each strip ending in an oval cellophane window. Once, looking down from the loft of a stable, I thought, That's not a horse's back, that's a cello.

Listen: this is quarazine. I am frightened.

Listen: my mother-in-law's lobster claw clamped around your wrist so you would not leave before she finished one of her interminably long, pointless stories. My mother-in-law, a muscled, all-dark-meat woman. Squeaky dentures, lipstick bleeding into the pleats around her mouth, nicotined fingers worked to the bone. She adored George, "my only child, my son, the diplomat." George was ashamed of her. "God's sake, Ma, if you have to label me, just say I'm with the State Department."

Every summer she visited us. The pipes rumbled as she bathed, five o'clock in the morning. The ironing was all finished when we returned at night from a party. No, she wouldn't come, no, she wouldn't "fit in. Besides, I'm allergic to Mexican food." That, George said, was a lot of bushwa. So she went with us to the Troups's in Mexico City. She ate tortillas and drank sangría until she was sick, o, o, *con fuoco* all over the Troups's bathroom.

In the middle of the night, I awoke. The guest-room door had blown open, and I heard her trying quietly to light a match. (Lord, I thought, someday I'll be old and visiting one of my married children, and they'll be whispering in bed, "When is she going home? Lord, I can't stand this much longer.") It wasn't love or pity that impelled me to walk into the guest room. I needed a talisman to ward off my own future. "Mrs. Manning," I said, "can I get you something?" A phlegmy, raspy laugh. Out came the lobster claw. "Listen," she said, "I know I'm a damn nuisance, but I can't seem to help it." The next morning at breakfast, she was the same, lipstick seeping, calliope laugh, trying to woo her son, her only child, the diplomat. The same and never the same again. Martin Buber would say the I-It relationship had changed to an I-Thou. Alan Watts would say the she-ness of she encountered the me-ness of me.

What do I say?

I say our journey is almost over, we're coming in over the airport, the landing gear is down and locked. Yesterday I went to the doctor's. I call him Chiclets for short and for spite. Why do I despise him? Fear, what else? He has wind-colored eyes, furry knuckles, and when he touches you his hands are deft and contemptuous, like a butcher handling meat. Why should a man so lacking in empathy become a doctor? Geld, more than likely, and status. God is his peer group. Pay homage to the doctor, oh yes, but forget the frank, insult, and mirth. His voice starts out in the lower abdomen, big and scornful, but after winding through fatty detours and truck routes, comes out of his rosebud mouth, minuscule, unvaliant, ridiculous somehow, like a tricycle batting it down the freeway.

"Ah, you have not started smoking again," he says, blowing smoke in my face. "Ah, you have courage." (Not enough, I wanted to say, not enough, you two-bit twot. I heard you browbeating that incontinent old wreck in the hospital.) "As I have said before, Mrs. Manning, quarazine is a powerful drug and your coagulating rate is at best erratic, but never in all my experience have I encountered a reaction such as yours." (Come off it, summer camper, sophomore in life, they should send you back to the worm, you're a waste of love and lust.) "My technician is getting married today, I will draw your blood, make a fist please." (How childish I was when my blood spurted on his shirt, so childishly delighted I found the nerve to ask that bitter-bile question.)

"Mrs. Manning, you may have to take quarazine all your life. It is more than likely, I should say, so you must resign yourself to that probability."

Resigned?

I ride down the elevator of the Medical Arts Building. The blind pencil vendor recognized my footsteps. "Your feet tapping weak today, Mrs. Manning." I say, "No, Mr. Holliday, I'm fine. How's the world treating you?" "Terrible. . . . No sense knocking it, is they?" Resigned, I can never be. Dead before I am docile. My neck aches from holding up the forest. I am dispersed. I have nightmares. I am frightened. Things frighten and attract me simultaneously.

The traffic island in front of me. I must cross the street to get a cab home. In the middle of the intersection, there's a pedestrian haven, a small raised triangle. When I'm lucky, I make it across the street without having the light change. Today I cannot walk fast enough. I stand on the traffic island, watching the cars arrel-bassing by, the trucks puffing smug and smog, wild-eyed buses so close they eat the breath from my mouth. I look down on my black alligator shoe. Put your little foot right there. Silly jingle. Right there, one inch, and it will all be over, Kate.

Stop pushing. Whoever is pushing me in the small of the back, *stop it*. No need to turn around. I know I am alone on the traffic island. I have no assurance that it would be quick, final, or painless. I could live all chewed up, fresh from the gristmill. Wouldn't that be loverly? When the light changes, I limp across to the cab stand. Be patient, patient. Be valid, invalid. Chop down the forest, but do not make me wait.

I've been waiting all afternoon. Look at the time, ten after three. The neighborhood children are coming home from school, sweater arms lashed around their waists. Elijah, a dilapidated coach dog, crawls out from under the hedge and gives a halfhearted hello.

"Hi, Elijah." I recognize the voice. The new little girl. Can't be five, wears mesh panty hose, and has the whole block in thrall. "Lijah, you know what?"

I pick up the phone before the second ring. It *is* Miss Franklin. I listen, repeat the new dosage, say thank you, hang up.

Lijah, you know what? I have to start taking twenty-two milligrams. *Madre de Dios.* In the hospital it was four milligrams. Then six, nine, eleven, fourteen, fifteen, eighteen. Twenty-two. I'll dissolve. I'll be in fragments.

Leaning on the white tree-stump cane, I walk into the bathroom. The wallpaper I've been meaning to change for years. It cloys— Cinderellas in hoopskirts stepping out of pumpkin coaches. I open the mirrored chest. Twenty-two. That's six peach. Six times five is twenty. One lavender is two. Twenty and two make twenty-two. I fill a cup from the dispenser with water. The pills go down smoothly. I close the medicine chest. Look, I say to the mirror, look old friend, you with the sags and bags, you've taken your quarazine today, so do not repeat. Repeat, do not repeat.

I say it.

There is no face in the mirror.

I can see the collar of a faded blue robe. I can see a corded neck. Above the neck? Nothing. Air. Where the face should be, a square of Cinderella wallpaper.

An optical illusion?

I turn on the light switch. I can hear that humming prelude fluorescent lights always make. I can hear the last trio from *Rosenkavalier* wisping down the hall. My tongue is wet. We have nice water, it's tart and tastes of fresh mermaids. The porcelain sink feels like a porcelain sink—cold, and eternal.

Alles in ordnung.

I look again in the mirror. The robe, the neck, the air, the wallpaper. I lean over, shaking. I grip my arms tight around my stomach. My heart roars like surf in my ears. Quarazine turned my head into a forest, now it has dissolved my face. Persona means mask. It melted my personal mask. The head, then the face, what comes next? The heart? The zero bone that registers encounters, that labels true feelings and looks ahead and wonders. How will I get through the rest of my days?

The house is cold. I should turn up the thermostat. Feeling the pull of the rug under my slippers, I back into my bedroom, my little mauve vegetable bin. When feelings go, I'll be a vegetable. Carrots, broccoli, O garland me with parsley. The worst has happened, I encountered me. There was no one there.

Memory nags, pulls on my sleeve. A ravenously rough trip to the Aran Islands, all of us strangers, so sopped by the rain we clung together in the snuggery while cows groaned and thudded in the hold. The Guinness flowed like buttermilk. A little runty Dubliner with a tweed cap and yardarm jaw apologized the first time the ship lurched and a wave of Guinness flipped from his glass into my lap. More lurches, more Guinness. There was no place to move to, nor did I saw any sign of dismay. Each time his apology was curter, less gracious, till in a fit of exasperation he growled, "Madame, ye've got to adjist to the whims of nature."

So I must. Nature never rejoices, mourns, never applauds, never condemns. Nature continues. I haven't the energy to cry. I sigh instead, a breathy sigh that nudges the walls like an airy puffball. Somehow it helps, when you are alone and no one can hear you, to sigh deeply, to say, "O dear. Dear me."

Dear me?

Dear nobody.

DIANE JOHNSON

AN APPLE, AN ORANGE

Twice a week Rosie Vedder got down on her knees, like a great blue and gold hassock, to scrub her kitchen floor, but she would not scrub another woman's floor in this position. That was a point she always carried at the outset.

"Too much work," she would say, looking at the lady with imperious, pale eyes as if challenging her to deny it. "You get me the kind of mop with the sponge on the end and the kind of thing you have not to wring out with your hands." And if the lady protested, which American ladies were mostly too timid to do, she would add, "If you can put your hands in it, the water is not hot enough. I am a very clean woman and I know. You got to use very hot water."

Her person inspired confident visions of cleanliness. She was big, heavily pink, with a knotted coronet of faded gold braids and the perennial odor of bleach, in which she seemed to slake herself, protecting against dirt the way one might use citronella against mosquitos. The indignant expression of her slightly protruding eyes had perhaps been caused by dirt; she pursued it like a vengeful goddess, and wore things down with cleaning. Rosie kept her house, and the houses of her ladies, the way she would have liked the whole world to be—shining, level, soap-tasting, safe.

In Los Angeles she had a better house than she had in Holland, and she had gotten it for herself, without a man. A little house with a kitchen and a bedroom, and a slatted porch in the back where the refrigerator was. All the floors, even in the living room, were green linoleum, and this was ugly but very easy to keep clean. Sometimes when the sun was hot on the windows the house had an old smell, so that Rosie would remember that many things had happened here before the house was hers, things with men, too, and a bitter feeling of helplessness would seal her ears and eyes, and she would trance-like scrub the place, trying not to think about the unassailable accretions of former lives within her rooms. But at other times when her kettle steamed too long and fogged the windows all around inside, and the steam trailed down in little mineral streaks which she would have to wash, some other day, she felt especially cozy. Her steam was permeating every crack and board and the whole house was some-how sealed and hers. Then she would be seized by a panic of precarious love.

In the evenings though she was very tired she would watch televi-sion and crochet and think of her special plan, to divorce her husband back in Holland. This was why she was taking in a boarder, though she hated the idea of a boarder, damp towels and alien tracks; it was to be a temporary arrangement only, just until she paid for her divorce. She had crossed an ocean to live alone, and would not abridge this priceless freedom except to win it absolutely. Free-dom, unrestraint, were passions seeded in her heart when she was young, had grown as she did in bulk, years and power, and now this flowering. At the age of fifty-three, her children scattered and breeding, she had said goodbye to the tyrannical old Dutch husband with his messy habits, thin legs, disgusting demands, and sailed to America. She was a woman of spirit, as they had found to their amazement. But she was a practical woman too. Sharing her little house with a refined, clean, nonsmoking, paying woman on a temporary basis would in the long run hasten her complete independence. She knew a divorce was probably unnecessary; poor spineless little Dutch men who think themselves too old to cross oceans are small threat to vigorous free women in America. She was being divorced because she would like the feeling. And someday, when perhaps a letter would come saying Papa is sick, it would have no claim on her. She would shrug.

What would she do when she was free? The idea hung unformed but luminous in her mind; she could imagine gazing unimpeded at broad landscapes, with, indistinctly, a person, some love or companion, perhaps the chic and witty woman she had seen once in a dove-grey suit alight from a train. Or someone, speaking to her at her elbow. She never could see this person, but she could hear her speaking. They leaned over a ship's rail, they peered from the little square golden windows of a westward-flying plane. Rosie smiled with a measure of self-tolerance at her own notions, so incompatible with her age and bulk, and yet she would not give them up. Boss of herself, traveler.

One of her daughters had followed her to America and had double-jumped the rules of cultural assimilation by marrying well and not minding that her mother was a scrub-lady. It had been this daughter who thought of the boarder, and found one. She represented the idea to her proud mother as "helpfulness"; Rosie would be helping a homeless woman who had been put out of her live-in housekeeping job. She had come all the way from China for this job and now had no place to go.

"A China woman? Here to *my* house?" Rosie had said at first, as if it were impossible, and then, "Is she a very clean woman?"

"She is a very clean woman, Mother, and the Foleys think very highly of her as a person, it's just that it hasn't worked out for them, she isn't too good with children or something."

"Hum," Rosie said, and secretly thought better of the China lady. And it would be somebody to talk to, as long as this was a clean woman. Ja, all right. "Thirty-five dollars a month she would have to pay, and half the light and water," and it was arranged.

She almost changed her mind on the day of Anna Lim's arrival, when it rained and she began to think about tracks on the bright floor, dripping puddles from the feet of strangers, damp luggage. She had not bargained for people bringing rain. Her hand was on the telephone when she saw the car pull up in front of the house, and then it was too late. She put some newspapers on the floor. Her daughter's neighbor, Mrs. Foley, a brisk anxious woman in a rain-coat, appeared at the door bearing apologies, thanks, spattered paper sacks full of clothing. Beyond, a face peered motionless out of the wet car window, watching Mrs. Foley carry satchels, and Rosie Vedder stood sourly at the door staring into the rain, making a barricade of her disapproving face.

The Chinese woman at length climbed out of the car and moved slowly up the walk, through the wet, without lifting her feet. She had the gait of the discouraged or the sick. Sickness occurred to Rosie in a rush of displeasure; she could not take care of someone complaining and helpless. The idea of sickness filled her with the same physical revulsion that dirt did, and she stared at the little woman as if she expected some affliction to show up luminous under her strong glare. The Chinese woman looked down at her own feet and at the puddles through which she indifferently sloshed, and did not meet Rosie's eyes.

Mrs. Foley led her in and sat her on the sofa, patted her, patted Rosie, hovered and finally dashed out into the rain again, wearing an expression of great relief. Rosie watched the disconsolate person huddled on the sofa, but said nothing until the neighbor drove away. Then she came closer, trying to decide about her. She at first seemed to be young, she was so little, but then Rosie saw that she was closer to her own age, tiny and pale, with a face of glass. She was not sick, Rosie saw, only timid. She had flat brown eyes, intent with fright, and the faintest of lines on her tight skin. She sat stiffly. Rosie was seized by an instinctive hospitable urge, something in her that did not want another person, however foreign and strange, to look so miserable in her house.

"Well, Anna Lim," she said, sitting down in her comfortable chair, as if for a good chat, "that woman did not like you at her house, eh? She was a bossy lady, I could tell." She expected that Anna would have a side to tell.

"No, I am no good," said Anna, and stirred inside her green coat.

"Ah? Well. A person in America does not have to live-in, like a slave. Work hard, you can have a house, like me, be free, be independent. But she wanted too much work, that one, I can always tell them. Yes?"

"Oh yes, she wanted everything. Cook, clean, iron. She even wanted me to polish the silver." A note of passion trembled in the flat voice, but she still stared at the floor. Rosie was mystified; to polish silver did not seem excessive. She tried to meet Anna on another ground.

"Well, you are China," she said, "but you speak English very good."

"Yes," said Anna. She spoke it with a perfect cultivated British accent.

"Better than me," laughed Rosie. "I learn it too old. But you aren't so young, are you?"

"I'm fifty," said Anna. She looked up, at this, for the first time, and seemed pleased to answer a personal question. Her face opened, and she seemed ready to answer more, but Rosie was on her feet.

"I will make you a cup of coffee," she said, and went to the kitchen.

Having decided to share her home, Rosie tried to do it handsomely. She kept to herself the bedroom and the bedroom closet, but she moved her umbrella and coat out of the entry closet so that Anna might put her few things there, and she allowed Anna to tape some pictures on the living-room wall above the sofa, her bed, even though they did not conform to Rosie's ideas of decoration. Two were photographs of a slim youth, Anna's nephew on Formosa, and one was a colored picture of Christ.

The nephew, as it appeared during the evenings that followed, was Anna's only relative, and in Rosie's opinion he was a poor excuse for one; there was nothing interesting about him and he never wrote. Still, he was something for them to talk about. They did not have much. They could not seem to speak of their own lives. Rosie thought China the strangest and most contrary country she had heard of, and could not bear to listen to such odd reminiscences. And Anna, infuriatingly, was too incurious and passive ever to ask about Holland. They tried once to talk about the war, but it was not interesting. Anna had not suffered much, she said, and that was all she would say. For Rosie the war always dissolved into one hard memory, something done to her by two German soldiers, which she could not think of yet without her breath quickening with impotent hatred.

"Germans are animals," was all she would say of it. "And there was no butter for five years."

Although they did not talk much, they were comfortable and companionable. A room with someone in it, female and clean, had a lighter, flowery feel. And Anna was as tidy as Rosie could wish. There were no signs of her unless you were looking right at her. When she had finished her bath, the tub would be dry, even; apparently she dried off the tub with her towel. Rosie would go to work in the morning and return at night to find Anna sitting in the spot where she had left her, nothing ever moved, nothing used or disarranged. It seemed as if Anna did nothing at all, all day. She was like a vase of faded blossoms, and like blossoms this was faintly easeful to the heart.

Her indolence was almost the only thing about Anna that bothered Rosie. She was incapable of indolence herself, and mistrustful of it in others; she nagged Anna to look for a job. She read to her aloud from the want ads and even composed a little advertisement for Anna to post at the supermarket. But Anna only shook her head and said in her British governess voice she would prefer to wait a little while. Rosie concluded from this that poor Anna's spirit was still bruised from her experience with Marie's neighbor, and did not press the matter much at first. She too had worked for difficult ladies.

She was concerned, though, about Anna's finances. She knew how they stood because Anna had entrusted her with the keeping of her savings, four hundred dollars—an impressive, fat fold of bills which Rosie counted admiringly and put away beneath her handkerchiefs in the top bureau drawer.

"Anna, you are a very sensible woman after all, I believe," she had said. "If I had four hundred dollars—well, what? Two hundred dollars for the divorce, then I am a free woman, no one can touch me. And then I would put the rest away, or maybe I would go someplace on a trip. Rosalinda Vedder, traveler." She had gone off to the kitchen for the coffeepot thinking about this. She was not a foolish woman, man-hunting on cruise ships. Not a foolish buyer of souvenirs. She had not yet thought of quite the right place to go, but she had the vision of it, heard the soft voice.

"Of course your money will be gone before you know it, if you get no job soon," she said, coming back. "Thirty-five dollars to me each month, half the food, half the lights. In four or five months it will be gone."

"That's a long time," said Anna. Her confidence in Providence seemed to Rosie unjustified, so because Anna did not seem to worry about her future, Rosie had to. Each time she lifted her handkerchiefs she felt the thickness of Anna's roll of money, and would warn and remind and scold Anna's complacency.

One day she put her hand in the drawer and was immediately aware that a lot of Anna's money was gone. She thought first of theft, and of being blamed herself, and let out a shriek that brought Anna running to her.

"Your money is gone! See, it is almost all gone." Her hand holding the flat packet was shaking. Anna, who had never touched her, reached out and took Rosie's hand. Her face was calm, in command, confident. The touch of her little hand was warm. Rosie found herself surprised at this.

"Don't worry, I know, I took the money myself, to give to my school. It's a surprise, you'll be so pleased."

"What school?" Rosie asked, withdrawing her hand, not liking the sound of this.

"It's a school for office work. I'll learn to type and use the telephone switchboard. Then I can get an office job," said Anna, smiling. "I have been planning to do this, you see, and now I will start on Monday."

"What's the matter with housekeeping jobs," said Rosie. "I can get you plenty of jobs."

"I just don't like—I'm no good. I suppose I don't have the strength," Anna said.

"No, you are too little," Rosie said, but then she tried to imagine Anna's thin little shoulders hunched above a typewriter—Anna, who never seemed to understand the simplest things, taking orders from a loud man in an office. She was filled with disgust for the pitiful notion and for a man who would take Anna's money and promise to teach the typewriter to a poor old woman.

"How much of your money gave you them?" she asked.

"Two hundred dollars. But of course when you have learned office work you can earn much more in one month."

"Oh, no," Rosie cried out, horrified. "You could get a divorce for two hundred dollars. You are just a stupid woman. You will never get an office job. You are fifty years old. You just throw the money away."

"No, it will be better," smiled Anna. "You'll see."

"*You* will see," said Rosie, much agitated, and stalked to the kitchen. She was unable to think of anything better to do for poor foolish Anna than to make her a cup of coffee.

Anna began school on Monday. They walked to the bus stop together every morning after that, and it was pleasant. Rosie held her golden head high, regarding with a cheerful fresh morning smile the early faces that they met, and Anna beside her took two of her tiny steps to keep pace. She wore her green coat, a foot too long for her, and her head was bent so that the knot of her hair at the nape of her neck was the tallest thing about her. She faithfully carried her little notebook under her arm, and Rosie felt as if she were walking a child to the school bus. She waved after Anna good-humoredly enough, but her resentment at the thieving school never vanished.

For one thing, besides being impractical and thieving, the school was making Anna very tired. When Rosie came home each evening at five-thirty, her steps scarcely slower than when she had gone out and her cheeks and hands bright red, she would find Anna waiting in the living room, bent over her notebook, frowning and pressing her forehead, exhausted. Rosie could not help but pity the poor little creature. She scowled and scolded about the school, but she fixed supper for them both without comment. Anna ate tremendously and was grateful. Her face was radiant through its weariness, it was as if no one had ever been good to her before.

"Thank you," she would always say. "That was a wonderful supper. You are very good to me. I can never repay you."

And she never did. Rosie began to notice this after a terrible day when she slipped and fell on the wet kitchen floor at work for Mrs. Baker. She didn't mention this to Mrs. Baker, nor to Anna, nor even to herself did she for a time admit it, but she had hurt her back. She noticed over the next few days that working was hard. There was one special pain that shot up her spine when she bent over, and another that tore into her shoulder blades when she straightened. It hurt to reach things on high shelves and it hurt to push a mop. At the end of a day she was exhausted by trying to modify her movements, and by the pain. Anna never seemed to notice this. She just sat at the table, working in her notebook, looking up at Rosie with a welcoming smile of dependence and joy.

By Wednesday Rosie allowed herself, as soon as she got home, the luxury of an ostentatious limp, but Anna did not notice this limp, nor hear aggrieved mutterings in the kitchen as she got supper. On Friday evening, in her resentment, Rosie was clumsy, dropped some potatoes too hard into boiling water and was scalded on the forearm by the splatter. She hissed in pain, and Anna came padding in.

"I have burned myself, do you see?" Rosie shrieked at her. "It is a wonder I have not burned myself before. Why can you not do this, cooking, when you know I am not feeling good?"

"No, I did not know," whispered Anna. "I am so sorry." She looked as if it were she who had been burned. "Please go in the living room. I will fix dinner. I am sorry, but I am so slow and stupid. I have been so unkind to my dear friend," she said.

Rosie limped off, nursing her arm and her resentment. She sat on the sofa and closed her eyes. Her bones seemed to settle and her legs were heavy. The burn smarted, the back pained.

"I am getting old," she said aloud; it was a frequent remark with her, but for almost the first time, a sense of her treacherous, ailing flesh made her believe it and distorted her image of herself as a woman free and unencumbered, before whom adventures lay. She suddenly wanted to see Kati and Peter, the two children left in Holland, of whom she seldom thought. The arm puffed and stung. Her eyes stung angrily.

Anna took her hand. Rosie had not heard her come. "Let me put some butter on your arm," she said, and gently rubbed soft butter over the burn stroking and stroking the poor arm. Rosie closed her eyes again.

"Thank you, Anna. I am just a poor old woman."

"Poor, poor Rosie," said Anna, in a soft, solicitous, crooning voice, like a Chinese song.

Anna was busy for a long time in the kitchen but she finally brought Rosie a plate of food. She gave her a napkin to spread over her lap.

"What is this?" Rosie asked, pleased at the attention.

"Meat and vegetables, prepared in the Chinese fashion," Anna said. Rosie ate slowly, watching the television, until she could not bear to keep still anymore.

"I have never eat such food!" she burst out. "The meat is all in little pieces mixed up in with the vegetables. The vegetables are hardly cooked. You don't even know how to cook! Oh, Anna, I tell you." She put her plate on the floor by her chair and adjusted herself to glare at Anna better. "You give all your money to the school, you are not strong enough to do housework and you cannot cook right—you are a completely foolish woman."

Anna sighed and shook her head. "When I get my office job, perhaps I can give you more money if you will do the cooking."

"Ach, no, I do not want your money. I am a very fair woman. I will tell you. You cook supper for you, I will cook supper for me. That is fair. Then we have no argument. And you help me clean on Saturdays. You have been here a month and never have you helped me clean on Saturday." And Anna agreed.

That night when they had gone to bed, Rosie heard a soft step in the bedroom, heard her own tiny gasp of fear, and then realized it was Anna. She whispered to her in the dark, to make sure. "Anna?"

"Yes," Anna whispered, "I could not go to sleep. I am so unhappy. Please tell me you are not unhappy with your Anna." The poor little old woman. She had a sweet smell, like an old doll out of an attic. Impulsively, Rosie clasped her, like a doll.

"No, you are all right," Rosie muttered, and turned away, ready for sleep again, and Anna crept off. But then Rosie lay awake, and felt a new anger press inside her, so that she could not sleep.

After that when Rosie came home from work she would fix a little plate of food for herself, a potato and a piece of meat and cabbage. Then Anna would go in and cook and eat whatever she ate, and wash her plate and put it away again, so that Rosie never knew what she ate. On Saturdays they would clean and then go to the market, each buy her groceries separately, take them home. Anna put hers in one side of the refrigerator, one end of the cupboard, Rosie the other. At the market Rosie would grumble to Anna of her extravagance. She ate odd things from little cans, very costly, and slices of expensive meat. "What will you do when the money is gone?" and Anna would smile archly and say, "An office job, remember, where I will not have to scrub and clean."

One afternoon Rosie came home late, nearly seven, because she had stayed late to fix supper for the family, and she was feeling tired, and her back still bothered her. She had been thinking of the nice cold baked apple waiting for her in the refrigerator, but when she looked for it it was gone. Her heart pounded, as if it were gold that was gone, or something precious, or as if she had found someone dead.

"Anna," she said, "an apple I was going to have for my supper . . ." Anna came into the kitchen with a strange, bright look on her face. Rosie's pale blue eyes were terrible. "Have you taken it?" Anna did not hesitate.

"Oh, my friend, I am sorry," she said. "Yes, I did. I ate it, and I did not think you would mind. I . . ."

"Well, I do mind," Rosie, very hungry, snapped at her. "By God, I do mind. Is stealing apples what they do in China?" She had supper of boiled potatoes in the kitchen and would not talk to Anna. Later in the night she thought she heard the little Chinese woman crying in her bed. She lay awake, half expecting Anna to come in to be forgiven, but this did not happen.

The next day as they walked to the bus, Anna put her hand on Rosie's arm.

"Stealing is what they do in China when they are hungry," she said in a low voice. "I suppose they do that anywhere. But I was wrong to take something from my only friend. It is just that I am so wicked."

Rosie had the awful idea that Anna would start to cry again right there on the bus stop, so she shook the little hand off and said, "Well, never mind, one apple is not so much. But you should not take things from me, in my house. But you should not be hungry either. We will talk of it tonight."

Then Anna's bus pulled up, and Rosie turned away, pretending not to notice that Anna had dropped her precious notebook into the wet gutter and had to carry it dripping and ruined onto the bus.

When Rosie got home she found Anna copying into a new notebook the little marks and squiggles she learned at school, like Chinese writing. Rosie had thought those lines would come easier to Anna than to an American woman. Anna's thin greying hair strayed from its knot and the tight skin across her flat little cheeks was damp with weariness and concentration.

"Have you not much money left now?" Rosie said, picking up the conversation as if it were her sharp sewing scissors to poke little Anna.

"No," Anna sighed, putting down her pen. "Soon I hope I will get my office job. I have three more weeks left at school."

"You have forty dollars left, ha?" Rosie said. She had kept careful track.

"No, only thirty. I gave ten dollars to my church."

"To your church! So you go hungry? So you steal from me? Is that what your church likes?!"

"Oh, no, I am sure it would not. I have said I am very sorry. You have forgiven me, and so will God." She smiled.

"Ah, don't bring it all up now. Thirty dollars! You have to give me that on Monday, also the light bill. What will you use for food?"

"I don't know," Anna said, still smiling.

"That's it! You don't plan! So it is, you give your money away, you have no job." Rosie's voice began to rise and shake in her wrath at the impracticality. "I never will understand you. You are so stupid." Anna shrugged and smiled, but when she spoke her soft voice also shook. She stood up and tightly held to the chair.

"Yes! I am 'so stupid.' No, I am not! You are always telling me that I am stupid and wasteful and wasted and weak. I am not. You despise me because I am not good at scrubbing floors, well scrubbing is good enough for you, you are a peasant anyway. I know about peasants, there are enough of them in China. But I am not one of them. I have had to do a lot of things, but I know what I am. I am not a young woman but I am not too old to make my life better. I am very good at my school, better than the young girls. The young girls laugh, but you should not laugh. You are a cruel uneducated woman. Well, I will work in an office and you will be a scrub-lady. Poor old Anna, she has no one, she has never had a man, she is 'China,' you said. But you will see!"

Rosie only gave one outraged cry and stamped off to her bedroom. "You tell me I am so old," Anna shouted outside the door. "I am the same, I am the same inside as I ever was, and I am trying. I am still trying. I have very much of my life yet to live."

"Go to bed," Rosie called in a terrible voice, and then when Anna said nothing more, she undressed herself in a trembling hurry, pulled her nightgown over her big body, over her big soft breasts, all in the blindest hurry, and covered herself up tightly in bed. In the morning she got up, made her bed and sat on the edge of it, waiting for Anna. She knew what to expect. Anna knocked and then crept in, very tiny and yellow in her long white nightgown. She knelt down at Rosie's knees and stared. She put her hands on Rosie's big knees, a gentle touch, like a healer's on the sore old knees.

"I am sorry," she began. "I am very wrong and very stupid. I have said cruel things to my only friend. Please forgive me. I am very old, and no one has ever loved me, and I have said stupid things to you. Look." She got up and went to the drawer in Rosie's chest and got her money. "Here is thirty dollars. I have some food and some bus tokens. Please let me stay a short time when this is gone. I will soon get a job, I will pay you more." Her lips were like a little line of Chinese writing.

Rosie took the money. She was frowning. She smoothed her dress over her knees. "I will tell Mrs. Baker I am sick today," she said. "You go work for her instead. Twelve dollars. See, I give you my work." Not a bad idea, it would be nice to stay home. But Anna shook her head. Her voice rose higher.

"No, I could not. But you are very kind. I do not deserve you. You are the best woman I know. Let me stay. Wouldn't you miss your Anna? I would miss you. We are old, and we should not be alone. It is a bad thing to be alone in life."

Something in this thin wail pierced Rosie further. It is a bad thing to be alone in life. She thought of Anna's light, warm fingers and old childlike face. "We are alone in life anyway," she said. "I am going to work now." She felt herself sigh, like a bellows, involuntarily.

Then she cleaned Mrs. Baker's house until no dirt could be spied in it anywhere and the windows shone like air, and rolls were in the oven, which made Mrs. Baker say she could never do without her. Rosie sniffed.

"You can never depend on other people," Rosie said. Then, before she left Mrs. Baker's, she called her daughter and told her to find another place for Anna.

Marie called two evenings later. Anna was studying as usual. "I think I should have glasses," she said, rubbing her eyes. "My eyes hurt, and sometimes my head aches so; do you think I should have glasses?"

"Glasses cost money," Rosie began, and then the phone rang.

"A woman up the street will take Anna. Martha Roberts. Her own girl had to leave, maybe for two months, sickness in the family. And Martha has five kids, so she needs somebody right away."

"That's good. This is a nice lady?"

"Oh, sure, she's all right. Anna will have a nice room and all. Martha could come after her tonight."

"Ja, thank you, I will tell her." Rosie hung up and turned to Anna.

"Well, I have a nice job for you," she said. Anna looked up, not understanding.

"That was my daughter. I told her you can stay here no longer and she finds you a nice lady to work for."

"What do you mean? You said I could stay here!"

"No, I did not say that. You did not understand. You have no money, you have to have work. Now comes a nice lady to take you. Nice house. She lives up by my daughter. My daughter lives on a nice street, and you will have a room to yourself. Plenty to eat."

"When? What are you saying?" Anna cried, pressing her little hands against her little flat chest.

"This lady will come for you tonight. It will be a good thing, Anna. You need to work."

"But I will get a job! I have told you. The school helps me to get a job when I graduate."

"Office work," Rosie snapped. "I told you not to throw your money away on that thing."

"Oh, I will not go," Anna said, her eyes darting with fear. "I have told you. I cannot go. I cannot miss my school, I . . ." She put out one hand and fumbled behind for her school notebook. Her voice became soft and quiet again.

"Please, Rosie dear, I know I have been such a trouble to you, but I love you, I am your friend. You are the only person who has ever been kind to me. I mean that. You mean more to me than my own nephew, my nephew, he has never done anything for me. You have done so much."

"Well, I do yet one more thing. I get you a good job. You better pack your things, Anna." But Anna sat still on the couch. Rosie went to Anna's closet and began to bring the clothes out, and put them in her suitcase. "You do this," Anna said presently, "so that I will not

graduate. Because you said I would never graduate." Her voice was
flat and her tears were gone. "You are a wicked woman. You take
away my life."

When Mrs. Roberts arrived Anna was nearly ready. Rosie was
carefully unsticking the photographs from the wall over the couch.
Anna watched, quiet, smiling at Mrs. Roberts, her eyes very blank.
"Shall I have my own room?" she asked Mrs. Roberts presently. The
woman liked the sound of Anna's cultivated British accent.

"Oh, yes!" she assured her, and was assiduous about carrying out
the suitcase, some sacks and boxes. Rosie watched them from the
door. Anna followed Mrs. Roberts to the car, holding herself
straight. Mrs. Roberts opened the door for her and carefully helped
her in. Anna was smiling her shy and fragile smile. She did not look
at Rosie anymore. Rosie with a heart like bitter stone scrubbed the
marks of tape from the wall where the pictures had hung, and then
she ate the orange Anna had left in the refrigerator.

SANDY BOUCHER

THE FIFTH GREAT DAY OF GOD

On the island of Mallorca, just off the unpaved road that leads from the village of Alcudia to the beach settlement of Mal-Pas, is an orchard and vegetable garden tended by an old woman. In Alcudia it is said that she remembers nothing—neither herself as a young girl nor the events of last week. The war, her wedding, the children she tended and loved—all have fallen from her like dead leaves from a tree. Yet she still exists, solid in her black dusty dress, her feet splayed and dry in cloth sandals; and in the shadow of her straw hat, brown eyes squint with an alertness neither interested nor indifferent, registering all about her.

The people in Alcudia murmur as they watch her pacing slowly in the street, speaking to no one. They do not understand her life without language, without a remembered time.

Beyond the orchard, a sheer cliff fronting the sea reddens before the falling sun. A stillness has settled on the trees. In the hut the old woman is busy placing the grapes in a basket against the cool stone wall. A black puppy lies near her, watching. She stoops beneath the low, smoke-blackened ceiling, and does not hear motor sounds from the road, footsteps across the yard.

A figure appears in the doorway, and the dog leaps up and yaps, his rangy body taut and straining against itself.

Are you . . . ? asks a hesitant voice, and the words are laid down in the old woman like a path leading back into brambles. Nuria Valentina Lizama de Colomer—her own full name that she has not heard in years, for the people in the village call her Tía Nuria if they address her at all. Who can he be to speak the name of a creature long abandoned?

She examines him, a square man with a bulge of flesh about his middle. His round face is young and flushed, and his eyes shine with moisture.

The dog falls silent under her warning hand, but remains rigid, his muzzle wrinkled up over his teeth.

Jorge, pleads the man. I am Jorge.

She crouches among the bags of potatoes, the peppers set out on a shelf, the baskets of grapes, the lumpy forms of shadow; and she watches him exactly as the dog watches him, with bright, wary eyes.

Awkwardly, the man turns and draws to him the young woman who has been standing behind him. She smiles down at the baby in her arms, looks up at the old woman shyly.

The old woman gazes at the child, whose sleeping face is round and placid as her own. Her lips open and she stares, fascinated. Then, seeing the mother's arms tighten about the baby's limp form, the old woman starts, shivering, and lowers her eyes to her rough twisted hands in her lap.

His voice constrained and low, the man is talking, but she does not hear the words, feels only his eagerness pressing unwanted against her, filling the space about her.

Now in the dark hut she lies staring upward. Her grandson has pitched a tent in the yard next to the dusty Citroen in which he arrived. The old woman feels in her bones the presence of the man and woman and child. The skin of her arms twitches, and it is as if a black shawl presses down over her bed, shutting out the high starry sky above the hut.

The murmured voices from the yard crawl like small animals over her skin. Fear makes her reach out in the darkness, and the dog pads to her side. But as her fingers touch his fur, a wisp of memory coils in her brain, faint inkling of muscle, bone and skin, the huddling of human creatures that was her life before. She draws away her hand and lies still, in agonized waiting for the night to take her.

But they told us in the village she was strange, the young woman says.

Jorge looks at his wife's face pale and blurred in the darkness of the tent. He shakes his head.

Perhaps in the morning . . . she goes on. She's a very old woman . . . maybe she doesn't yet understand who you are. . . .

He raises himself on one elbow to look at the baby asleep in its plastic traveling basket. Then he lies back to stare at the canvas roof. For a time he is silent, and she thinks he has gone to sleep. Then he says in a low, incredulous voice, She didn't seem to *care*.

Tomorrow, says his wife, hoping to comfort him. In the morning she'll be different.

For three days they camp in the yard, and the old woman rises each morning to chew on the stale bread that is her breakfast and light the fire under the huge blackened pot in the yard. She stands with her back toward the tent and cuts up potatoes to put in the pot. Then she empties a pan of scraps over the top bar of the pigs' pen, watching potatoes and bread crusts bounce on the rough hide of their backs. Going into the hut, she returns carrying her broad-brimmed hat, and having put it on her head above the single sparse braid of grey hair, she sets off in her rocking stride down the path to the vineyard. In all of this she does not look at the young woman kneeling over the kicking, naked baby or the man leaning against the fence breaking twigs with nervous fingers.

The dog, who would normally stay behind to guard the hut, goes with her down the path, running close against the hem of her skirt, whining now and then, and stays near her as she works in the field.

María-Celia, says the man, and his voice is jolted as he trips on the stones and ruts of the path. . . . My mother . . . when I was growing up . . . she was always sure you were still alive somewhere. . . .

He trails behind her as she goes between the rows of vines, finds the spot at which she stopped picking yesterday. She unfolds the bag of faded grey cloth and takes the knife from the pocket of her dress.

A light cool breeze comes from the sea, but the sun is very hot and the man has begun to sweat. She wanted to find you. But after they escaped across the mountains, they were in a camp for emigrés in southern France. After that they were very poor . . . and the babies . . . Joaquin and myself and Valentina and María-Montserrat . . . it wasn't possible. . . .

The old woman watches her hands at work. The brim of the hat hides his face from her, though she cannot help seeing from the corner of her eye his sturdy form in the sweat-stained white shirt, his hands helpless at his sides. She drops bunch after bunch of grapes into the bag and feels it grow heavy at her side.

Two years ago she died. She had been ill . . . had been ill . . . for a long time. Papa lives by himself now. On our way here I tried to find Uncle Joaquin in Barcelona . . . but he . . . there was no trace of him. . . .

Jorge stoops with the habitual carefulness of the city man concerned with his clothes, and leans against one of the stakes. After a time he lapses into silence, and his downturned face is grey-shadowed and discouraged. He has hoped, by saying the names, to draw from her a word, even a gesture, that would acknowledge him. But she moves down the row, snapping the grape stems, only her labored breathing breaking the silence, her back as impervious as the trunk of a tree.

He cannot know the panic rising in her, how she struggles not to hear the names. She who has learned to desire nothing now wishes with all her strength that he should go away. Her life that is sun and dark, the motion of her limbs, the smell of dust and leaves, she knows to be threatened. As if her movement were the grass soughing under the sea wind or the afternoon light driving shadow from the cliff. Between herself and this movement he tries to throw a net of names; he suffers there not ten feet away, while suffering for her is hard work in the heat, the chill of evening settling in her muscles, the pain sometimes in her chest. This is all. Only this moment as she forces the knife through the stringy stem, lifts the heaviness of grapes.

The dog lies in the short grass under the vines, his coat dappled with leaf shadows, his tongue lolling pink over his teeth. His eyes never leave her as she moves down the row. The dog responds somewhere in himself to what the man cannot know, and his hide twitches.

On the third night Jorge sits at the opening of the tent, holding the sleeping child. The trees, the hut, are black huddled masses before him. High above, stars hang in icy solitude.

We're going tomorrow, he says.

The young woman, lying inside the tent, reaches to lay her hand on his thigh.

I've tried everything. It's useless. He lowers his head, his face hardening. Crazy old woman. Crazy old . . . bitch.

For he expected an aged woman plump and smiling, in a room hung with relics and brittle photographs, who would weep when he spoke of her daughter, and afterwards clasp his hand in both her own and gaze at him in wonder. This picture he had held in his mind for years, until it became a recurrent dream from which he would awake smiling and comforted; as if in the night he had been taken to a good land where all was gentle, safe. At his mother's death he knew he would set about finding the woman of impassioned tenderness, whose life was somehow stronger, deeper than his own.

But he has found nothing of himself or his mother in this old woman. She is a stone, a tree, an animal. She does not hear him, and her eyes gaze stupid and flat at him. He stares at the black bulk of the hut, and feels himself, even with the warm limp bundle of the child in his arms, monstrously alone in the night, trapped in his present life, helpless in its smallness.

The old woman lies in deep exhaustion on her bed against the wall. She will not admit that she has heard the names, seen the baby kicking fat exuberant legs in the air, the young woman calling up an echo of something far down in her spine. Yet in sleep she is taken and rolls under a groundswell of cheeks lips hair thighs hands, all that was cherished and lost, all her dead emerging to moan and beckon. She does not know that as she sleeps the tears slide down her brown old cheeks, wetting her hair.

The noise of the retreating car has long ago died, and the morning is so still that she can hear the faint murmuring wash of the waves against the cliff, or perhaps it is the leaves brushing together in the breeze.

She is seated on the ground in the doorway of the hut. Head hung forward, hand motionless in her lap, she is lost to the light and shade, the odors of dirt and stone and leaves that were her mind's element, her own body that was no entity or age but only movement as unquestioned as the bending of a branch, the knowledge not of self but of the wind's direction, the sea's foreboding. She has been drawn from this into the creature Jorge sought.

Slowly she rises, brushing at her cheeks with a roughened hand, and goes to light the fire, to feed the pigs. But her brown face is wizened with regret, and she moves with the faltering steps of the very old.

Nuria Valentina Lizama de Colomer—returned, and heavy with the festering past. The people of Alcudia will come to love her soon, will speak of her fondly; when she comes to town they will inquire of her ailments, familiarly at last.

THE WOMAN | BURNING SONG

I knew love and I knew evil
woke to the burning song and the tree burning blind

—Muriel Rukeyser, "Night Feeding" (1935)

CHARLOTTE PERKINS GILMAN

THE YELLOW WALLPAPER

It is very seldom that mere ordinary people like John and myself secure ancestral halls for the summer.

A colonial mansion, a hereditary estate, I would say a haunted house, and reach the height of romantic felicity—but that would be asking too much of fate!

Still I will proudly declare that there is something queer about it.

Else, why should it be let so cheaply? And why have stood so long untenanted?

John laughs at me, of course, but one expects that in [him]. John is practical in the extreme. He has no patience with faith, an intense horror of superstition, and he scoffs openly at any talk of things not to be felt and seen and put down in figures.

John is a physician, and *perhaps*—(I would not say it to a living soul, of course, but this is dead paper and a great relief to my mind)—*perhaps* that is one reason I do not get well faster.

You see he does not believe I am sick! And what can one do?

If a physician of high standing, and one's own husband, assures friends and relatives that there is really nothing the matter with one but temporary nervous depression—a slight hysterical tendency—what is one to do?

My brother is also a physician, and also of high standing, and he says the same thing.

So I take phosphates or phosphites—whichever it is—and tonics, and journeys, and air, and exercise, and am absolutely forbidden to "work" until I am well again.

Personally, I disagree with their ideas.

Personally, I believe that congenial work, with excitement and change, would do me good.

But what is one to do?

I did write for a while in spite of them; but it *does* exhaust me a good deal—having to be so sly about it, or else meet with heavy opposition.

I sometimes fancy that in my condition if I had less opposition and more society and stimulus—but John says the very worst thing I can do is to think about my condition, and I confess it always makes me feel bad.

So I will let it alone and talk about the house.

The most beautiful place! It is quite alone, standing well back from the road, quite three miles from the village. It makes me think of English places that you read about, for there are hedges and walls and gates that lock, and lots of separate little houses for the gardeners and people.

There is a *delicious* garden! I never saw such a garden—large and shady, full of box-bordered paths, and lined with long grape-covered arbors with seats under them.

There were greenhouses, too, but they are all broken now.

There was some legal trouble, I believe, something about the heirs and coheirs; anyhow, the place has been empty for years.

That spoils my ghostliness, I am afraid, but I don't care—there is something strange about the house—I can feel it.

I even said so to John one moonlight evening, but he said what I felt was a draft, and shut the window.

I get unreasonably angry with John sometimes. I'm sure I never used to be so sensitive. I think it is due to this nervous condition.

But John says if I feel so I shall neglect proper self-control; so I take pains to control myself—before him, at least, and that makes me very tired.

I don't like our room a bit. I wanted one downstairs that opened on the piazza and had roses all over the window, and such pretty old-fashioned chintz hangings! But John would not hear of it.

He said there was only one window and not room for two beds, and no near room for him if he took another.

He is very careful and loving, and hardly lets me stir without special direction.

I have a schedule prescription for each hour in the day; he takes all care from me, and so I feel basely ungrateful not to value it more.

He said we came here solely on my account, that I was to have perfect rest and all the air I could get. "Your exercise depends on your strength, my dear," said he, "and your food somewhat on your appetite; but air you can absorb all the time." So we took the nursery at the top of the house.

It is a big, airy room, the whole floor nearly, with windows that look all ways, and air and sunshine galore. It was nursery first and then playroom and gymnasium, I should judge; for the windows are barred for little children, and there are rings and things in the walls.

The paint and paper look as if a boys' school had used it. It is stripped off—the paper—in great patches all around the head of my bed, about as far as I can reach, and in a great place on the other side of the room low down. I never saw a worse paper in my life.

One of those sprawling flamboyant patterns committing every artistic sin.

It is dull enough to confuse the eye in following, pronounced enough constantly to irritate and provoke study, and when you follow the lame uncertain curves for a little distance they suddenly commit suicide—plunge off at outrageous angles, destroy themselves in unheard of contradictions.

The color is repellant, almost revolting; a smoldering unclean yellow, strangely faded by the slow-turning sunlight.

It is a dull yet lurid orange in some places, a sickly sulphur tint in others.

No wonder the children hated it! I should hate it myself if I had to live in this room long.

There comes John, and I must put this away—he hates to have me write a word.

We have been here two weeks, and I haven't felt like writing before, since that first day.

I am sitting by the window now, up in this atrocious nursery, and there is nothing to hinder my writing as much as I please, save lack of strength.

John is away all day, and even some nights when his cases are serious.

I am glad my case is not serious!

But these nervous troubles are dreadfully depressing.

John does not know how much I really suffer. He knows there is no *reason* to suffer, and that satisfies him.

Of course it is only nervousness. It does weigh on me so not to do my duty in any way!

I meant to be such a help to John, such a real rest and comfort, and here I am a comparative burden already!

Nobody would believe what an effort it is to do what little I am able—to dress and entertain, and order things.

It is fortunate Mary is so good with the baby. Such a dear baby!

And yet I *cannot* be with him, it makes me so nervous.

I suppose John never was nervous in his life. He laughs at me so about this wallpaper!

At first he meant to repaper the room, but afterwards he said that I was letting it get the better of me, and that nothing was worse for a nervous patient than to give way to such fancies.

He said that after the wallpaper was changed it would be the heavy bedstead, and then the barred windows, and then that gate at the head of the stairs, and so on.

"You know the place is doing you good," he said, "and really, dear, I don't care to renovate the house just for a three-months' rental."

"Then do let us go downstairs," I said, "there are such pretty rooms there."

Then he took me in his arms and called me a blessed little goose, and said he would go down cellar, if I wished, and have it whitewashed into the bargain.

But he is right enough about the beds and windows and things.

It is an airy and comfortable room as any one need wish, and, of course, I would not be so silly as to make him uncomfortable just for a whim.

I'm really getting quite fond of the big room, all but that horrid paper.

Out of one window I can see the garden, those mysterious deep-shaded arbors, the riotous old-fashioned flowers, and bushes and gnarly trees.

Out of another I get a lovely view of the bay and a little private wharf belonging to the estate. There is a beautiful shaded lane that runs down there from the house. I always fancy I see people walking in these numerous paths and arbors, but John has cautioned me not to give way to fancy in the least. He says that with my imaginative power and habit of story-making, a nervous weakness like mine is sure to lead to all manner of excited fancies, and that I ought to use my will and good sense to check the tendency. So I try.

I think sometimes that if I were only well enough to write a little it would relieve the press of ideas and rest me.

But I find I get pretty tired when I try.

It is so discouraging not to have any advice and companionship about my work. When I get really well, John says we will ask Cousin Henry and Julia down for a long visit; but he says he would as soon put fireworks in my pillowcase as to let me have those stimulating people about now.

I wish I could get well faster.

But I must not think about that. This paper looks to me as if it *knew* what a vicious influence it had!

There is a recurrent spot where the pattern lolls like a broken neck and two bulbous eyes stare at you upside down.

I get positively angry with the impertinence of it and the everlastingness. Up and down and sideways they crawl, and those absurd, unblinking eyes are everywhere. There is one place where two breadths didn't match, and the eyes go all up and down the line, one a little higher than the other.

I never saw so much expression in an inanimate thing before, and we all know how much expression they have! I used to lie awake as a child and get more entertainment and terror out of blank walls and plain furniture than most children could find in a toy store.

I remember what a kindly wink the knobs of our big, old bureau used to have, and there was one chair that always seemed like a strong friend.

I used to feel that if any of the other things looked too fierce I could always hop into that chair and be safe.

The furniture in this room is no worse than inharmonious, however, for we had to bring it all from downstairs. I suppose when this was used as a playroom they had to take the nursery things out, and no wonder! I never saw such ravages as the children have made here.

The wallpaper, as I said before, is torn off in spots, and it sticketh closer than a brother—they must have had perseverance as well as hatred.

Then the floor is scratched and gouged and splintered, the plaster itself is dug out here and there, and this great heavy bed which is all we found in the room, looks as if it had been through the wars.

But I don't mind it a bit—only the paper.

There comes John's sister. Such a dear girl as she is, and so careful of me! I must not let her find me writing.

She is a perfect and enthusiastic housekeeper, and hopes for no better profession. I verily believe she thinks it is the writing which made me sick!

But I can write when she is out, and see her a long way off from these windows.

There is one that commands the road, a lovely shaded winding road, and one that just looks off over the country. A lovely country, too, full of great elms and velvet meadows.

This wallpaper has a kind of subpattern in a different shade, a particularly irritating one, for you can only see it in certain lights, and not clearly then.

But in the places where it isn't faded and where the sun is just so—I can see a strange, provoking, formless sort of figure, that seems to skulk about behind that silly and conspicuous front design.

There's sister on the stairs!

Well, the Fourth of July is over! The people are all gone and I am tired out. John thought it might do me good to see a little company, so we just had mother and Nellie and the children down for a week.

Of course I didn't do a thing. Jennie sees to everything now.

But it tired me all the same.

John says if I don't pick up faster he shall send me to Weir Mitchell in the fall.

But I don't want to go there at all. I had a friend who was in his hands once, and she says he is just like John and my brother, only more so!

Besides, it is such an undertaking to go so far.

I don't feel as if it was worth while to turn my hand over for anything, and I'm getting dreadfully fretful and querulous.

I cry at nothing, and cry most of the time.

Of course I don't when John is here, or anybody else, but when I am alone.

And I am alone a good deal just now. John is kept in town very often by serious cases, and Jennie is good and lets me alone when I want her to.

So I walk a little in the garden or down that lovely lane, sit on the porch under the roses, and lie down up here a good deal.

I'm getting really fond of the room in spite of the wallpaper. Perhaps *because* of the wallpaper.

It dwells in my mind so!

I lie here on this great immovable bed—it is nailed down, I believe—and follow that pattern about by the hour. It is as good as gymnastics, I assure you. I start, we'll say, at the bottom, down in the corner over there where it has not been touched, and I determine for the thousandth time that I *will* follow that pointless pattern to some sort of a conclusion.

I know a little of the principle of design, and I know this thing was not arranged on any laws of radiation, or alternation, or repetition, or symmetry, or anything else that I ever heard of.

It is repeated, of course, by the breadths, but not otherwise.

Looked at in one way each breadth stands alone, the bloated curves and flourishes—a kind of "debased Romanesque" with delirium tremens—go waddling up and down in isolated columns of fatuity.

But, on the other hand, they connect diagonally, and the sprawling outlines run off in great slanting waves of optic horror, like a lot of wallowing seaweeds in full chase.

The whole thing goes horizontally, too, at least it seems so, and I exhaust myself trying to distinguish the order of its going in that direction.

They have used a horizontal breadth for a frieze, and that adds wonderfully to the confusion.

There is one end of the room where it is almost intact, and there, when the crosslights fade and the low sun shines directly upon it, I can almost fancy radiation after all—the interminable grotesques seem to form around a common center and rush off in headlong plunges of equal distraction.

It makes me tired to follow it. I will take a nap I guess.

I don't know why I should write this.

I don't want to.

I don't feel able.

And I know John would think it absurd. But I *must* say what I feel and think in some way—it is such a relief!

But the effort is getting to be greater than the relief.

Half the time now I am awfully lazy, and lie down ever so much.

John says I mustn't lose my strength, and has me take cod liver oil and lots of tonics and things, to say nothing of ale and wine and rare meat.

Dear John! He loves me very dearly, and hates to have me sick. I tried to have a real earnest reasonable talk with him the other day, and tell him how I wish he would let me go and make a visit to Cousin Henry and Julia.

But he said I wasn't able to go, nor able to stand it after I got there; and I did not make out a very good case for myself, for I was crying before I had finished.

It is getting to be a great effort for me to think straight. Just this nervous weakness I suppose.

And dear John gathered me up in his arms, and just carried me upstairs and laid me on the bed, and sat by me and read to me till it tired my head.

He said I was his darling and his comfort and all he had, and that I must take care of myself for his sake, and keep well.

He says no one but myself can help me out of it, that I must use my will and self-control and not let any silly fancies run away with me.

There's one comfort, the baby is well and happy, and does not have to occupy this nursery with the horrid wallpaper.

If we had not used it, that blessed child would have! What a fortunate escape! Why, I wouldn't have a child of mine, an impressionable little thing, live in such a room for worlds.

I never thought of it before, but it is lucky that John kept me here after all, I can stand it so much easier than a baby, you see.

Of course I never mention it to them anymore—I am too wise—but I keep watch for it all the same.

There are things in that paper that nobody knows but me, or ever will.

Behind that outside pattern the dim shapes get clearer every day.

It is always the same shape, only very numerous.

And it is like a woman stooping down and creeping about behind that pattern. I don't like it a bit. I wonder—I begin to think—I wish John would take me away from here!

It is so hard to talk with John about my case, because he is so wise, and because he loves me so.

But I tried it last night.

It was moonlight. The moon shines in all around just as the sun does.

I hate to see it sometimes, it creeps so slowly, and always comes in by one window or another.

John was asleep and I hated to waken him, so I kept still and watched the moonlight on that undulating wallpaper till I felt creepy.

The faint figure behind seemed to shake the pattern, just as if she wanted to get out.

I got up softly and went to feel and see if the paper *did* move, and when I came back John was awake.

"What is it, little girl?" he said. "Don't go walking about like that—you'll get cold."

I thought it was a good time to talk so I told him that I really was not gaining here, and that I wished he would take me away.

"Why darling!" said he, "our lease will be up in three weeks, and I can't see how to leave before.

"The repairs are not done at home, and I cannot possibly leave town just now. Of course if you were in any danger, I could and would, but you really are better, dear, whether you can see it or not. I am a doctor, dear, and I know. You are gaining flesh and color, your appetite is better, I feel really much easier about you."

"I don't weigh a bit more," said I, "nor as much; and my appetite may be better in the evening when you are here, but it is worse in the morning when you are away!"

"Bless her little heart!" said he with a big hug, "she shall be as sick as she pleases! But now let's improve the shining hours by going to sleep, and talk about it in the morning!"

"And you won't go away?" I asked gloomily.

"Why, how can I, dear? It is only three weeks more and then we will take a nice little trip of a few days while Jennie is getting the house ready. Really, dear, you are better!"

"Better in body perhaps—" I began, and stopped short, for he sat up straight and looked at me with such a stern, reproachful look that I could not say another word.

"My darling," said he, "I beg of you, for my sake and for our child's sake, as well as for your own, that you will never for one instant let that idea enter your mind! There is nothing so dangerous, so fascinating, to a temperament like yours. It is a false and foolish fancy. Can you not trust me as a physician when I tell you so?"

So of course I said no more on that score, and we went to sleep before long. He thought I was asleep first, but I wasn't, and lay there for hours trying to decide whether that front pattern and the back pattern really did move together or separately.

On a pattern like this, by daylight, there is a lack of sequence, a defiance of law, that is a constant irritant to a normal mind.

The color is hideous enough, and unreliable enough, and infuriating enough, but the pattern is torturing.

You think you have mastered it, but just as you get well underway in following, it turns a back-somersault and there you are. It slaps you in the face, knocks you down, and tramples upon you. It is like a bad dream.

The outside pattern is a florid arabesque, reminding one of a fungus. If you can imagine a toadstool in joints, an interminable string of toadstools, budding and sprouting in endless convolutions —why, that is something like it.

That is, sometimes!

There is one marked peculiarity about this paper, a thing nobody seems to notice but myself, and that is that it changes as the light changes.

When the sun shoots in through the east window—I always watch for that first, long, straight ray—it changes so quickly that I never can quite believe it.

That is why I watch it always.

By moonlight—the moon shines in all night when there is a moon—I wouldn't know it was the same paper.

At night in any kind of light, in twilight, candlelight, lamplight, and worst of all by moonlight, it becomes bars! The outside pattern I mean, and the woman behind it is as plain as can be.

I didn't realize for a long time what the thing was that showed behind, that dim subpattern, but now I am quite sure it is a woman.

By daylight she is subdued, quiet. I fancy it is the pattern that keeps her so still. It is so puzzling. It keeps me quiet by the hour.

I lie down ever so much now. John says it is good for me, and to sleep all I can.

Indeed he started the habit by making me lie down for an hour after each meal.

It is a very bad habit I am convinced, for you see I don't sleep.

And that cultivates deceit, for I don't tell them I'm awake—O, no!

The fact is I am getting a little afraid of John.

He seems very queer sometimes, and even Jennie has an inexplicable look.

It strikes me occasionally, just as a scientific hypothesis, that perhaps it is the paper!

I have watched John when he did not know I was looking, and come into the room suddenly on the most innocent excuses, and I've caught him several times *looking at the paper!* And Jennie too, I caught Jennie with her hand on it once.

She didn't know I was in the room, and when I asked her in a quiet, a very quiet voice, with the most restrained manner possible, what she was doing with the paper—she turned around as if she had been caught stealing, and looked quite angry—asked me why I should frighten her so!

Then she said that the paper stained everything it touched, that she had found yellow smooches on all my clothes and John's, and she wished we would be more careful!

Did not that sound innocent? But I know she was studying that pattern, and I am determined that nobody shall find it out but myself!

Life is very much more exciting now than it used to be. You see, I have something more to expect, to look forward to, to watch. I really do eat better, and am more quiet than I was.

John is so pleased to see me improve! He laughed a little the other day, and said I seemed to be flourishing in spite of my wallpaper.

I turned it off with a laugh. I had no intention of telling him it was *because* of the wallpaper—he would make fun of me. He might even want to take me away.

I don't want to leave now until I have found it out. There is a week more, and I think that will be enough.

I'm feeling ever so much better! I don't sleep much at night, for it is so interesting to watch developments; but I sleep a good deal in the daytime.

In the daytime it is tiresome and perplexing.

There are always new shoots on the fungus, and new shades of yellow all over it. I cannot keep count of them, though I have tried conscientiously.

It is the strangest yellow, that wallpaper! It makes me think of all the yellow things I ever saw—not beautiful ones like buttercups, but old foul, bad yellow things.

But there is something else about that paper—the smell! I noticed it the moment we came into the room, but with so much air and sun it was not bad. Now we have had a week of fog and rain, and whether the windows are open or not, the smell is here.

It creeps all over the house.

I find it hovering in the dining room, skulking in the parlor, hiding in the hall, lying in wait for me on the stairs.

It gets into my hair.

Even when I go to ride, if I turn my head suddenly and surprise it—there is that smell!

Such a peculiar odor, too! I have spent hours in trying to analyze it, to find what it smelled like.

It is not bad—at first, and very gentle, but quite the subtlest, most enduring odor I ever met.

In this damp weather it is awful, I wake up in the night and find it hanging over me.

It used to disturb me at first. I thought seriously of burning the house—to reach the smell.

But now I am used to it. The only thing I can think of that it is like is the *color* of the paper! A yellow smell.

There is a very funny mark on this wall, low down, near the mopboard. A streak that runs round the room. It goes behind every piece of furniture, except the bed, a long, straight, even *smooch*, as if it had been rubbed over and over.

I wonder how it was done and who did it, and what they did it for. Round and round and round—round and round and round—it makes me dizzy!

I really have discovered something at last.

Through watching so much at night, when it changes so, I have finally found out.

The front pattern *does* move—and no wonder! The woman behind shakes it!

Sometimes I think there are a great many women behind, and sometimes only one, and she crawls around fast, and her crawling shakes it all over.

Then in the very bright spots she keeps still, and in the very shady spots she just takes hold of the bars and shakes them hard.

And she is all the time trying to climb through. But nobody could climb through that pattern—it strangles so; I think that is why it has so many heads.

They get through, and then the pattern strangles them off and turns them upside down, and makes their eyes white!

If those heads were covered or taken off it would not be half so bad.

I think that woman gets out in the daytime!

And I'll tell you why—privately—I've seen her!

I can see her out of every one of my windows!

It is the same woman, I know, for she is always creeping, and most women do not creep by daylight.

I see her in that long shaded lane, creeping up and down, I see her in those dark grape arbors, creeping all around the garden.

I see her on that long road under the trees, creeping along, and when a carriage comes she hides under the blackberry vines.

I don't blame her a bit. It must be very humiliating to be caught creeping by daylight!

I always lock the door when I creep by daylight. I can't do it at night, for I know John would suspect something at once.

And John is so queer now, that I don't want to irritate him. I wish he would take another room! Besides, I don't want anybody to get that woman out at night but myself.

I often wonder if I could see her out of all the windows at once.

But, turn as fast as I can, I can only see out of one at one time.

And though I always see her, she *may* be able to creep faster than I can turn!

I have watched her sometimes away off in the open country, creeping as fast as a cloud shadow in a high wind.

If only that top pattern could be gotten off from the under one! I mean to try it, little by little.

I have found out another funny thing, but I shan't tell it this time! It does not do to trust people too much.

There are only two more days to get this paper off, and I believe John is beginning to notice. I don't like the look in his eyes.

And I heard him ask Jennie a lot of professional questions about me. She had a very good report to give.

She said I slept a good deal in the daytime.

John knows I don't sleep very well at night, for all I'm so quiet!

He asked me all sorts of questions, too, and pretended to be very loving and kind.

As if I couldn't see through him!

Still, I don't wonder he acts so, sleeping under this paper for three months.

It only interests me, but I feel sure John and Jennie are secretly affected by it.

Hurrah! This is the last day, but it is enough. John is to stay in town overnight, and won't be out until this evening.

Jennie wanted to sleep with me—the sly thing! But I told her I should undoubtedly rest better for a night all alone.

That was clever, for really I wasn't alone a bit! As soon as it was moonlight and that poor thing began to crawl and shake the pattern, I got up and ran to help her.

I pulled and she shook, I shook and she pulled, and before morning we had peeled off yards of that paper.

A strip about as high as my head and half around the room.

And then when the sun came and that awful pattern began to laugh at me, I declared I would finish it today!

We go away tomorrow, and they are moving all my furniture down again to leave things as they were before.

Jennie looked at the wall in amazement, but I told her merrily that I did it out of pure spite at the vicious thing.

She laughed and said she wouldn't mind doing it herself, but I must not get tired.

How she betrayed herself that time!

But I am here, and no person touches this paper but Me—not *alive!*

She tried to get me out of the room—it was too patent! But I said it was so quiet and empty and clean now that I believed I would lie down again and sleep all I could; and not to wake me even for dinner—I would call when I woke.

So now she is gone, and the servants are gone, and the things are gone, and there is nothing left but that great bedstead nailed down, with the canvas mattress we found on it.

We shall sleep downstairs tonight, and take the boat home tomorrow.

I quite enjoy the room, now it is bare again.

How those children did tear about here!

This bedstead is fairly gnawed!

But I must get to work.

I have locked the door and thrown the key down into the front path.

I don't want to go out, and I don't want to have anybody come in, till John comes.

I want to astonish him.

I've got a rope up here that even Jennie did not find. If that woman does get out, and tries to get away, I can tie her!

But I forgot I could not reach far without anything to stand on! This bed will *not* move!

I tried to lift and push it until I was lame, and then I got so angry I bit off a little piece at one corner—but it hurt my teeth.

Then I peeled off all the paper I could reach standing on the floor. It sticks horribly and the pattern just enjoys it! All those strangled heads and bulbous eyes and waddling fungus growths just shriek with derision!

I am getting angry enough to do something desperate. To jump out of the window would be admirable exercise, but the bars are too strong even to try.

Besides I wouldn't do it. Of course not. I know well enough that a step like that is improper and might be misconstrued.

I don't like to *look* out of the windows even—there are so many of those creeping women, and they creep so fast.

I wonder if they all come out of that wallpaper as I did?

But I am securely fastened now by my well-hidden rope—you don't get *me* out in the road there!

I suppose I shall have to get back behind the pattern when it comes night, and that is hard!

It is so pleasant to be out in this great room and creep around as I please!

I don't want to go outside. I won't, even if Jennie asks me to.

For outside you have to creep on the ground, and everything is green instead of yellow.

But here I can creep smoothly on the floor, and my shoulder just fits in that long smooch around the wall, so I cannot lose my way.

Why there's John at the door!

It is no use, young man, you can't open it!

How he does call and pound!

Now he's crying for an ax.

It would be a shame to break down that beautiful door!

"John dear!" said I in the gentlest voice, "the key is down by the front steps, under a plantain leaf!"

That silenced him for a few moments.

Then he said, very quietly indeed, "Open the door, my darling!"

"I can't," said I. "The key is down by the front door under a plantain leaf!"

And then I said it again, several times, very gently and slowly, and said it so often that he had to go and see, and he got it of course, and came in. He stopped short by the door.

"What is the matter?" he cried. "For God's sake, what are you doing!"

I kept on creeping just the same, but I looked at him over my shoulder.

"I've got out at last," said I, "in spite of you and Jennie. And I've pulled off most of the paper, so you can't put me back!"

Now why should that man have fainted? But he did, and right across my path by the wall, so that I had to creep over him every time!

KATHERINE MANSFIELD

A CUP OF TEA

Rosemary Fell was not exactly beautiful. No, you couldn't have called her beautiful. Pretty? Well, if you took her to pieces . . . But why be so cruel as to take anyone to pieces? She was young, brilliant, extremely modern, exquisitely well dressed, amazingly well read in the newest of the new books, and her parties were the most delicious mixture of the really important people and . . . artists—quaint creatures, discoveries of hers, some of them too terrifying for words, but others quite presentable and amusing.

Rosemary had been married two years. She had a duck of a boy. No, not Peter—Michael. And her husband absolutely adored her. They were rich, really rich, not just comfortably well off, which is odious and stuffy and sounds like one's grandparents. But if Rosemary wanted to shop she would go to Paris as you and I would go to Bond Street. If she wanted to buy flowers, the car pulled up at that perfect shop in Regent Street, and Rosemary inside the shop just gazed in her dazzled, rather exotic way, and said: "I want those and those and those. Give me four bunches of those. And that jar of roses. Yes, I'll have all the roses in the jar. No, no lilac. I hate lilac. It's got no shape." The attendant bowed and put the lilac out of sight, as though this was only too true; lilac was dreadfully shapeless. "Give me those stumpy little tulips. Those red and white ones." And she was followed to the car by a thin shopgirl staggering under an immense white paper armful that looked like a baby in long clothes. . . .

One winter afternoon she had been buying something in a little antique shop in Curzon Street. It was a shop she liked. For one thing, one usually had it to oneself. And then the man who kept it was ridiculously fond of serving her. He beamed whenever she came in. He clasped his hands; he was so gratified he could scarcely speak. Flattery, of course. All the same, there was something . . .

"You see, madam," he would explain in his low respectful tones, "I love my things. I would rather not part with them than sell them to someone who does not appreciate them, who has not that fine feeling which is so rare. . . ." And, breathing deeply, he unrolled a tiny square of blue velvet and pressed it on the glass counter with his pale fingertips.

Today it was a little box. He had been keeping it for her. He had shown it to nobody as yet. An exquisite little enamel box with a glaze so fine it looked as though it had been baked in cream. On the lid a minute creature stood under a flowery tree, and a more minute creature still had her arms around his neck. Her hat, really no bigger than a geranium petal, hung from a branch; it had green ribbons. And there was a pink cloud like a watchful cherub floating above their heads. Rosemary took her hands out of her long gloves. She always took off her gloves to examine such things. Yes, she liked it very much. She loved it; it was a great duck. She must have it. And, turning the creamy box, opening and shutting it, she couldn't help noticing how charming her hands were against the blue velvet. The shopman, in some dim cavern of his mind, may have dared to think so too. For he took a pencil, leant over the counter, and his pale bloodless fingers crept timidly towards those rosy, flashing ones, as he murmured gently: "If I may venture to point out to madam, the flowers on the little lady's bodice."

"Charming!" Rosemary admired the flowers. But what was the price? For a moment the shopman did not seem to hear. Then a murmur reached her. "Twenty-eight guineas, madame."

"Twenty-eight guineas." Rosemary gave no sign. She laid the little box down; she buttoned her gloves again. Twenty-eight guineas. Even if one is rich . . . She looked vague. She stared at a plump teakettle like a plump hen above the shopman's head, and her voice was dreamy as she answered: "Well, keep it for me—will you? I'll . . ."

But the shopman had already bowed as though keeping it for her was all any human being could ask. He would be willing, of course, to keep it for her forever.

The discreet door shut with a click. She was outside on the step, gazing at the winter afternoon. Rain was falling, and with the rain it seemed the dark came too, spinning down like ashes. There was a cold bitter taste in the air, and the new-lighted lamps looked sad. Sad were the lights in the houses opposite. Dimly they burned as if regretting something. And people hurried by, hidden under their hateful umbrellas. Rosemary felt a strange pang. She pressed her muff to her breast; she wished she had the little box, too, to cling to. Of course, the car was there. She'd only to cross the pavement. But still she waited. There are moments, horrible moments in life, when one emerges from shelter and looks out, and it's awful. One oughtn't to give way to them. One ought to go home and have an extra-special tea. But at the very instant of thinking that, a young girl, thin, dark, shadowy—where had she come from?—was standing at Rosemary's elbow and a voice like a sigh, almost like a sob, breathed: "Madame, may I speak to you a moment?"

"Speak to me?" Rosemary turned. She saw a little battered creature with enormous eyes, someone quite young, no older than herself, who clutched at her coat collar with reddened hands, and shivered as though she had just come out of the water.

"M-madame," stammered the voice. "Would you let me have the price of a cup of tea?"

"A cup of tea?" There was something simple, sincere in that voice; it wasn't in the least the voice of a beggar. "Then have you no money at all?" asked Rosemary.

"None, madam," came the answer.

"How extraordinary!" Rosemary peered through the dusk, and the girl gazed back at her. How more than extraordinary! And suddenly it seemed to Rosemary such an adventure. It was like something out of a novel by Dostoevski, this meeting in the dusk. Supposing she took the girl home? Supposing she did do one of those things she was always reading about or seeing on the stage, what would happen? It would be thrilling. And she heard herself saying afterwards to the amazement of her friends: "I simply took her home with me," as she stepped forward and said to that dim person beside her: "Come home to tea with me."

The girl drew back startled. She even stopped shivering for a moment. Rosemary put out a hand and touched her arm. "I mean it," she said, smiling. And she felt how simple and kind her smile was. "Why won't you? Come home with me now in my car and have tea."

"You—you don't mean it, madam," said the girl, and there was pain in her voice.

"But I do," cried Rosemary. "I want you to. To please me. Come along."

The girl put her fingers to her lips and her eyes devoured Rosemary. "You're—you're not taking me to the police station?" she stammered.

"The police station!" Rosemary laughed out. "Why should I be so cruel? No, I only want to make you warm and to hear—anything you care to tell me."

Hungry people are easily led. The footman held the door of the car open, and a moment later they were skimming through the dusk.

"There!" said Rosemary. She had a feeling of triumph as she slipped her hand through the velvet strap. She could have said, "Now I've got you," as she gazed at the little captive she had netted. But of course she meant it kindly. Oh, more than kindly. She was going to prove to this girl that—wonderful things did happen in life, that—fairy godmothers were real, that—rich people had hearts, and that women *were* sisters. She turned impulsively, saying: "Don't be frightened. After all, why shouldn't you come back with me? We're both women. If I'm the more fortunate, you ought to expect . . ."

But happily at that moment, for she didn't know how the sentence was going to end, the car stopped. The bell was rung, the door opened, and with a charming, protecting, almost embracing movement, Rosemary drew the other into the hall. Warmth, softness, light, a sweet scent, all those things so familiar to her she never even thought about them, she watched that other receive. It was fascinating. She was like the little rich girl in her nursery with all the cupboards to open, all the boxes to unpack.

"Come, come upstairs," said Rosemary, longing to begin to be generous. "Come up to my room." And, besides, she wanted to spare this poor little thing from being stared at by the servants; she decided as they mounted the stairs she would not even ring for Jeanne, but take off her things by herself. The great thing was to be natural!

And "There!" cried Rosemary again, as they reached her beautiful big bedroom with the curtains drawn, the fire leaping on her wonderful lacquer furniture, her gold cushions and the primrose and blue rugs.

The girl stood just inside the door; she seemed dazed. But Rosemary didn't mind that.

"Come and sit down," she cried, dragging her big chair up to the fire, "in this comfy chair. Come and get warm. You look so dreadfully cold."

"I daren't, madam," said the girl, and she edged backwards.

"Oh, please"—Rosemary ran forward—"you mustn't be frightened, you mustn't, really. Sit down, and when I've taken off my things we shall go into the next room and have tea and be cosy. Why are you afraid?" And gently she half pushed the thin figure into its deep cradle.

But there was no answer. The girl stayed just as she had been put, with her hands by her sides and her mouth slightly open. To be quite sincere, she looked rather stupid. But Rosemary wouldn't acknowledge it. She leant over her, saying: "Won't you take off your hat? Your pretty hair is all wet. And one is so much more comfortable without a hat, isn't one?"

There was a whisper that sounded like "Very good, madam," and the crushed hat was taken off.

"Let me help you off with your coat, too," said Rosemary.

The girl stood up. But she held on to the chair with one hand and let Rosemary pull. It was quite an effort. The other scarcely helped her at all. She seemed to stagger like a child, and the thought came and went through Rosemary's mind that if people wanted helping they must respond a little, just a little, otherwise it became very difficult indeed. And what was she to do with the coat now? She left it on the floor, and the hat too. She was just going to take a cigarette off the mantelpiece when the girl said quickly, but so lightly and strangely: "I'm very sorry, madam, but I'm going to faint. I shall go off, madam, if I don't have something."

"Good heavens, how thoughtless I am!" Rosemary rushed to the bell.

"Tea! Tea at once! And some brandy immediately!"

The maid was gone again, but the girl almost cried out. "No, I don't want no brandy. I never drink brandy. It's a cup of tea I want, madam." And she burst into tears.

It was a terrible and fascinating moment. Rosemary knelt beside her chair.

"Don't cry, poor little thing," she said. "Don't cry." And she gave the other her lace handkerchief. She really was touched beyond words. She put her arm round those thin, birdlike shoulders.

Now at last the other forgot to be shy, forgot everything except that they were both women, and gasped out: "I can't go on no longer like this. I can't bear it. I shall do away with myself. I can't bear no more."

"You shan't have to. I'll look after you. Don't cry anymore. Don't you see what a good thing it was that you met me? We'll have tea and you'll tell me everything. And I shall arrange something. I promise. *Do* stop crying. It's so exhausting. Please!"

The other did stop just in time for Rosemary to get up before the tea came. She had the table placed between them. She plied the poor little creature with everything, all the sandwiches, all the bread and butter, and every time her cup was empty she filled it with tea, cream, and sugar. People always said sugar was so nourishing. As for herself she didn't eat; she smoked and looked away tactfully so that the other should not be shy.

And really the effect of that slight meal was marvelous. When the tea table was carried away a new being, a light, frail creature with tangled hair, dark lips, deep, lighted eyes, lay back in the big chair in a kind of sweet languor, looking at the blaze. Rosemary lit a fresh cigarette; it was time to begin.

"And when did you have your last meal?" she asked softly.

But at that moment the door handle turned.

"Rosemary, may I come in?" It was Philip.

"Of course."

He came in. "Oh, I'm so sorry," he said, and stopped and stared.

"It's quite all right," said Rosemary smiling. "This is my friend, Miss—"

"Smith, madam," said the languid figure, who was strangely still and unafraid.

"Smith," said Rosemary. "We are going to have a little talk."

"Oh, yes," said Philip. "Quite," and his eye caught sight of the coat and hat on the floor. He came over to the fire and turned his back to it. "It's a beastly afternoon," he said curiously, still looking at that listless figure, looking at its hands and boots, and then at Rosemary again.

"Yes, isn't it?" said Rosemary enthusiastically. "Vile."

Philip smiled his charming smile. "As a matter of fact," said he, "I wanted you to come into the library for a moment. Would you? Will Miss Smith excuse us?"

The big eyes were raised to him, but Rosemary answered for her. "Of course she will." And they went out of the room together.

"I say," said Philip, when they were alone. "Explain. Who is she? What does it all mean?"

Rosemary, laughing, leaned against the door and said: "I picked her up in Curzon Street. Really. She's a real pickup. She asked me for the price of a cup of tea, and I brought her home with me."

"But what on earth are you going to do with her?" cried Philip.

"Be nice to her," said Rosemary quickly. "Be frightfully nice to her. Look after her. I don't know how. We haven't talked yet. But show her—treat her—make her feel—"

"My darling girl," said Philip, "you're quite mad, you know. It simply can't be done."

"I knew you'd say that," retorted Rosemary. "Why not? I want to. Isn't that a reason? And besides, one's always reading about these things. I decided—"

"But," said Philip slowly, and he cut the end of a cigar, "she's so astonishingly pretty."

"Pretty?" Rosemary was so surprised that she blushed. "Do you think so? I—I hadn't thought about it."

"Good Lord!" Philip struck a match. "She's absolutely lovely. Look again, my child. I was bowled over when I came into your room just now. However . . . I think you're making a ghastly mistake. Sorry, darling, if I'm crude and all that. But let me know if Miss Smith is going to dine with us in time for me to look up *The Milliner's Gazette*."

"You absurd creature!" said Rosemary, and she went out of the library, but not back to her bedroom. She went to her writing room and sat down at her desk. Pretty! Absolutely lovely! Bowled over! Her heart beat like a heavy bell. Pretty! Lovely! She drew her checkbook towards her. But no, checks would be no use, of course. She opened a drawer and took out five pound notes, looked at them, put two back, and holding the three squeezed in her hand, she went back to her bedroom.

Half an hour later Philip was still in the library, when Rosemary came in.

"I only wanted to tell you," said she, and she leaned against the door again and looked at him with her dazzled exotic gaze, "Miss Smith won't dine with us tonight."

Philip put down the paper. "Oh, what's happened? Previous engagement?"

Rosemary came over and sat down on his knee. "She insisted on going," said she, "so I gave the poor little thing a present of money. I couldn't keep her against her will, could I?" she added softly.

Rosemary had just done her hair, darkened her eyes a little, and put on her pearls. She put up her hands and touched Philip's cheeks.

"Do you like me?" said she, and her tone, sweet, husky, troubled him.

"I like you awfully," he said, and he held her tighter. "Kiss me."

There was a pause.

Then Rosemary said dreamily, "I saw a fascinating little box today. It cost twenty-eight guineas. May I have it?"

Philip jumped her on his knee. "You may, little wasteful one," said he.

But that was not really what Rosemary wanted to say.

"Philip," she whispered, and she pressed his head against her bosom, "am I *pretty*?"

EUDORA WELTY

A PIECE OF NEWS

She had been out in the rain. She stood in front of the cabin fireplace, her legs wide apart, bending over, shaking her wet yellow head crossly, like a cat reproaching itself for not knowing better. She was talking to herself—only a small fluttering sound, hard to lay hold of in the sparsity of the room.

"The pouring-down rain, the pouring-down rain"—was that what she was saying over and over, like a song? She stood turning in little quarter turns to dry herself, her head bent forward and the yellow hair hanging out streaming and tangled. She was holding her skirt primly out to draw the warmth in.

Then, quite rosy, she walked over to the table and picked up a little bundle. It was a sack of coffee, marked "Sample" in red letters, which she unwrapped from a wet newspaper. But she handled it tenderly.

"Why, how come he wrapped it in a newspaper!" she said, catching her breath, looking from one hand to the other. She must have been lonesome and slow all her life, the way things would take her by surprise.

She set the coffee on the table, just in the center. Then she dragged the newspaper by one corner in a dreamy walk across the floor, spread it all out, and lay down full length on top of it in front of the fire. Her little song about the rain, her cries of surprise, had been only a preliminary, only playful pouting with which she amused herself when she was alone. She was pleased with herself now. As she sprawled close to the fire, her hair began to slide out of its damp tangles and hung all displayed down her back like a piece of bargain silk. She closed her eyes. Her mouth fell into a deepness, into a look of unconscious cunning. Yet in her very stillness and pleasure she seemed to be hiding there, all alone. And at moments when the fire stirred and tumbled in the grate, she would tremble, and her hand would start out as if in impatience or despair.

Presently she stirred and reached under her back for the newspaper. Then she squatted there, touching the printed page as if it were fragile. She did not merely look at it—she watched it, as if it were unpredictable, like a young girl watching a baby. The paper was still wet in places where her body had lain. Crouching tensely and patting the creases away with small cracked red fingers, she frowned now and then at the blotched drawing of something and big letters that spelled a word underneath. Her lips trembled, as if looking and spelling so slowly had stirred her heart.

All at once she laughed.

She looked up.

"Ruby Fisher!" she whispered.

An expression of utter timidity came over her flat blue eyes and her soft mouth. Then a look of fright. She stared about.... What eye in the world did she feel looking in on her? She pulled her dress down tightly and began to spell through a dozen words in the newspaper.

The little item said:

"Mrs. Ruby Fisher had the misfortune to be shot in the leg by her husband this week."

As she passed from one word to the next she only whispered; she left the long word, "misfortune," until the last, and came back to it, then she said it all over out loud, like conversation.

"That's me," she said softly, with deference, very formally.

The fire slipped and suddenly roared in the house already deafening with the rain which beat upon the roof and hung full of lightning and thunder outside.

"You Clyde!" screamed Ruby Fisher at last, jumping to her feet. "Where are you, Clyde Fisher?"

She ran straight to the door and pulled it open. A shudder of cold brushed over her in the heat, and she seemed striped with anger and bewilderment. There was a flash of lightning, and she stood waiting, as if she half thought that would bring him in, a gun leveled in his hand.

She said nothing more and, backing against the door, pushed it closed with her hip. Her anger passed like a remote flare of elation. Neatly avoiding the table where the bag of coffee stood, she began to walk nervously about the room, as if a teasing indecision, an untouched mystery, led her by the hand. There was one window, and she paused now and then, waiting, looking out at the rain. When she was still, there was a passivity about her, or a deception of passivity, that was not really passive at all. There was something in her that never stopped.

At last she flung herself onto the floor, back across the newspaper, and looked at length into the fire. It might have been a mirror in the cabin, into which she could look deeper and deeper as she pulled her fingers through her hair, trying to see herself and Clyde coming up behind her.

"Clyde?"

But of course her husband, Clyde, was still in the woods. He kept a thick brushwood roof over his whisky still, and he was mortally afraid of lightning like this, and would never go out in it for anything.

And then, almost in amazement, she began to comprehend her predicament: it was unlike Clyde to take up a gun and shoot her.

She bowed her head toward the heat, onto her rosy arms, and began to talk and talk to herself. She grew voluble. Even if he heard about the coffee man, with a Pontiac car, she did not think he would shoot her. When Clyde would make her blue, she would go out onto the road, some car would slow down, and if it had a Tennessee license, the lucky kind, the chances were that she would spend the afternoon in the shed of the empty gin. (Here she rolled her head about on her arms and stretched her legs tiredly behind her, like a cat.) And if Clyde got word, he would slap her. But the account in the paper was wrong. Clyde had never shot her, even once. There had been a mistake made.

A spark flew out and nearly caught the paper on fire. Almost in fright she beat it out with her fingers. Then she murmured and lay back more firmly upon the pages.

There she stretched, growing warmer and warmer, sleepier and sleepier. She began to wonder out loud how it would be if Clyde shot her in the leg. . . . If he were truly angry, might he shoot her through the heart?

At once she was imagining herself dying. She would have a night-gown to lie in, and a bullet in her heart. Anyone could tell, to see her lying there with that deep expression about her mouth, how strange and terrible that would be. Underneath a brand new nightgown her heart would be hurting with every beat, many times more than her toughened skin when Clyde slapped at her. Ruby began to cry softly, the way she would be crying from the extremity of pain; tears would run down in a little stream over the quilt. Clyde would be standing there above her, as he once looked, with his wild black hair hanging to his shoulders. He used to be very handsome and strong!

He would say, "Ruby, I done this to you."

She would say—only a whisper—"That is the truth, Clyde—you done this to me."

Then she would die; her life would stop right there.

She lay silently for a moment, composing her face into a look which would be beautiful, desirable, and dead.

Clyde would have to buy her a dress to bury her in. He would have to dig a deep hole behind the house, under the cedar, a grave. He would have to nail her up a pine coffin and lay her inside. Then he would have to carry her to the grave, lay her down, and cover her up. All the time he would be wild, shouting, and all distracted, to think he could never touch her one more time.

She moved slightly, and her eyes turned toward the window. The white rain splashed down. She could hardly breathe for thinking that this was the way it was to fall on her grave, where Clyde would come and stand, looking down in the tears of some repentance.

A whole tree of lightning stood in the sky. She kept looking out the window, suffused with the warmth from the fire and with the pity and beauty and power of her death. The thunder rolled.

Then Clyde was standing there, with dark streams flowing over the floor where he had walked. He poked at Ruby with the butt of his gun, as if she were asleep.

"What's keepin' supper?" he growled.

She jumped up and darted away from him. Then, quicker than lightning, she put away the paper. The room was dark, except for the firelight. From the long shadow of his steamy presence she spoke to him glibly and lighted the lamp.

He stood there with a stunned, yet rather good-humored look of delay and patience on his face, and kept on standing there. He stamped his mud-red boots, and his enormous hands seemed weighted with the rain that fell from him and dripped down the barrel of the gun. Presently he sat down with dignity in the chair at the table, making a little tumult of his rightful wetness and hunger. Small streams began to flow from him everywhere.

Ruby was going through the preparations for the meal gently. She stood almost on tiptoe in her bare, warm feet. Once as she knelt at the safe, getting out the biscuits, she saw Clyde looking at her and she smiled and bent her head tenderly. There was some way she began to move her arms that was mysteriously sweet and yet abrupt and tentative, a delicate and vulnerable manner, as though her breasts gave her pain. She made many unnecessary trips back and forth across the floor, circling Clyde where he sat in his steamy silence, a knife and fork in his fists.

"Well, where you been, anyway?" he grumbled at last, as she set the first dish on the table.

"Nowheres special."

"Don't you talk back to me. You been hitchhikin' again, ain't you?" He almost chuckled.

She gave him a quick look straight into his eyes. She had not even heard him. She was filled with happiness. Her hand trembled when she poured the coffee. Some of it splashed on his wrist.

At that he let his hand drop heavily down upon the table and made the plates jump.

"Someday I'm goin' to smack the livin' devil outa you," he said.

Ruby dodged mechanically. She let him eat. Then, when he had crossed his knife and fork over his plate, she brought him the newspaper. Again she looked at him in delight. It excited her even to touch the paper with her hand, to hear its quiet secret noise when she carried it, the rustle of surprise.

"A newspaper!" Clyde snatched it roughly and with a grabbing disparagement. "Where'd you git that? Hussy."

"Look at this-here," said Ruby in her small singsong voice. She opened the paper while he held it and pointed gravely to the paragraph.

Reluctantly, Clyde began to read it. She watched his damp bald head slowly bend and turn.

Then he made a sound in his throat and said, "It's a lie."

"That's what's in the newspaper about me," said Ruby, standing up straight. She took up his plate and gave him that look of joy.

He put his big crooked finger on the paragraph and poked at it.

"Well, I'd just like to see the place I shot you!" he cried explosively. He looked up, his face blank and bold.

But she drew herself in, still holding the empty plate, faced him straightened and hard, and they looked at each other. The moment filled full with their helplessness. Slowly they both flushed, as though with a double shame and a double pleasure. It was as though Clyde might really have killed Ruby, and as though Ruby might really have been dead at his hand. Rare and wavering, some possibility stood timidly like a stranger between them and made them hang their heads.

Then Clyde walked over in his water-soaked boots and laid the paper on the dying fire. It floated there a moment and then burst into flame. They stood still and watched it burn. The whole room was bright.

"Look," said Clyde suddenly. "It's a Tennessee paper. See 'Tennessee'? That wasn't none of you it wrote about." He laughed, to show that he had been right all the time.

"It was Ruby Fisher!" cried Ruby. "My name is Ruby Fisher!" she declared passionately to Clyde.

"Oho, it was another Ruby Fisher—in Tennessee," cried her husband. "Fool me, huh? Where'd you get that paper?" He spanked her good-humoredly across her backside.

Ruby folded her still trembling hands into her skirt. She stood stooping by the window until everything, outside and in, was quieted before she went to her supper.

It was dark and vague outside. The storm had rolled away to faintness like a wagon crossing a bridge.

DORIS LESSING

THE DE WETS COME TO KLOOF GRANGE

The verandah, which was lifted on stone pillars, jutted forward over the garden like a box in the theater. Below were luxuriant masses of flowering shrubs, and creepers whose shiny leaves, like sequins, reflected light from a sky stained scarlet and purple and apple-green. This splendiferous sunset filled one half of the sky, fading gently through shades of mauve to a calm expanse of ruffling grey, blown over by tinted cloudlets; and in this still evening sky, just above a clump of darkening conifers, hung a small crystal moon.

There sat Major Gale and his wife, as they did every evening at this hour, side by side trimly in deck chairs, their sundowners on small tables at their elbows, critically watching, like connoisseurs, the pageant presented for them.

Major Gale said, with satisfaction: "Good sunset tonight," and they both turned their eyes to the vanquishing moon. The dusk drew veils across sky and garden; and punctually, as she did every day, Mrs. Gale shook off nostalgia like a terrier shaking off water and rose, saying: "Mosquitoes!" She drew her deck chair to the wall, where she neatly folded and stacked it.

"Here is the post," she said, her voice quickening; and Major Gale went to the steps, waiting for the native who was hastening towards them through the tall shadowing bushes. He swung a sack from his back and handed it to Major Gale. A sour smell of raw meat rose from the sack. Major Gale said with a kindly contempt he used for his native servants: "Did the spooks get you?" and laughed. The native, who had panted the last mile of his ten-mile journey through a bush filled with unnameable phantoms, ghosts of ancestors, wraiths of tree and beast, put on a pantomime of fear and chattered and shivered for a moment like an ape, to amuse his master. Major Gale dismissed the boy. He ducked thankfully around the corner of the house in the back, where there were lights and companionship.

Mrs. Gale lifted the sack and went into the front room. There she lit the oil lamp and called for the houseboy, to whom she handed the groceries and meat she removed. She took a fat bundle of letters from the very bottom of the sack and wrinkled her nose slightly; blood from the meat had stained them. She sorted the letters into two piles; and then husband and wife sat themselves down opposite each other to read their mail.

It was more than the ordinary farm living room. There were koodoo horns branching out over the fireplace, and a bundle of knobkerries hanging on a nail; but on the floor were fine rugs, and the furniture was two hundred years old. The table was a pool of softly reflected lights; it was polished by Mrs. Gale herself every day before she set on it an earthenware crock filled with thorny red flowers. Africa and the English eighteenth century mingled in this room and were at peace.

From time to time Mrs. Gale rose impatiently to attend to the lamp, which did not burn well. It was one of those terrifying paraffin things that have to be pumped with air to a whiter-hot flame from time to time, and which in any case emit a continuous soft hissing noise. Above the heads of the Gales a light cloud of flying insects wooed their fiery death and dropped one by one, plop, plop, plop to the table among the letters.

Mrs. Gale took an envelope from her own heap and handed it to her husband. "The assistant," she remarked abstractedly, her eyes bent on what she held. She smiled tenderly as she read. The letter was from her oldest friend, a woman doctor in London, and they had written to each other every week for thirty years, ever since Mrs. Gale came to exile in Southern Rhodesia. She murmured half aloud: "Why, Betty's brother's daughter is going to study economics," and though she had never met Betty's brother, let alone the daughter, the news seemed to please and excite her extraordinarily. The whole of the letter was about people she had never met and was not likely ever to meet—about the weather, about English politics. Indeed, there was not a sentence in it that would not have struck an outsider as having been written out of a sense of duty; but when Mrs. Gale had finished reading it, she put it aside gently and sat smiling quietly: she had gone back half a century to her childhood.

Gradually sight returned to her eyes, and she saw her husband where previously she had sat looking through him. He appeared disturbed; there was something wrong about the letter from the assistant.

Major Gale was a tall and still military figure, even in his khaki bush-shirt and shorts. He changed them twice a day. His shorts were creased sharp as folded paper, and the six pockets of his shirt were always buttoned up tight. His small head, with its polished surface of black hair, his tiny jaunty black moustache, his farmer's hands with their broken but clean nails—all these seemed to say that it was no easy matter not to let oneself go, not to let this damned disintegrating gaudy easygoing country get under one's skin. It wasn't easy, but he did it; he did it with the conscious effort that had slowed his movements and added the slightest touch of caricature to his appearance: one finds a man like Major Gale only in exile.

He rose from his chair and began pacing the room, while his wife watched him speculatively and waited for him to tell her what was the matter. When he stood up, there was something not quite right —what was it? Such a spruce and tailored man he was; but the disciplined shape of him was spoiled by a curious fatness and softness: the small rounded head was set on a thickening neck; the buttocks were fattening too, and quivered as he walked. Mrs. Gale, as these facts assailed her, conscientiously excluded them: she had her own picture of her husband, and could not afford to have it destroyed.

At last he sighed, with a glance at her; and when she said: "Well, dear?" he replied at once. "The man has a wife."

"Dear me!" she exclaimed, dismayed.

At once, as if he had been waiting for her protest, he returned briskly: "It will be nice for you to have another woman about the place."

"Yes, I suppose it will," she said humorously. At this most familiar note in her voice, he jerked his head up and said aggressively: "You always complain I bury you alive."

And so she did. Every so often, but not so often now, she allowed herself to overflow into a mood of gently humorous bitterness; but it had not carried conviction for many years; it was more, really, of an attention to him, like remembering to kiss him good night. In fact, she had learned to love her isolation, and she felt aggrieved that he did not know it.

"Well, but they can't come to the house. That I really couldn't put up with." The plan had been for the new assistant—Major Gale's farming was becoming too successful and expanding for him to manage any longer by himself—to have the spare room, and share the house with his employers.

"No, I suppose not, if there's a wife." Major Gale sounded doubtful; it was clear he would not mind another family sharing with them. "Perhaps they could have the old house?" he enquired at last.

"I'll see to it," said Mrs. Gale, removing the weight of worry off her husband's shoulders. Things he could manage: people bothered him. That they bothered her, too, now, was something she had become resigned to his not understanding. For she knew he was hardly conscious of her; nothing existed for him outside his farm.

And this suited her well. During the early years of their marriage, with the four children growing up, there was always a little uneasiness between them, like an unpaid debt. Now they were friends and could forget each other. What a relief when he no longer "loved" her! (That was how she put it.) Ah, that "love"—she thought of it with a small humorous distaste. Growing old had its advantages.

When she said "I'll see to it," he glanced at her, suddenly, directly, her tone had been a little too comforting and maternal. Normally his gaze wavered over her, not seeing her. Now he really observed her for a moment; he saw an elderly Englishwoman, as thin and dry as a stalk of maize in September, sitting poised over her letters, one hand touching them lovingly, and gazing at him with her small flower-blue eyes. A look of guilt in them troubled him. He crossed to her and kissed her cheek. "There!" she said, inclining her face with a sprightly, fidgety laugh. Overcome with embarrassment he stopped for a moment, then said determinedly: "I shall go and have my bath."

After his bath, from which he emerged pink and shining like an elderly baby, dressed in flannels and a blazer, they ate their dinner under the wheezing oil lamp and the cloud of flying insects. Immediately the meal was over he said "Bed," and moved off. He was always in bed before eight and up by five. Once Mrs. Gale had adapted herself to his routine. Now, with the four boys out sailing the seven seas in the navy, and nothing really to get her out of bed (her servants were perfectly trained), she slept until eight, when she joined her husband at breakfast. She refused to have that meal in bed; nor would she have dreamed of appearing in her dressing gown. Even as things were she was guilty enough about sleeping those three daylight hours, and found it necessary to apologize for her slackness. So, when her husband had gone to bed she remained under the lamp, rereading her letters, sewing, reading, or simply dreaming about the past, the very distant past, when she had been Caroline Morgan, living near a small country town, a country squire's daughter. That was how she liked best to think of herself.

Tonight she soon turned down the lamp and stepped on to the verandah. Now the moon was a large, soft, yellow fruit caught in the top branches of the blue gums. The garden was filled with glamor, and she let herself succumb to it. She passed quietly down the steps and beneath the trees, with one quick solicitous glance back at the bedroom window: her husband hated her to be out of the house by herself at night. She was on her way to the old house that lay half a mile distant over the veld.

Before the Gales had come to this farm, two brothers had it, South Africans by birth and upbringing. The houses had then been separated by a stretch of untouched bush, with not so much as a fence or a road between them; and in this state of guarded independence the two men had lived, both bachelors, both quite alone. The thought of them amused Mrs. Gale. She could imagine them sending polite notes to each other, invitations to meals or to spend an evening. She imagined them loaning each other books by native bearer, meeting at a neutral point between their homes. She was amused, but she respected them for a feeling she could understand. She made up all kinds of pretty ideas about these brothers, until one day she learned from a neighbor that in fact the two men had quarreled continually, and had eventually gone bankrupt because they could not agree how the farm was to be run. After this discovery Mrs. Gale ceased to think about them; a pleasant fancy had become a distasteful reality.

The first thing she did on arriving was to change the name of the farm from Kloof Nek to Kloof Grange, making a link with home. One of the houses was denuded of furniture and used as a storage space. It was a square, bare box of a place, stuck in the middle of the. bare veld, and its shut windows flashed back light to the sun all day. But her own home had been added to and extended, and surrounded with verandahs and fenced; inside the fence were two acres of garden, that she had created over years of toil. And what a garden! These were what she lived for: her flowering African shrubs, her vivid English lawns, her water garden with the goldfish and water lilies. Not many people had such a garden.

She walked through it this evening under the moon, feeling herself grow lightheaded and insubstantial with the influence of the strange greenish light, and of the perfumes from the flowers. She touched the leaves with her fingers as she passed, bending her face to the roses. At the gate, under the hanging white trumpets of the moonflower she paused, and lingered for a while, looking over the space of empty veld between her and the other house. She did not like going outside her garden at night. She was not afraid of natives, no: she had contempt for women who were afraid, for she regarded Africans as rather pathetic children, and was very kind to them. She did not know what made her afraid. Therefore she took a deep breath, compressed her lips, and stepped carefully through the gate, shutting it behind her with a sharp click. The road before her was a glimmering white ribbon, the hard-crusted sand sending up a continuous small sparkle of light as she moved. On either side were sparse stumpy trees, and their shadows were deep and black. A nightjar cut across the stars with crooked trailing wings, and she set her mouth defiantly: why, this was only the road she walked over every afternoon, for her constitutional! There were the trees she had pleaded for, when her husband was wanting to have them cut for firewood: in a sense, they were her trees. Deliberately slowing her steps, as a discipline, she moved through the pits of shadow, gaining each stretch of clear moonlight with relief, until she came to the house. It looked dead, a dead thing with staring eyes, with those blank windows gleaming pallidly back at the moon. Nonsense, she told herself. Nonsense. And she walked to the front door, unlocked it, and flashed her torch over the floor. Sacks of grain were piled to the rafters, and the brick floor was scattered with loose mealies. Mice scurried invisibly to safety, and flocks of cockroaches blackened the walls. Standing in a patch of moonlight on the brick, so that she would not unwittingly walk into a spiderweb or a jutting sack, she drew in deep breaths of the sweetish smell of maize, and made a list in her head of what had to be done; she was a very capable woman.

Then something struck her: if the man had forgotten, when applying for the job, to mention a wife, he was quite capable of forgetting children too. If they had children it wouldn't do: no, it wouldn't. She simply couldn't put up with a tribe of children—for Afrikaners never had less than twelve—running wild over her beautiful garden and teasing her goldfish. Anger spurted in her. De Wet—the name was hard on her tongue. Her husband should not have agreed to take on an Afrikaner. Really, really, Caroline, she chided herself humorously, standing there in the deserted moonlit house, don't jump to conclusions, don't be unfair.

She decided to arrange the house for a man and his wife, ignoring the possibility of children. She would arrange things, in kindness, for a woman who might be unused to living in loneliness; she would be good to this woman; so she scolded herself, to make atonement for her short fit of pettiness. But when she tried to form a picture of this woman who was coming to share her life, at least to the extent of taking tea with her in the mornings, and swapping recipes (so she supposed), imagination failed her. She pictured a large Dutch frau, all homely comfort and sweating goodness, and was repulsed. For the first time the knowledge that she must soon, next week, take another woman into her life, came home to her; and she disliked it intensely.

Why must she? Her husband would not have to make a friend of the man. They would work together, that was all; but because they, the wives, were two women on an isolated farm, they would be expected to live in each other's pockets. All her instincts toward privacy, the distance which she had put between herself and other people, even her own husband, rebelled against it. And because she rebelled, rejecting this imaginary Dutch woman, to whom she felt so alien, she began to think of her friend Betty, as if it were she who would be coming to the farm.

Still thinking of her friend Betty she returned through the silent veld to her home, imagining them walking together over this road and talking as they had been used to do. The thought of Betty, who had turned into a shrewd, elderly woman doctor with kind eyes, sustained her through the frightening silences. At the gate she lifted her head to sniff the heavy perfume of the moonflowers, and became conscious that something else was invading her dream: it was a very bad smell, an odor of decay mingled with the odor from the flowers. Something had died on the veld, and the wind had changed and was bringing the smell towards the house. She made a mental note: I must send the boy in the morning to see what it is. Then the conflict between her thoughts of her friend and her own life presented itself sharply to her. You are a silly woman, Caroline, she said to herself. Three years before they had gone on holiday to England, and she had found she and Betty had nothing to say to each other. Their lives were so far apart, and had been for so long, that the weeks they spent together were an offering to a friendship that had died years before. She knew it very well, but tried not to think of it. It was necessary to her to have Betty remain, in imagination at least, as a counterweight to her loneliness. Now she was being made to realize the truth. She resented that too, and somewhere the resentment was chalked up against Mrs. De Wet, the Dutch woman who was going to invade her life with impertinent personal claims.

And next day, and the days following, she cleaned and swept and tidied the old house, not for Mrs. De Wet, but for Betty. Otherwise she could not have gone through with it. And when it was all finished, she walked through the rooms which she had furnished with things taken from her own home, and said to a visionary Betty (but Betty as she had been thirty years before): "Well, what do you think of it?" The place was bare but clean now, and smelling of sunlight and air. The floors had colored coconut matting over the brick; the beds, standing on opposite sides of the room, were covered with gaily striped counterpanes. There were vases of flowers everywhere. "You would like living here," Mrs. Gale said to Betty, before locking the house up and returning to her own, feeling as if she had won a victory over herself.

The De Wets sent a wire saying they would arrive on Sunday after lunch. Mrs. Gale noted with annoyance that this would spoil her rest, for she slept every day, through the afternoon heat. Major Gale, for whom every day was a working day (he hated idleness and found odd jobs to occupy him on Sundays), went off to a distant part of the farm to look at his cattle. Mrs. Gale laid herself down on her bed with her eyes shut and listened for a car, all her nerves stretched. Flies buzzed drowsily over the windowpanes; the breeze from the garden was warm and scented. Mrs. Gale slept uncomfortably, warring all the afternoon with the knowledge that she should be awake. When she woke at four she was cross and tired, and there was still no sign of a car. She rose and dressed herself, taking a frock from the cupboard without looking to see what it was: her clothes were often fifteen years old. She brushed her hair absentmindedly; and then, recalled by a sense that she had not taken enough trouble, slipped a large gold locket round her neck, as a conscientious mark of welcome. Then she left a message with the houseboy that she would be in the garden and walked away from the verandah with a strong excitement growing in her. This excitement rose as she moved through the crowding shrubs under the walls, through the rose garden with its wide green lawns where water sprayed all the year round, and arrived at her favorite spot among the fountains and the pools of water lilies. Her watergarden was an extravagance, for the pumping of the water from the river cost a great deal of money.

She sat herself on a shaded bench; and on one side were the glittering plumes of the fountains, the roses, the lawns, the house, and beyond them the austere wind-bitten high veld; on the other, at her feet, the ground dropped hundreds of feet sharply to the river. It was a rocky shelf thrust forward over the gulf, and here she would sit for hours, leaning dizzily outwards, her short grey hair blown across her face, lost in adoration of the hills across the river. Not of the river itself, no, she thought of that with a sense of danger, for there, below her, in that green-crowded gully, were suddenly the tropics: palm trees, a slow brown river that eddied into reaches of marsh or curved round belts of reeds twelve feet high. There were crocodiles, and leopards came from the rocks to drink. Sitting there on her exposed shelf, a smell of sun-warmed green, of hot decaying water, of luxurious growth, an intoxicating heady smell, rose in waves to her face. She had learned to ignore it, and to ignore the river, while she watched the hills. They were *her* hills: that was how she felt. For years she had sat here, hours every day, watching the cloud shadows move over them, watching them turn blue with distance or come close after rain so that she could see the exquisite brushwork of trees on the lower slopes. They were never the same half an hour together. Modulating light created them anew for her as she looked, thrusting one peak forward and withdrawing another, moving them back so that they were hazed on a smoky horizon, crouched in sullen retreat, or raising them so that they towered into a brilliant cleansed sky. Sitting here, buffeted by winds, scorched by the sun or shivering with cold, she could challenge anything. They were her mountains; they were what she was; they had made her, had crystallized her loneliness into a strength, had sustained her and fed her. And now she almost forgot the De Wets were coming, and were hours late. Almost, not quite. At last, understanding that the sun was setting (she could feel its warmth striking below her shoulders), her small irritation turned to anxiety. Something might have happened to them? They had taken the wrong road, perhaps? The car had broken down? And there was the Major, miles away with their own car, and so there was no means of looking for them. Perhaps she should send out natives along the roads? If they had taken the wrong turning, to the river, they might be bogged in mud to the axles. Down there, in the swampy heat, they could be bitten by mosquitoes and then . . .

Caroline, she said to herself severely (thus finally withdrawing from the mountains), don't let things worry you so. She stood up and shook herself, pushed the hair out of her face, and gripped her whipping skirts in a thick bunch. She stepped backwards away from the wind that raked the edges of the cliff, sighed a goodbye to her garden for that day, and returned to the house. There, outside the front door, was a car, an ancient jalopy bulging with luggage, its back doors tied with rope. And children! She could see a half-grown girl on the steps. No, really, it was too much. On the other side of the car stooped a tall, thin, fairheaded man, burnt as brown as toffee, looking for someone to come. He must be the father. She approached, adjusting her face to a smile, looking apprehensively about her for the children. The man slowly came forward, the girl after him. "I expected you earlier," began Mrs. Gale briskly, looking reproachfully into the man's face. His eyes were cautious, blue, assessing. He looked her casually up and down and seemed not to take her into account. "Is Major Gale about?" he asked. "I am Mrs. Gale," she replied. Then, again: "I expected you earlier." Really, four hours late and not a word of apology!

"We started late," he remarked. "Where can I put our things?"

Mrs. Gale swallowed her annoyance and said: "I didn't know you had a family. I didn't make arrangements."

"I wrote to the Major about my wife," said De Wet. "Didn't he get my letter?" He sounded offended.

Weakly Mrs. Gale said: "Your wife?" and looked in wonderment at the girl, who was smiling awkwardly behind her husband. It could be seen, looking at her more closely, that she might perhaps be eighteen. She was a small creature, with delicate brown legs and arms, a brush of dancing black curls, and large excited black eyes. She put both hands round her husband's arm, and said, giggling: "I am Mrs. De Wet."

De Wet put her away from him, gently, but so that she pouted and said: "We got married last week."

"Last week," said Mrs. Gale, conscious of dislike.

The girl said, with an extraordinary mixture of effrontery and shyness: "He met me in a cinema and we got married next day." It seemed as if she were in some way offering herself to the older woman, offering something precious of herself.

"Really," said Mrs. Gale politely, glancing almost apprehensively at this man, this slow-moving, laconic, shrewd South African, who had behaved with such violence and folly. Distaste twisted her again.

Suddenly the man said, grasping the girl by the arm, and gently shaking her to and fro, in a sort of controlled exasperation: "Thought I had better get myself a wife to cook for me, all this way out in the blue. No restaurants here, hey Doodle?"

"Oh, Jack," pouted the girl, giggling. "All he thinks about is his stomach," she said to Mrs. Gale, as one girl to another, and then glanced with delicious fear up at her husband.

"Cooking is what I married you for," he said, smiling down at her intimately.

There stood Mrs. Gale opposite them, and she saw that they had forgotten her existence; and that it was only by the greatest effort of will that they did not kiss. "Well," she remarked drily, "this is a surprise."

They fell apart, their faces changing. They became at once what they had been during the first moments: two hostile strangers. They looked at her across the barrier that seemed to shut the world away from them. They saw a middle-aged English lady, in a shapeless old-fashioned blue silk dress, with a gold locket sliding over a flat bosom, smiling at them coldly, her blue, misted eyes critically. narrowed.

"I'll take you to your house," she said energetically. "I'll walk, and you go in the car—no, I walk it often." Nothing would induce her to get into the bouncing rattletrap that was bursting with luggage and half-suppressed intimacies.

As stiff as a twig, she marched before them along the road, while the car jerked and ground along in bottom gear. She knew it was ridiculous; she could feel their eyes on her back, could feel their astonished amusement; but she could not help it.

When they reached the house, she unlocked it, showed them briefly what arrangements had been made, and left them. She walked back in a tumult of anger, caused mostly because of her picture of herself, walking along that same road, meekly followed by the car, and refusing to do the only sensible thing, which was to get into it with them.

She sat on the verandah for half an hour, looking at the sunset sky without seeing it, and writhing with various emotions, none of which she classified. Eventually she called the houseboy, and gave him a note, asking the two to come to dinner. No sooner had the boy left, and was trotting off down the bushy path to the gate, than she called him back. "I'll go myself," she said. This was partly to prove that she made nothing of walking the half mile, and partly from contrition. After all, it was no crime to get married, and they seemed very fond of each other. That was how she put it.

When she came to the house, the front room was littered with luggage, paper, pots and pans. All the exquisite order she had created was destroyed. She could hear voices from the bedroom.

"But, Jack, I don't want you to. I want you to stay with me." And then his voice, humorous, proud, slow, amorous: "You'll do what I tell you, my girl. I've got to see the old man and find out what's cooking. I start work tomorrow, don't forget."

"But, Jack . . ." Then came sounds of scuffling, laughter, and a sharp slap.

"Well," said Mrs. Gale, drawing in her breath. She knocked on the wood of the door, and all sound ceased. "Come in," came the girl's voice. Mrs. Gale hesitated, then went into the bedroom.

Mrs. De Wet was sitting in a bunch on the bed, her flowered frock spread all around her, combing her hair. Mrs. Gale noted that the two beds had already been pushed together. "I've come to ask you to dinner," she said briskly. "You don't want to have to cook when you've just come."

Their faces had already become blank and polite.

"Oh no, don't trouble, Mrs. Gale," said De Wet, awkwardly. "We'll get ourselves something, don't worry." He glanced at the girl, and his face softened. He said, unable to resist it: "She'll get busy with the tin-opener in a minute, I expect. That's her idea of feeding a man."

"Oh Jack," pouted his wife.

De Wet turned back to the washstand, and proceeded to swab lather on his face. Waving the brush at Mrs. Gale, he said: "Thanks all the same. But tell the Major I'll be over after dinner to talk things over."

"Very well," said Mrs. Gale, "just as you like."

She walked away from the house. Now she felt rebuffed. After all, they might have had the politeness to come; yet she was pleased they hadn't; yet if they preferred making love to getting to know the people who were to be their close neighbors for what might be years, it was their own affair . . .

Mrs. De Wet was saying, as she painted her toenails, with her knees drawn up to her chin, and the bottle of varnish gripped between her heels: "Who the hell does she think she is, anyway? Surely she could give us a meal without making such a fuss when we've just come."

"She came to ask us, didn't she?"

"Hoping we would say no."

And Mrs. Gale knew quite well that this what they were thinking, and felt it was unjust. She would have liked them to come: the man wasn't a bad sort, in his way; a simple soul, but pleasant enough; as for the girl, she would have to learn, that was all. They should have come; it was their fault. Nevertheless she was filled with that discomfort that comes of having done a job badly. If she had behaved differently they would have come. She was cross throughout dinner; and that meal was not half finished when there was a knock on the door. De Wet stood there, apparently surprised they had not finished, from which it seemed that the couple had, after all, dined off sardines and bread and butter.

Major Gale left his meal and went out to the verandah to discuss business. Mrs. Gale finished her dinner in state, and then joined the two men. Her husband rose politely at her coming, offered her a chair, sat down and forgot her presence. She listened to them talking for some two hours. Then she interjected a remark (a thing she never did, as a rule, for women get used to sitting silent when men discuss farming) and did not know herself what made her say what she did about the cattle; but when De Wet looked round absently as if to say she should mind her own business, and her husband remarked absently, "Yes, dear," when a Yes dear did not fit her remark at all, she got up angrily and went indoors. Well, let them talk, then, she did not mind.

As she undressed for bed, she decided she was tired, because of her broken sleep that afternoon. But she could not sleep then, either. She listened to the sound of the men's voices, drifting brokenly round the corner of the verandah. They seemed to be thoroughly enjoying themselves. It was after twelve when she heard De Wet say, in that slow facetious way of his: "I'd better be getting home. I'll catch it hot, as it is." And, with rage, Mrs. Gale heard her husband laugh. He actually laughed. She realized that she herself had been planning an acid remark for when he came to the bedroom; so when he did enter, smelling of tobacco smoke, and grinning, and then proceeded to walk jauntily about the room in his underclothes, she said nothing, but noted that he was getting fat, in spite of all the hard work he did.

"Well, what do you think of the man?"

"He'll do very well indeed," said Major Gale, with satisfaction. "Very well. He knows his stuff all right. He's been doing mixed farming in the Transvaal for years." After a moment he asked politely, as he got with a bounce into his own bed on the other side of the room? "And what is she like?"

"I haven't seen much of her, have I? But she seems pleasant enough." Mrs. Gale spoke with measured detachment.

"Someone for you to talk to," said Major Gale, turning himself over to sleep. "You had better ask her over to tea."

At this Mrs. Gale sat straight up in her own bed with a jerk of annoyance. Someone for her to talk to, indeed! But she composed herself, said good night with her usual briskness, and lay awake. Next day she must certainly ask the girl to morning tea. It would be rude not to. Besides, that would leave the afternoon free for her garden and her mountains.

Next morning she sent a boy across with a note, which read: "I shall be so pleased if you will join me for morning tea." She signed it: Caroline Gale.

She went herself to the kitchen to cook scones and cakes. At eleven o'clock she was seated on the verandah in the green-dappled shade from the creepers, saying to herself that she believed she was in for a headache. Living as she did, in a long, timeless abstraction of growing things and mountains and silence, she had become very conscious of her body's responses to weather and to the slow advance of age. A small ache in her ankle when rain was due was like a cherished friend. Or she would sit with her eyes shut, in the shade, after a morning's pruning in the violent sun, feeling waves of pain flood back from her eyes to the back of her skull, and say with satisfaction: "You deserve it, Caroline!" It was right she should pay for such pleasure with such pain.

At last she heard lagging footsteps up the path, and she opened her eyes reluctantly. There was the girl, preparing her face for a social occasion, walking primly through the bougainvillea arches, in a flowered frock as vivid as her surroundings. Mrs. Gale jumped to her feet and cried gaily: "I am so glad you had time to come." Mrs. De Wet giggled irresistibly and said: "But I had nothing else to do, had I?" Afterwards she said scornfully to her husband: "She's nuts. She writes me letters with stuck down envelopes when I'm five minutes away, and says Have I the time? What the hell else did she think I had to do?" And then, violently: "She can't have anything to do. There was enough food to feed ten."

"Wouldn't be a bad idea if you spent more time cooking," said De Wet fondly.

The next day Mrs. Gale gardened, feeling guilty all the time, because she could not bring herself to send over another note of invitation. After a few days, she invited the De Wets to dinner, and through the meal made polite conversation with the girl while the men lost themselves in cattle diseases. What could one talk to a girl like that about? Nothing! Her mind, as far as Mrs. Gale was concerned, was a dark continent, which she had no inclination to explore. Mrs. De Wet was not interested in recipes, and when Mrs. Gale gave helpful advice about ordering clothes from England, which was so much cheaper than buying them in the local towns, the reply came that she had made all her own clothes since she was seven. After that there seemed nothing to say, for it was hardly possible to remark that these strapped sun-dresses and bright slacks were quite unsuitable for the farm, besides being foolish, since bare shoulders in this sun were dangerous. As for her shoes! She wore corded sandals which had already turned dust color from the roads.

There were two more tea parties; then they were allowed to lapse. From time to time Mrs. Gale wondered uneasily what on earth the poor child did with herself all day, and felt it was her duty to go and find out. But she did not.

One morning she was pricking seedlings into a tin when the houseboy came and said the little missus was on the verandah and she was sick.

At once dismay flooded Mrs. Gale. She thought of a dozen tropical diseases, of which she had had unpleasant experience, and almost ran to the verandah. There was the girl, sitting screwed up in a chair, her face contorted, her eyes red, her whole body shuddering violently. "Malaria," thought Mrs. Gale at once, noting that trembling.

"What is the trouble, my dear?" Her voice was kind. She put her hand on the girl's shoulder. Mrs. De Wet turned and flung her arms round her hips, weeping, weeping, her small curly head buried in

Mrs. Gale's stomach. Holding herself stiffly away from this dismaying contact, Mrs. Gale stroked the head and made soothing noises.

"Mrs. Gale, Mrs. Gale . . ."

"What is it?"

"I can't stand it. I shall go mad. I simply can't stand it."

Mrs. Gale, seeing that this was not a physical illness, lifted her up, led her inside, laid her on her own bed, and fetched cologne and handkerchiefs. Mrs. De Wet sobbed for a long while, clutching the older woman's hand, and then at last grew silent. Finally she sat up with a small rueful smile, and said pathetically: "I am a fool."

"But what *is* it, dear?"

"It isn't anything, really. I am so lonely. I wanted to get my mother up to stay with me, only Jack said there wasn't room, and he's quite right, only I got mad, because I thought he might at least have had my mother . . ."

Mrs. Gale felt guilt like a sword: she could have filled the place of this child's mother.

"And it isn't anything, Mrs. Gale, not really. It's not that I'm not happy with Jack. I am, but I never see him. I'm not used to this kind of thing. I come from a family of thirteen counting my parents, and I simply can't stand it."

Mrs. Gale sat and listened, and thought of her own loneliness when she first began this sort of life.

"And then he comes in late, not till seven sometimes, and I know he can't help it, with the farm work and all that, and then he has supper and goes straight off to bed. I am not sleepy then. And then I get up sometimes and I walk along the road with my dog . . ."

Mrs. Gale remembered how, in the early days after her husband had finished with his brief and apologetic embraces, she used to rise with a sense of relief and steal to the front room, where she lighted the lamp again and sat writing letters, reading old ones, thinking of her friends and of herself as a girl. But that was before she had her first child. She thought: This girl should have a baby; and could not help glancing downwards at her stomach.

Mrs. De Wet, who missed nothing, said resentfully: "Jack says I should have a baby. That's all he says." Then, since she had to include Mrs. Gale in this resentment, she transformed herself all at once from a sobbing baby into a gauche but armored young woman with whom Mrs. Gale could have no contact. "I am sorry," she said formally. Then, with a grating humor: "Thank you for letting me blow off steam." She climbed off the bed, shook her skirts straight, and tossed her head. "Thank you. I am a nuisance." With painful brightness she added: "So, that's how it goes. Who would be a woman, eh?"

Mrs. Gale stiffened. "You must come and see me whenever you are lonely," she said, equally bright and false. It seemed to her incredible that this girl should come to her with all her defenses down, and then suddenly shut her out with this facetious nonsense. But she felt more comfortable with the distance between them, she couldn't deny it.

"Oh, I will, Mrs. Gale. Thank you so much for asking me." She lingered for a moment, frowning at the brilliantly polished table in the front room, and then took her leave. Mrs. Gale watched her go. She noted that at the gate the girl started whistling gaily, and smiled comically. Letting off steam! Well, she said to herself, well . . . And she went back to her garden.

That afternoon she made a point of walking across to the other house. She would offer to show Mrs. De Wet the garden. The two women returned together, Mrs. Gale wondering if the girl regretted her emotional lapse of the morning. If so, she showed no signs of it. She broke into bright chatter when a topic mercifully occurred to her; in between were polite silences full of attention to what she seemed to hope Mrs. Gale might say.

Mrs. Gale was relying on the effect of her garden. They passed the house through the shrubs. There were the fountains, sending up their vivid showers of spray, there the cool mats of water lilies, under which the colored fishes slipped, there the irises, sunk in green turf.

"This must cost a packet to keep up," said Mrs. De Wet. She stood at the edge of the pool, looking at her reflection dissolving among the broad green leaves, glanced obliquely up at Mrs. Gale, and dabbled her exposed red toenails in the water.

Mrs. Gale saw that she was thinking of herself as her husband's employer's wife. "It does, rather," she said drily, remembering that the only quarrels she ever had with her husband were over the cost of pumping up water. "You are fond of gardens?" she asked. She could not imagine anyone not being fond of gardens.

Mrs. De Wet said sullenly: "My mother was always too busy having kids to have time for gardens. She had her last baby early this year." An ancient and incommunicable resentment dulled her face. Mrs. Gale, seeing that all this beauty and peace meant nothing to her companion that she would have it mean, said, playing her last card: "Come and see my mountains." She regretted the pronoun as soon as it was out—*so* exaggerated.

But when she had the girl safely on the rocky verge of the escarpment, she heard her say: "There's my river." She was leaning forward over the great gulf, and her voice was lifted with excitement. "Look," she was saying. "Look, there it is." She turned to Mrs. Gale, laughing, her hair spun over her eyes in a fine iridescent rain, tossing her head back, clutching her skirts down, exhilarated by the tussle with the wind.

"Mind, you'll lose your balance." Mrs. Gale pulled her back. "You have been down to the river, then?"

"I go there every morning."

Mrs. Gale was silent. The thing seemed preposterous. "But it is four miles there and four back."

"Oh, I'm used to walking."

"But . . ." Mrs. Gale heard her own sour, expostulating voice and stopped herself. There was after all no logical reason why the girl should not go to the river. "What do you do there?"

"I sit on the edge of a big rock and dangle my legs in the water, and I fish, sometimes. I caught a barble last week. It tasted foul, but it was fun catching it. And I pick water lilies."

"There are crocodiles," said Mrs. Gale sharply. The girl was wrong-headed; anyone was who could like that steamy bath of vapors, heat, smells, and—what? It was an unpleasant place. "A native girl was taken there last year, at the ford."

"There couldn't be a crocodile where I go. The water is clear, right down. You can see right under the rocks. It is a lovely pool. There's a kingfisher, and waterbirds, all colors. They are so pretty. And when you sit there and look, the sky is a long narrow slit. From here it looks quite far across the river to the other side, but really it isn't. And the trees crowding close make it narrower. Just think how many millions of years it must have taken for the water to wear down the rock so deep."

"There's bilharzia, too."

"Oh, bilharzia!"

"There's nothing funny about bilharzia. My husband had it. He had injections for six months before he was cured."

The girl's face dulled. "I'll be careful," she said irrationally, turning away, holding her river and her long hot dreamy mornings away from Mrs. Gale, like a secret.

"Look at the mountains," said Mrs. Gale, pointing. The girl glanced over the chasm at the foothills, then bent forward again, her face reverent. Through the mass of green below were glimpses of satiny brown. She breathed deeply: "Isn't it a lovely smell?" she said.

"Let's go and have some tea," said Mrs. Gale. She felt cross and put out; she had no notion why. She could not help being brusque with the girl. And so at last they were quite silent together; and in silence they remained on that verandah above the beautiful garden, drinking their tea and wishing it was time for them to part.

Soon they saw the two husbands coming up the garden. Mrs. De Wet's face lit up; and she sprang to her feet and was off down the path, running lightly. She caught her husband's arm and clung there. He put her away from him, gently. "Hullo," he remarked good-humoredly. "Eating again?" And then he turned back to Major Gale and went on talking. The girl lagged up the path behind her husband like a sulky small girl, pulling at Mrs. Gale's beloved roses and scattering crimson petals everywhere.

On the verandah the men sank at once into chairs, took large cups of tea, and continued talking as they drank thirstily. Mrs. Gale listened and smiled. Crops, cattle, disease; weather, crops and cattle. Mrs. De Wet perched on the verandah wall and swung her legs. Her face was petulant, her lips trembled, her eyes were full of tears. Mrs.

Gale was saying silently under her breath, with ironical pity, in which there was also cruelty: You'll get used to it, my dear; you'll get used to it. But she respected the girl, who had courage: walking to the river and back, wandering round the dusty flower beds in the starlight, trying to find peace—at least, she was trying to find it.

She said sharply, cutting into the men's conversation: "Mr. De Wet, did you know your wife spends her mornings at the river?"

The man looked at her vaguely, while he tried to gather the sense of her words: his mind was on the farm. "Sure," he said at last. "Why not?"

"Aren't you afraid of bilharzia?"

He said laconically: "If we were going to get it, we would have got it long ago. A drop of water can infect you, touching the skin."

"Wouldn't it be wiser not to let the water touch you in the first place?" she enquired with deceptive mildness.

"Well, I told her. She wouldn't listen. It is too late now. Let her enjoy it."

"But . . ."

"About that red heifer," said Major Gale, who had not been aware of any interruption.

"No," said Mrs. Gale sharply. "You are not going to dismiss it like that." She saw the three of them look at her in astonishment. "Mr. De Wet, have you ever thought what it means to a woman being alone all day, with not enough to do. It's enough to drive anyone crazy."

Major Gale raised his eyebrows; he had not heard his wife speak like that for so long. As for De Wet, he said with a slack good humor that sounded brutal: "And what do you expect me to do about it."

"You don't realize," said Mrs. Gale futilely, knowing perfectly well there was nothing he could do about it. "You don't understand how it is."

"She'll have a kid soon," said De Wet. "I hope so, at any rate. That will give her something to do."

Anger raced through Mrs. Gale like a flame along petrol. She was trembling. "She might be that red heifer," she said at last.

"What's the matter with having kids?" asked De Wet. "Any objection?"

"You might ask me first," said the girl bitterly.

Her husband blinked at her, comically bewildered. "Hey, what is this?" he enquired. "What have I done? You said you wanted to have kids. Wouldn't have married you otherwise."

"I never said I didn't."

"Talking about her as if she were . . ."

"When, then?" Mrs. Gale and the man were glaring at each other.

"There's more to women than having children," said Mrs. Gale at last, and flushed because of the ridiculousness of her words.

De Wet looked her up and down, up and down. "I want kids," he said at last. "I want a large family. Make no mistake about that. And when I married her"—he jerked his head at his wife—"I told her I wanted them. She can't turn round now and say I didn't."

"Who is turning round and saying anything?" asked the girl, fine and haughty, staring away over the trees.

"Well, if no one is blaming anyone for anything," asked Major Gale, jauntily twirling his little moustache, "what is all this about?"

"God knows, I don't," said De Wet angrily. He glanced sullenly at Mrs. Gale. "I didn't start it."

Mrs. Gale sat silent, trembling, feeling foolish, but so angry she could not speak. After a while she said to the girl: "Shall we go inside, my dear?" The girl, reluctantly, and with a lingering backward look at her husband, rose and followed Mrs. Gale. "He didn't mean anything," she said awkwardly, apologizing for her husband to her husband's employer's wife. This room, with its fine old furniture, always made her apologetic. At this moment, De Wet stooped into the doorway and said: "Come on, I am going home."

"Is that an order?" asked the girl quickly, backing so that she came side by side with Mrs. Gale: she even reached for the older woman's hand. Mrs. Gale did not take it: this was going too far.

"What's got into you?" he said, exasperated. "Are you coming, or are you not?"

"I can't do anything else, can I?" she replied, and followed him from the house like a queen who has been insulted.

Major Gale came in after a few moments. "Lovers' quarrel," he said, laughing awkwardly. This phrase irritated Mrs. Gale. "That man!" she exclaimed. "That man!"

"Why, what is wrong with him?" She remained silent, pretending to arrange her flowers. This silly scene, with its hinterlands of emotion, made her furious. She was angry with herself, angry with her husband, and furious at that foolish couple who had succeeded in upsetting her and destroying her peace. At last she said: "I am going to bed. I've such a headache I can't think."

"I'll bring you a tray, my dear," said Major Gale, with a touch of exaggeration in his courtesy that annoyed her even more. "I don't want anything, thank you," she said, like a child, and marched off to the bedroom.

There she undressed and went to bed. She tried to read, found she was not following the sense of the words, put down the book, and blew out the light. Light streamed into the room from the moon; she could see the trees along the fence banked black against stars. From next door came the clatter of her husband's solitary meal.

Later she heard voices from the verandah. Soon her husband came into the room and said: "De Wet is asking whether his wife has been here."

"What!" exclaimed Mrs. Gale, slowly assimilating the implications of this. "Why, has she gone off somewhere?"

"She's not at home," said the Major uncomfortably. For he always became uncomfortable and very polite when he had to deal with situations like this.

Mrs. Gale sank back luxuriously on her pillows. "Tell that fine young man that his wife often goes for long walks by herself when he's asleep. He probably hasn't noticed it." Here she gave a deadly look at her husband. "Just as I used to," she could not prevent herself adding.

Major Gale fiddled with his moustache, and gave her a look which seemed to say: "Oh lord, don't say we are going back to all that business again?" He went out, and she heard him saying: "Your wife might have gone for a walk, perhaps?" Then the young man's voice: "I know she does sometimes. I don't like her being out at night, but she just walks around the house. And she takes the dogs with her. Maybe she's gone further this time—being upset, you know."

"Yes, I know," said Major Gale. Then they both laughed. The laughter was of a quite different quality from the sober responsibility of their tone a moment before: and Mrs. Gale found herself sitting up in bed, muttering: "How *dare* he?"

She got up and dressed herself. She was filled with premonitions of unpleasantness. In the main room her husband was sitting reading, and since he seldom read, it seemed he was also worried. Neither of them spoke. When she looked at the clock, she found it was just past nine o'clock.

After an hour of tension, they heard the footsteps they had been waiting for. There stood De Wet, angry, worried sick, his face white, his eyes burning.

"We must get the boys out," he said, speaking directly to Major Gale, and ignoring Mrs. Gale.

"I am coming too," she said.

"No, my dear," said the Major cajolingly. "You stay here."

"You can't go running over the veld at this time of night," said De Wet to Mrs. Gale, very blunt and rude.

"I shall do as I please," she returned.

The three of them stood on the verandah, waiting for the natives. Everything was drenched in moonlight. Soon they heard a growing clamor of voices from over the ridge, and a little later the darkness there was lightened by flaring torches held high by invisible hands: it seemed as if the night were scattered with torches advancing of their own accord. Then a crowd of dark figures took shape under the broken lights. The farm natives, excited by the prospect of a night's chasing over the veld, were yelling as if they were after a small buck or a hare.

Mrs. Gale sickened. "Is it necessary to have all these natives in it?" she asked. "After all, have we even considered the possibilities? Where can a girl run to on a place like this?"

"That is the point," said Major Gale frigidly.

"I can't bear to think of her being—pursued, like this, by a crowd of natives. It's horrible."

"More horrible still if she has hurt herself and is waiting for help," said De Wet. He ran off down the path, shouting to the natives and waving his arms. The Gales saw them separate into three bands, and soon there were three groups of lights jerking away in different directions through the hazy dark, and the yells and shouting came back to them on the wind.

Mrs. Gale thought: "She could have taken the road back to the station, in which case she could be caught by car, even now."

She commanded her husband: "Take the car along the road and see."

"That's an idea," said the Major, and went off to the garage. She heard the car start off, and watched the rear light dwindle redly into the night.

But that was the least ugly of the possibilities. What if she had been so blind with anger, grief, or whatever emotion it was that had driven her away, that she had simply run off into the veld not knowing where she went? There were thousands of acres of trees, thick grass, gullies, *kopjes*. She might at this moment be lying with a broken arm or leg; she might be pushing her way through grass higher than her head, stumbling over roots and rocks. She might be screaming for help somewhere for fear of wild animals, for if she crossed the valley into the hills there were leopards, lions, wild dogs. Mrs. Gale suddenly caught her breath in an agony of fear: the valley! What if she had mistaken her direction and walked over the edge of the escarpment in the dark? What if she had forded the river and been taken by a crocodile? There were so many things: she might even be caught in a game trap. Once, taking her walk, Mrs. Gale herself had come across a tall sapling by the path where the spine and ribs of a large buck dangled, and on the ground were the pelvis and legs, fine eroded bones of an animal trapped and forgotten by its trapper. Anything might have happened. And worse than any of the actual physical dangers was the danger of falling a victim to fear: being alone on the veld, at night, knowing oneself lost: this was enough to send anyone off balance.

The silly little fool, the silly little fool: anger and pity and terror confused in Mrs. Gale until she was walking crazily up and down her garden through the bushes, tearing blossoms and foliage to pieces in trembling fingers. She had no idea how time was passing; until Major Gale returned and said that he had taken the ten miles to the station at seven miles an hour, turning his lights into the bush this way and that. At the station everyone was in bed, but the police were standing on the alert for news.

It was long after twelve. As for De Wet and the bands of searching natives, there was no sign of them. They would be miles away by this time.

"Go to bed," said Major Gale at last.

"Don't be ridiculous," she said. After a while she held out her hand to him, and said: "One feels so helpless."

There was nothing to say; they walked together under the stars, their minds filled with horrors. Later she made some tea and they drank it standing; to sit would have seemed heartless. They were so tired they could hardly move. Then they got their second wind and continued walking. That night Mrs. Gale hated her garden, that highly cultivated patch of luxuriant growth, stuck in the middle of a country that could do this sort of thing to you suddenly. It was all the fault of the country! In a civilized sort of place, the girl would have caught the train to her mother, and a wire would have put everything right. Here, she might have killed herself, simply because of a passing fit of despair. Mrs. Gale began to get hysterical. She was weeping softly in the circle of her husband's arms by the time the sky lightened and the redness of dawn spread over the sky.

As the sun rose, De Wet returned alone over the veld. He said he had sent the natives back to their huts to sleep. They had found nothing. He stated that he also intended to sleep for an hour, and that he would be back on the job by eight. Major Gale nodded: he recognized this as a necessary discipline against collapse. But after the young man had walked off across the veld towards his house, the two older people looked at each other and began to move after him. "He must not be alone," said Mrs. Gale sensibly. "I shall make him some tea and see that he drinks it."

"He wants sleep," said Major Gale. His own eyes were red and heavy.

"I'll put something in his tea," said Mrs. Gale. "He won't know it is there." Now she had something to do, she was much more cheerful. Planning De Wet's comfort, she watched him turn in at his gate and vanish inside the house: they were some two hundred yards behind.

Suddenly there was a shout, and then a commotion of screams and yelling. The Gales ran fast along the remaining distance and burst into the front room, white-faced and expecting the worst, in whatever form it might choose to present itself.

There was De Wet, his face livid with rage, bending over his wife, who was huddled on the floor and shielding her head with her arms, while he beat her shoulders with his closed fists.

Mrs. Gale exclaimed: "Beating your wife!"

De Wet flung the girl away from him, and staggered to his feet. "She was here all the time," he said, half in temper, half in sheer wonder. "She was hiding under the bed. She told me so. When I came in she was sitting on the bed and laughing at me."

The girl beat her hands on the floor and said, laughing and crying together: "Now you have to take some notice of me. Looking for me all night over the veld with your silly natives! You looked so stupid, running about like ants, looking for me."

"My God," said De Wet simply, giving up. He collapsed backwards into a chair and lay there, his eyes shut, his face twitching.

"So now you have to notice me," she said defiantly, but beginning to look scared. "I have to pretend to run away, but then you sit up and take notice."

"Be quiet," said De Wet, breathing heavily. "Be quiet, if you don't want to get hurt bad."

"Beating your wife," said Mrs. Gale. "Savages behave better."

"Caroline, my dear," said Major Gale awkwardly. He moved towards the door.

"Take that woman out of here if you don't want me to beat her too," said De Wet to Major Gale.

Mrs. Gale was by now crying with fury. "I'm not going," she said. "I'm not going. This poor child isn't safe with you."

"But what was it all about?" said Major Gale, laying his hand kindly on the girl's shoulder. "What was it, my dear? What did you have to do it for, and make us all so worried?"

She began to cry. "Major Gale, I am so sorry. I forgot myself. I got so mad. I told him I was going to have a baby. I told him when I got back from your place. And all he said was: That's fine. That's the first of them, he said. He didn't love me, or say he was pleased, or nothing."

"Dear Christ in hell," said De Wet wearily, with the exasperation strong in his voice, "what do you make me do these things for? Do you think I want to beat you? Did you think I wasn't pleased: I keep telling you I want kids, I love kids."

"But you don't care about me," she said, sobbing bitterly.

"Don't I?" he said helplessly.

"Beating your wife when she is pregnant," said Mrs. Gale. "You ought to be ashamed of yourself." She advanced on the young man with her own fists clenched, unconscious of what she was going. "You ought to be beaten yourself, that's what you need."

Mrs. De Wet heaved herself off the floor, rushed on Mrs. Gale, pulled her back so that she nearly lost balance, and then flung herself on her husband. "Jack," she said, clinging to him desperately. "I am so sorry. I am so sorry, Jack."

He put his arms round her. "There," he said simply, his voice thick with tiredness, "don't cry. We got mixed up, that's all."

Major Gale, who had caught and steadied his wife as she staggered back, said to her in a low voice: "Come, Caroline. Come. Leave them to sort it out."

"And what if he loses his temper again and decides to kill her this time?" demanded Mrs. Gale, her voice shrill.

De Wet got to his feet, lifting his wife with him. "Go away now, Mrs. Major," he said. "Get out of here. You've done enough damage."

"I've done enough damage?" she gasped. "And what have I done?"

"Oh nothing, nothing at all," he said with ugly sarcasm. "Nothing at all. But please go and leave my wife alone in future, Mrs. Major."

"Come, Caroline, *please*," said Major Gale.

She allowed herself to be drawn out of the room. Her head was aching so that the vivid morning light invaded her eyes in a wave of pain. She swayed a little as she walked.

"Mrs. Major," she said, "Mrs. Major!"

"He was upset," said her husband judiciously.

She snorted. Then, after a silence: "So, it was all my fault."

"He didn't say so."

"I thought that was what he was saying. He behaves like a brute and then says it is my fault."

"It was no one's fault," said Major Gale, patting her vaguely on shoulders and back as they stumbled back home.

They reached the gate, and entered the garden, which was now musical with birds.

"A lovely morning," remarked Major Gale.

"Next time you get an assistant," she said finally, "get people of our kind. These might be savages, the way they behave."

And that was the last word she would ever say on the subject.

SYLVIA PLATH

THE FIFTEEN-DOLLAR EAGLE

There are other tattoo shops in Madigan Square, but none of them a
patch on Carmey's place. He's a real poet with the needle and dye, an
artist with a heart. Kids, dock bums, the out-of-town couples in for a
beer put on the brakes in front of Carmey's, nose-to-the-window,
one and all. You got a dream, Carmey says, without saying a word,
you got a rose on the heart, an eagle in the muscle, you got the sweet
Jesus himself, so come in to me. Wear your heart on your skin in this
life, I'm the man can give you a deal. Dogs, wolves, horses, and lions
for the animal lover. For the ladies, butterflies, birds of paradise,
baby heads smiling or in tears, take your choice. Roses, all sorts,
large, small, bud, and full bloom, roses with name scrolls, roses with
thorns, roses with dresden-doll heads sticking up in dead center,
pink petal, green leaf, set off smart by a lead-black line. Snakes and
dragons for Frankenstein. Not to mention cowgirls, hula girls, mer-

maids, and movie queens, ruby-nippled and bare as you please. If you've got a back to spare, there's Christ on the cross, a thief at either elbow, and angels overhead to right and left holding up a scroll with "Mount Calvary" on it in Old English script, close as yellow can get to gold.

Outside they point at the multicolored pictures plastered on Carmey's three walls, ceiling to floor. They mutter like a mob scene, you can hear them through the glass:

"Honey, take a looka those peacocks!"

"That's crazy, paying for tattoos. I only paid for one I got, a panther on my arm."

"You want a heart, I'll tell him where."

I see Carmey in action for the first time courtesy of my steady man, Ned Bean. Lounging against a wall of hearts and flowers, waiting for business, Carmey is passing the time of day with a Mr. Tomolillo, an extremely small person wearing a wool jacket that drapes his nonexistent shoulders without any attempt at fit or reformation. The jacket is patterned with brown squares the size of cigarette packs, each square boldly outlined in black. You could play tick-tack-toe on it. A brown fedora hugs his head just above the eyebrows like the cap on a mushroom. He has the thin, rapt, triangular face of a praying mantis. As Ned introduces me, Mr. Tomolillo snaps over from the waist in a bow neat as the little moustache hairlining his upper lip. I can't help admiring this bow because the shop is so crowded there's barely room for the four of us to stand up without bumping elbows and knees at the slightest move.

The whole place smells of gunpowder and some fumey antiseptic. Ranged along the back wall from left to right are: Carmey's worktable, electric needles hooked to a rack over a Lazy Susan of dye pots, Carmey's swivel chair facing the show window, a straight customer's chair facing Carmey's chair, a waste bucket, and an orange crate covered with scraps of paper and pencil stubs. At the front of the shop, next to the glass door, there is another straight chair, with the big placard of Mount Calvary propped on it, and a cardboard file-drawer on a scuffed wooden table. Among the babies and daisies on the wall over Carmey's chair hang two faded sepia daguerre-otypes of a boy from the waist up, one front-view, one back. From the distance he seems to be wearing a long-sleeved, skintight black lace shirt. A closer look shows he is stark naked, covered only with a creeping ivy of tattoos.

In a jaundiced clipping from some long-ago rotogravure, these Oriental men and women are sitting cross-legged on tasseled cushions, back to the camera and embroidered with seven-headed dragons, mountain ranges, cherry trees, and waterfalls. "These people have not a stitch of clothing on," the blurb points out. "They belong to a society in which tattoos are required for membership. Sometimes a full job costs as much as $300." Next to this, a photograph of a bald man's head with the tentacles of an octopus just rounding the top of the scalp from the rear.

"Those skins are valuable as many a painting, I imagine," says Mr. Tomolillo. "If you had them stretched on a board."

But the Tattooed Boy and those clubby Orientals have nothing on Carmey, who is himself a living advertisement of his art—a schooner in full sail over a rose-and-holly leaf ocean on his right biceps, Gypsy Rose Lee flexing her muscled belly on the left, forearms jammed with hearts, stars, and anchors, lucky numbers and namescrolls, indigo edges blurred so he reads like a comic strip left out in a Sunday rainstorm. A fan of the Wild West, Carmey is rumored to have a bronco reared from navel to collarbone, a thistle-stubborn cowboy stuck to its back. But that may be a mere fable inspired by his habit of wearing tooled leather cowboy boots, finely heeled, and a Bill Hickok belt studded with red stones to hold up his black chino slacks. Carmey's eyes are blue. A blue in no way inferior to the much-sung-about skies of Texas.

"I been at it sixteen years now," Carmey says, leaning back against his picturebook wall, "and you might say I'm still learning. My first job was in Maine, during the war. They heard I was a tattooist and called me out to this station of Wacs. . . ."

"To tat*too* them?" I ask.

"To tattoo their numbers on, nothing more or less."

"Weren't some of them *scared*?"

"Oh, sure, sure. But some of them came back. I got two Wacs in one day for a tattoo. Well they hemmed. And they hawed. 'Look,' I tell them, 'you came in the other day and you knew which one you wanted, what's the trouble?' "

" 'Well, it's not what we want but where we want it,' one of them pipes up. 'Well if that's all it is you can trust me,' I say. 'I'm like a doctor, see? I handle so many women it means nothing.' 'Well I want three roses,' this one says: 'one on my stomach and one on each cheek of my butt.' So the other one gets up courage, you know how it is, and asks for one rose . . ."

"Little ones or big ones?" Mr. Tomolillo won't let a detail slip.

"About like that up there." Carmey points to a card of roses on the wall, each bloom the size of a Brussels sprout. "The biggest going. So I did the roses and told them: 'Ten dollars off the price if you come back and show them to me when the scab's gone.' "

"Did they come?" Ned wants to know.

"You bet they did." Carmey blows a smoke ring that hangs wavering in the air a foot from his nose, the blue, vaporous outline of a cabbage rose.

"You wanta know," he says, "a crazy law? I could tattoo you anywhere," he looks me over with great care, "anywhere at all. Your back. Your rear." His eyelids droop, you'd think he was praying. "Your breasts. Anywhere at all but your face, hands and feet."

Mr. Tomolillo asks: "Is that a *Fed*eral law?"

Carmey nods. "A Federal law. I got a blind," he juts a thumb at the dusty-slatted venetian blind drawn up in the display window. "I let the blind down, and I can do privately any part of the body. Except face, hands and feet."

"I bet it's because they *show*," I say.

"Sure. Take in the Army, at drill. The guys wouldn't look right. Their faces and hands would stand out, they couldn't cover up."

"However that may be," Mr. Tomolillo says, "I think it is a shocking law, a totalitarian law. There should be a freedom about personal adornment in any democracy. I mean, if a lady *wants* a rose on the back of her hand, I should think . . ."

"She should *have* it," Carmey finishes with heat. "People should have what they want, regardless. Why, I had a little lady in here the other day," Carmey levels the air with the flat of his hand not five feet from the floor. "So high. Wanted Calvary, the whole works, on her back, and I gave it to her. Eighteen hours it took."

I eye the thieves and angels on the poster of Mount Calvary with some doubt. "Didn't you have to shrink it down a bit?"

"Nope."

"Or leave off an angel?" Ned wonders. "Or a bit of the foreground?"

"Not a bit of it. A thirty-five dollar job in full color, thieves, angels, Old English—the works. She went out of the shop proud as punch. It's not every little lady's got all Calvary in full color on her back. Oh, I copy photos people bring in, I copy movie stars. Anything they want, I do it. I've got some designs I wouldn't put up on the wall on account of offending some of the clients. I'll show you." Carmey opens the cardboard file-drawer on the table at the front of the shop. "The wife's got to clean this up," he says. "It's a terrible mess."

"Does your wife help you?" I ask with interest.

"Oh, Laura, she's in the shop most of the day." For some reason Carmey sounds all at once solemn as a monk on Sunday. I wonder, does he use her for a come-on: Laura, the Tattooed Lady, a living masterpiece, sixteen years in the making. Not a white patch on her, ladies and gentlemen—look all you want to. "You should drop by and keep her company, she likes talk." He is rummaging around in the drawer, not coming up with anything, when he stops in his tracks and stiffens like a pointer.

This big guy is standing in the doorway.

"What can I do for you?" Carmey steps forward, the maestro he is.

"I want that eagle you showed me."

Ned and Mr. Tomolillo and I flatten ourselves against the side walls to let the guy into the middle of the room. He'll be a sailor out of uniform in his pea jacket and plaid wool shirt. His diamond-shaped head, width all between the ears, tapers up to a narrow plateau of cropped black hair.

"The nine-dollar or the fifteen?"

"The fifteen."

Mr. Tomolillo sighs in gentle admiration.

The sailor sits down in the chair facing Carmey's swivel, shrugs out of his pea jacket, unbuttons his left shirt cuff, and begins slowly to roll up the sleeve.

"You come right in here," Carmey says to me in a low, promising voice, "where you can get a good look. You've never seen a tattooing before." I squinch up and settle on the crate of papers in the corner at the left of Carmey 's chair, careful as a hen on eggs.

Carmey flicks through the cardboard file again and this time digs out a square piece of plastic. "Is this the one?"

The sailor looks at the eagle pricked out on the plastic. Then he says: "That's right," and hands it back to Carmey.

"Mmmm," Mr. Tomolillo murmurs in honor of the sailor's taste.

Ned says: "That's a fine eagle."

The sailor straightens with a certain pride. Carmey is dancing round him now, laying a dark-stained burlap cloth across his lap, arranging a sponge, a razor, various jars with smudged-out labels, and a bowl of antiseptic on his worktable—finicky as a priest whetting his machete for the fatted calf. Everything has to be just so. Finally he sits down. The sailor holds out his right arm and Ned and Mr. Tomolillo close in behind his chair, Ned leaning over the sailor's right shoulder and Mr. Tomolillo over his left. At Carmey's elbow I have the best view of all.

With a close, quick swipe of the razor, Carmey clears the sailor's forearm of its black springing hair, wiping the hair off the blade's edge and onto the floor with his thumb. Then he anoints the area of bared flesh with vaseline from a small jar on top of his table. "You ever been tattooed before?"

"Yeah." The sailor is no gossip. "Once." Already his eyes are locked in a vision of something on the far side of Carmey's head, through the walls and away in the thin air beyond the four of us in the room.

Carmey is sprinkling a black powder on the face of the plastic square and rubbing the powder into the pricked holes. The outline of the eagle darkens. With one flip, Carmey presses the plastic square powder-side against the sailor's greased arm. When he peels the plastic off, easy as skin off an onion, the outline of an eagle, wings spread, claws hooked for action, frowns up from the sailor's arm.

"Ah!" Mr. Tomolillo rocks back on his cork heels and casts a meaning look at Ned. Ned raises his eyebrows in approval. The sailor allows himself a little quirk of the lip. On him it is as good as a smile.

"Now," Carmey takes down one of the electric needles, pitching it rabbit-out-of-the-hat, "I am going to show you how we make a nine-dollar eagle a fifteen-dollar eagle."

He presses a button on the needle. Nothing happens.

"Well," he sighs, "it's not working."

Mr. Tomolillo groans. "Not again?"

Then something strikes Carmey and he laughs and flips a switch on the wall behind him. This time when he presses the needle it buzzes and sparks blue. "No connection, that's what it was."

"Thank heaven," says Mr. Tomolillo.

Carmey fills the needle from a pot of black dye on the Lazy Susan. "This same eagle," Carmey lowers the needle to the eagle's right wingtip, "for nine dollars is only black and red. For fifteen dollars you're going to see a blend of four colors." The needle steers along the lines laid by the powder. "Black, green, brown and red. We're out of blue at the moment or it'd be five colors." The needle skips and backtalks like a pneumatic drill but Carmey's hand is steady as a surgeon's. "How I *love* eagles!"

"I believe you *live* on Uncle Sam's eagles," says Mr. Tomolillo.

Black ink seeps over the curve of the sailor's arm and into the stiff, stained butcher's-apron canvas covering his lap, but the needle travels on, scalloping the wing feathers from tip to root. Bright beads of red are rising through the ink, heart's-blood bubbles smearing out into the black stream.

"The guys complain," Carmey singsongs. "Week after week I get the same complaining: What have you got new? We don't want the same type eagle, red and black. So I figure out this blend. You wait. A solid-color eagle."

The eagle is losing itself in a spreading thundercloud of black ink.

Carmey stops, sloshes his needle in the bowl of antiseptic, and a geyser of white blooms up to the surface from the bowl's bottom. Then Carmey dips a big, round, cinnamon-colored sponge in the bowl and wipes away the ink from the sailor's arm. The eagle emerges from its hood of bloodied ink, a raised outline on the raw skin.

"Now you're gonna see something." Carmey twirls the Lazy Susan till the pot of green is under his thumb and picks another needle from the rack.

The sailor is gone from behind his eyes now, off somewhere in Tibet, Uganda, or the Barbados, oceans and continents away from the blood drops jumping in the wake of the wide green swaths Carmey is drawing in the shadow of the eagle's wings.

About this time I notice an odd sensation. A powerful sweet perfume is rising from the sailor's arm. My eyes swerve from the mingling red and green and I find myself staring intently into the waste bucket by my left side. As I watch the calm rubble of colored candy wrappers, cigarette butts, and old wads of muddily stained kleenex, Carmey tosses a tissue soaked with fresh red onto the heap. Behind the silhouetted heads of Ned and Mr. Tomolillo the panthers, roses, and red-nippled ladies wink and jitter. If I fall forward or to the right, I will jog Carmey's elbow and make him stab the sailor and ruin a perfectly good fifteen-dollar eagle, not to mention disgracing my sex. The only alternative is a dive into the bucket of bloody papers.

"I'm doing the brown now," Carmey sings out a mile away, and my eyes rivet again on the sailor's blood-sheened arm. "When the eagle heals, the colors will blend right into each other, like on a painting."

Ned's face is a scribble of blank India ink on a seven-color crazy-quilt.

"I'm going . . ." I make my lips move, but no sound comes out.

Ned starts toward me but before he gets there the room switches off like a light.

The next thing is, I am looking into Carmey's shop from a cloud with the X-ray eyes of an angel and hearing the tiny sound of a bee spitting blue fire.

"The blood get her?" It is Carmey's voice, small and far.

"She looks all white," says Mr. Tomolillo. "And her eyes are funny."

Carmey passes something to Mr. Tomolillo. "Have her sniff that." Mr. Tomolillo hands something to Ned. "But not too much."

Ned holds something to my nose.

I sniff, and I am sitting in the chair at the front of the shop with Mount Calvary as a backrest. I sniff again. Nobody looks angry so I have not bumped Carmey's needle. Ned is screwing the cap on a little flask of yellow liquid. Yardley's smelling salts.

"Ready to go back?" Mr. Tomolillo points kindly to the deserted orange crate.

"Almost." I have a strong instinct to stall for time. I whisper in Mr. Tomolillo's ear which is very near to me, he is so short, "Do *you* have any tattoos?"

Under the mushroom brim of his fedora Mr. Tomolillo's eyes roll heavenward. "My gracious no! I'm only here to see about the springs. The springs in Mr. Carmichael's machine have a way of breaking in the middle of a customer."

"How annoying."

"That's what I'm here for. We're testing out a new spring now, a much heavier spring. You know how distressing it is when you're in the dentist's chair and your mouth is full of whatnot. . . ."

"Balls of cotton and little metal siphons. . . ?"

"Precisely. And in the middle of this the dentist turns away," Mr. Tomolillo half-turns his back in illustration and makes an evil, secretive face, "and buzzes about in the corner for ten minutes with the machinery, you don't know what." Mr. Tomolillo's face smooths out like linen under a steam iron. "That's what I'm here to see about, a stronger spring. A spring that won't let the customer down."

By this time I am ready to go back to my seat of honor on the orange crate. Carmey has just finished with the brown and in my absence the inks have indeed blended into one another. Against the shaven skin, the lacerated eagle is swollen in tricolored fury, claws curved sharp as butcher's hooks.

"I think we could redden the eye a little?"

The sailor nods, and Carmey opens the lid on a pot of dye the color of tomato ketchup. As soon as he stops working with the needle, the sailor's skin sends up its blood beads, not just from the bird's black outline now, but from the whole rasped, rainbowed body.

"Red," Carmey says, "really picks things up."

"Do you save the blood?" Mr. Tomolillo asks suddenly.

"I should think," says Ned, "you might well have some arrangement with the Red Cross."

"With the blood bank!" The smelling salts have blown my head clear as a blue day on Monadnock. "Just put a little basin on the floor to catch the drippings."

Carmey is picking out a red eye on the eagle. "We vampires don't share our blood." The eagle's eye reddens but there is now no telling blood from ink. "You never heard of a vampire do that, did you?"

"Nooo. . . ." Mr. Tomolillo admits.

Carmey floods the flesh behind the eagle with red and the finished eagle poises on a red sky, born and baptized in the blood of its owner.

The sailor drifts back from parts unknown.

"Nice?" With his sponge Carmey clears the eagle of the blood filming its colors the way a sidewalk artist might blow the pastel dust from a drawing of the White House, Liz Taylor, or Lassie-Come-Home.

"I always say," the sailor remarks to nobody in particular, "when you get a tattoo, get a good one. Nothing but the best." He looks down at the eagle, which has begun in spite of Carmey's swabbing to bleed again. There is a little pause. Carmey is waiting for something and it isn't money. "How much to write Japan under that?"

Carmey breaks into a pleased smile. "One dollar."

"Write Japan, then."

Carmey marks out the letters on the sailor's arm, an extra flourish to the J's hook, the loop of the P, and the final N, a love letter to the eagle-conquered Orient. He fills the needle and starts on the J.

"I under*stand*," Mr. Tomolillo observes in his clear, lecturer's voice, "Japan is a center of tattooing."

"Not when *I* was there," the sailor says. "It's banned."

"Banned!" says Ned. "What for?"

"Oh, they think it's *bar*barous nowadays." Carmey doesn't lift his eyes from the second A, the needle responding like a broken-in bronc under his masterly thumb. "There are operators, of course. Sub rosa. There always are." He puts the final curl on the N and sponges off the wellings of blood which seem bent on obscuring his artful lines. "That what you wanted?"

"That's it."

Carmey folds a wad of kleenex into a rough bandage and lays it over the eagle and Japan. Spry as a shopgirl wrapping a gift package he tapes the tissue into place.

The sailor gets up and hitches into his pea jacket. Several school-boys, lanky, with pale, pimply faces, are crowding the doorway, watching. Without a word the sailor takes out his wallet and peels sixteen dollar bills off a green roll. Carmey transfers the cash to his wallet. The schoolboys fall back to let the sailor pass into the street.

"I hope you didn't mind my getting dizzy."

Carmey grins. "Why do you think I've got those salts so close to hand? I have big guys passing out cold. They get egged in here by their buddies and don't know how to get out of it. I got people getting sick to their ears in that bucket."

"She's never got like that before," Ned says. "She's seen all sorts of blood. Babies born. Bullfights. Things like that."

"You was all worked up." Carmey offers me a cigarette, which I accept, takes one himself, and Ned takes one, and Mr. Tomolillo says no-thank-you. "You was all tensed, that's what did it."

"How much is a heart?"

The voice comes from a kid in a black leather jacket in the front of the shop. His buddies nudge each other and let out harsh, puppy-barks of laughter. The boy grins and flushes all at once under his purple stipple of acne. "A heart with a scroll under it and a name on the scroll."

Carmey leans back in his swivel chair and digs his thumbs into his belt. The cigarette wobbles on his bottom lip. "Four dollars," he says without batting an eye.

"Four dollars?" The boy's voice swerves up and cracks in shrill disbelief. The three of them in the doorway mutter among themselves and shuffle back and forth.

"Nothing here in the heart line under three dollars." Carmey doesn't kowtow to the tightfisted. You want a rose, you want a heart in this life, you pay for it. Through the nose.

The boy wavers in front of the placards of hearts on the wall, pink, lush hearts, hearts with arrows through them, hearts in the center of buttercup wreaths. "How much," he asks in a small, craven voice, "for just a name?"

"One dollar." Carmey's tone is strictly business.

The boy holds out his left hand. "I want Ruth." He draws an imaginary line across his left wrist. "Right here . . . so I can cover it up with a watch if I want to."

His two friends guffaw from the doorway.

Carmey points to the straight chair and lays his half-smoked cigarette on the Lazy Susan between two dye pots. The boy sits down, schoolbooks balanced on his lap.

"What happens," Mr. Tomolillo asks of the world in general, "if you choose to change a name? Do you just cross it off and write the next above it?"

"You could," Ned suggests, "wear a watch over the old name so only the new name showed."

"And then another watch," I say, "over that, when there's a third name."

"Until your arm," Mr. Tomolillo nods, "is up to the shoulder with watches."

Carmey is shaving the thin scraggly growth of hairs from the boy's wrist. "You're taking a lot of ragging from somebody."

The boy stares at his wrist with a self-conscious and unsteady smile, a smile that is maybe only a public substitute for tears. With his right hand he clutches his schoolbooks to keep them from sliding off his knee.

Carmey finishes marking R-U-T-H on the boy's wrist and holds the needle poised. "She'll bawl you out when she sees this." But the boy nods him to go ahead.

"Why?" Ned asks. "Why should she bawl him out?"

"Gone and got yourself tattooed!" Carmey mimicks a mincing disgust. "And with just a name! Is *that* all you think of me?—She'll be wanting roses, birds, butterflies. . . ." The needle sticks for a second and the boy flinches like a colt. "And if you *do* get all that stuff to please her—roses . . ."

"Birds and butterflies," Mr. Tomolillo puts in.

". . . she'll say, sure as rain at a ball game: What'd you want to go and spend all that *money* for?" Carmey whizzes the needle clean in the bowl of antiseptic. "You can't beat a woman." A few meager blood drops stand up along the four letters—letters so black and plain you can hardly tell it's a tattoo and not just inked in with a pen. Carmey tapes a narrow bandage of kleenex over the name. The whole operation lasts less than ten minutes.

The boy fishes a crumpled dollar bill from his back pocket. His friends cuff him fondly on the shoulder and the three of them crowd out the door, all at the same time, nudging, pushing, tripping over their feet. Several faces, limpet-pale against the window, melt away as Carmey's eye lingers on them.

"No wonder he doesn't want a heart, that kid, he wouldn't know what to do with it. He'll be back next week asking for a Betty or a Dolly or some such, you wait." He sighs, and goes to the cardboard file and pulls out a stack of those photographs he wouldn't put on the wall and passes them around. "One picture I would like to get." Carmey leans back in the swivel chair and props his cowboy boots on a little carton. "The butterfly. I got pictures of the rabbit hunt. I got pictures of ladies with snakes winding up their legs and into them, but I could make a lot of sweet dough if I got a picture of the butterfly on a woman."

"Some queer kind of butterfly nobody wants?" Ned peers in the general direction of my stomach as at some high-grade salable parchment.

"It's not what, it's where. One wing on the front of each thigh. You know how butterflies on a flower make their wings flutter, ever so little? Well, any move a woman makes, these wings look to be going in and out, in and out. I'd like a photograph of that so much I'd practically do a butterfly for free."

I toy, for a second, with the thought of a New Guinea Golden, wings extending from hipbone to kneecap, ten times life-size, but drop it fast. A fine thing if I got tired of my own skin sooner than last year's sack.

"Plenty of women *ask* for butterflies in that particular spot," Carmey goes on, "but you know what, not one of them will let a photograph be taken after the job's done. Not even from the waist down. Don't imagine I haven't asked. You'd think everybody over the whole United States would recognize them from the way they carry on when it's even mentioned."

"Couldn't," Mr. Tomolillo ventures shyly, "the wife oblige? Make it a little family affair?"

Carmey's face skews up in a pained way. "Naw," he shakes his head, his voice weighted with an old wonder and regret. "Naw, Laura won't hear of the needle. I used to think the idea of it'd grow on her after a bit, but nothing doing. She makes me feel, sometimes, what do I see in it all. Laura's white as the day she was born. Why, she *hates* tattoos."

Up to this moment I have been projecting, fatuously, intimate visits with Laura at Carmey's place. I have been imagining a lithe, supple Laura, a butterfly poised for flight on each breast, roses blooming on her buttocks, a gold-guarding dragon on her back, and Sinbad the Sailor in six colors on her belly, a woman with Experience written all over her, a woman to learn from in this life. I should have known better.

The four of us are slumped there in a smog of cigarette smoke, not saying a word, when a round, muscular woman comes into the shop, followed closely by a greasy-haired man with a dark, challenging expression. The woman is wrapped to the chin in a woolly electric-blue coat; a fuchsia kerchief covers all but the pompadour of her glinting blond hair. She sits down in the chair in front of the window regardless of Mount Calvary and proceeds to stare fixedly at

Carmey. The man stations himself next to her and keeps a severe eye on Carmey too, as if expecting him to bolt without warning.

There is a moment of potent silence.

"Why," Carmey says pleasantly, but with small heart, "here's the Wife now."

I take a second look at the woman and rise from my comfortable seat on the crate at Carmey's elbow. Judging from his watchdog stance, I gather the strange man is either Laura's brother or her bodyguard or a low-class private detective in her employ. Mr. Tomolillo and Ned are moving with one accord toward the door.

"We must be running along," I murmur, since nobody else seems inclined to speak.

"Say hello to the people, Laura," Carmey begs, back to the wall. I can't help but feel sorry for him, even a little ashamed. The starch is gone out of Carmey now, and the gay talk.

Laura doesn't say a word. She is waiting with the large calm of a cow for the three of us to clear out. I imagine her body, death-lily-white and totally bare—the body of a woman immune as a nun to the eagle's anger, the desire of the rose. From Carmey's wall the world's menagerie howls and ogles at her alone.

MARGE PIERCY

DYNASTIC ENCOUNTER

When the knocking came, Maud was taking a sponge bath. Grabbing
the sheet from the daybed she stuck her head out. One of the old
men from the first floor stood there looking sore. "You got a phone
call—why don't you come down when I call? All the way up here on
account of you don't listen . . ."

Clutching the sheet she ran for the extension. Hearing Duncan's
voice she was sure it was all off. "Duncan, what is it? He can't make it?
He won't meet me?"

"Of course, Maud, don't get excited. Didn't I tell you it's all
arranged?" His voice playing cool and dependable. "Just a little
change of plans. First, we're not meeting at my place."

"Oh." Goodbye to his wife's potato salad, the rye bread and
cheeses—port salut, roquefort, camembert. All day she had been

figuring the odds on salami, slicing those virgin cheeses. Gorgon-zola, gouda, crema danica.

"Bill wants to meet us in town, at the Low Blow. There's a jazz group he wants to hear." The familiarity of the first name hung on the telephone wire as if with clothes pins.

She had an urge to add the last name. The lumpy old man from downstairs had not hung up. He would not know who W. Saltzman was. They hated her in the rooming house, her and the two still sexual men up on three: said they were noisy, said they used the phone too much. Doors opened eye-wide behind her in the halls, but when she spoke, the old men answered with suspiciously pursed lips, if at all.

Duncan was warning briskly that she not be late. He would pick her up—he and his wife, chuckle. Damp under the sheet she ran for her room. Duncan was eager to make her, would like to set up an extracurricular lay on Fridays after his last class. He taught at the College but lived in a house adorned with oriental carpets in an older suburb. With lumbering sauveness he tried to nudge her guilty for lunches at his expense in an off-campus Italian restaurant. Often he spoke of his friendship with the poet W. Saltzman, discovering in her work even more influence than there was, quoting the great man on trivial occasions. Introducing Saltzman was an attempt to net her in obligation: rubbing herself dry, she grinned.

Rhoda, his wife, was an excellent cook. Rhoda: chicken gently sautéed in white-wine sauce, roast sesame lamb, avocado salad. She would move in if Rhoda would cook for her. But Duncan was a beefy milk-fed professor; from dead men's bones he ground plastic bread. He was so sure she was his proper prey, a rootless, nameless arty girl half nuts and outside the pale: because it never, never occurred to him that she might be right.

She put on her good dress—the shade of blue was good, anyhow. The refrigerator held about a glass of milk and something in a napkin. She had babysat for a couple she'd known during her stint teaching at the College. Besides babyfood, she'd turned up mara-schino cherries, cocktail onions, and half a box of animal crackers. She had consumed the cherries and onions and carried off the box.

She poured out a little milk and sat slowly chewing the crackers, eating each animal paw by paw and the head last.

She crossed to the john then. The light was on, the door ajar. The toilet was filled to the brim, splashing over to puddle the floor. Lazily like a carp in the bowl a long cigar-brown turd floated. She backed out.

She had as landlady an ex-inmate of Treblinka. She would go down tomorrow to complain, and Mrs. Goldman would show her her tattoo: Mr. Goldman and the little Goldmen long since ashes. Mrs. Goldman would assure her she was lucky to be in the United States and alive. She would retreat apologizing. Nothing was commensurate, and the plumbing broke down every two weeks. Mrs. Goldman would hint she was flushing tampax down the toilet, and she would deny it. Mrs. Goldman would bat her large weak eyes in disbelief. She and Mrs. Goldman would continue the argument as she backed up the staircase. Then Mrs. Goldman would utter a few Yiddish curses for women of loose morals and retire, slamming her door. She would piss in the sink as she did now and go over to the College whenever possible. The College, where she had taught until replaced by a Ph.D., had useful facilities.

She reread the poems she had gone through five times. Saltzman could tell her where to send stuff, give her introductions, even help her find a job, point her out to editors, tell her how to get a book published. He was power. Besides it was getting to be winter. Though he was not her only literary pa, surely he would not mind the other influences. He was the local boy and everybody claimed to know him or his ex-girl friend or his dentist. Imagining this meeting had soothed her to sleep bitter nights. She felt she was moving in darkness about to come round a corner into blinding light and be—not consumed—transfigured. Someday she would make it, why not now? She had to: how else could she survive?

The buzzer rasped. She jumped up. Turned, grabbed the envelope of poems. Clearly saw herself in the bar bearing down on him poems in hand. She took out the bottom three, her cream, shoved them in her purse. Just happened to have on me. Well, shit, he can ask. Shrugging on her mouton coat.

Going slowly down—if she hurried she would fall—she felt the weight of the coat. It had been Sandy's. A year in the state hatch, insulin, electric shock, and hydrotherapy had dulled her, but not enough. When Mrs. Gross decided Sandy was getting too wild and must be put away again, Sandy went up on the apartment-house roof and jumped. She saw Sandy's long curious face, her tea-brown hair, her freckled hands with the chewed nails, so vividly she could not take in Duncan. Docilely she followed him to the small Mercedes and got in back.

"What, Rhoda?" She came to. "Oh, Harry the Tailor got robbed. No, they didn't smash the window when they robbed him, it was a man and a woman and they cut him up." She sat with head ducked, assuming Sandy's old position with hands knit, foot tapping shyly. Dead, stone dead. "No, some kids smashed the window, after." Mrs. Gross had acted funny when she gave her the coat. Maud had not wanted it, but she did need a coat. Further, she felt a right to Sandy's things. What she wanted was Sandy's books, but Mrs. Gross brought out the coat. Mrs. Gross kept talking about how much she had paid for it, what good condition it was in, how little Sandy had worn it, till Maud had taken it to please her.

She sat up, her knuckles bumping her teeth. Mrs. Gross had wanted her to pay for the coat. Then she began to laugh, covering her mouth so they would not hear.

Rhoda was sitting turned from Duncan. Her coat had a high fur collar, her reddish hair was done up in smooth whorls, and she radiated a faint smell of hair spray and spicy perfume. Rhoda did not like her because she was young, single and therefore presumably scheming. She and Rhoda were always talking in oblique boring sideways conversations. If they were to talk straight out:

RHODA: See my house! See my pretty things! They cost a lot! See how expensive I am.
MAUD: If you can't get out the door, have you tried the window?
RHODA: See my man. No Trespassing! Keep Off the Grass!
MAUD: It's only lunch I want. I swear it'll never happen while I'm conscious.

Duncan was of middle height but he sat tall: the Man behind the Desk. A sandy thirty-eight, his jaw was square and he thrust it forward like a girl proud of her bosom. "Did you call Julie Norman about the seventeenth? I want her at the party."

"Duncan, I hardly know her," Rhoda whined.

"What do you mean, you don't know her? What do you do at those meetings?"

"You know what I mean." Rhoda's neck arched from the collar: angry goose neck stretching. "She won't remember me."

"Well, make her remember. Doesn't Susan play with her kid?"

"Let's leave Susan out of this."

"Out of what?" Duncan reared back from the wheel. "Can't you make a simple phone call?"

Williams Saltzman (Bill, Duncan had called him: hello, Bill, help!) made and broke reputations. His earlier poems were in the newer college anthologies. He had put out a paperback of younger poets, and why not me, dear god. Would he be queer? He was supposed to have had that affair with a woman anthropologist. Besides, his poems were full of breasts. She reached down the neck of her dress and jerked the bra straps tighter. Made a langorous face of surrender and giggled in disgust.

"There's the Low Blow." She leaned over Rhoda's shoulder to point.

"Yes, love, but do you think I can check the car with the hatgirl?"

Dashboard clock read five to nine. Her stomach dropped.

"There's a lot," Rhoda sang out.

"We're paying through the nose for a sitter. Hold on. Plenty of onstreet parking."

They passed the Low Blow again. If it were like other jazz spots there would be nothing to eat. The rock music she went to hear with her last man never came there. Maybe afterward sandwiches, roast beef or pastrami. The clock hand slipped down from nine.

"Maybe he won't wait, Duncan, if we're late."

"What do you think he'll do, go home? He'll be there."

Around the block again past the Mad Place, past the Squaw Man All Night Hairdressers, past the Low Blow and Orvieto's Pizzeria and Ron's Ale House and around the other corner. She sank back, cradling her cheek in her coat. Open the door and make a break for it. "There's somebody pulling out!" she yelled. He jammed on the brakes and backed jerkily into position, ignoring a Lincoln leaning on its horn.

"See," he said, expansive on the sidewalk with an arm guiding each woman, "why pay a couple of bucks, could be three? A little patience. Keep cool."

She dodged free of Duncan's arm entering and shrank behind him. What was the use, he wouldn't like her stuff. He must have his own protégées.

Duncan got tense, solider. "There he is."

"Where? Which one?" From behind she poked his arm.

"By the bar, talking with that big colored fellow."

Peeking around him, she studied Saltzman. Over what looked like someone else's army fatigues he wore what had been a good leather jacket, lined with fleece. He ought to feel hot in the close room. He was tall with a gaunt face, a short kinky mustard-yellow beard streaked with grey and a paunch sloping somewhat over the trousers.

His gaze on them, when finally he ended the conversation and started over, was cold and cat green. She thought him a fine-looking man, because he was W. Saltzman and she knew his poems backwards, and because his cheeks and forehead were textured like weathered bark, and also because he had a satyr's paunch and must like food. But his eyes were cold as the sidewalks outside. Shuffling behind came a man his age and seedier, broader built, with a ruddy face, strong white hair and a knowing grin. Saltzman came at a slow deliberate amble, looked at Duncan's outstretched hand for a moment, touched it.

Duncan said nervously, "How are you making it?"

W. Saltzman grunted. He said hello to Rhoda, looked then at Maud, was introduced. "We need a table, Ed," he said to the person, who asked how many of them there were.

"Sure, Willy, right up front." They hung back in brief conversation. The table was tiny and near the stand. Saltzman and his friend, still unintroduced, lolled on one side, and the three of them huddled on the other. The set was starting.

"Uh, Bill," Duncan began.

Saltzman looked with his eyelids lowered and then raised in disbelief. He motioned they should listen. The first round of drinks was on the house: Saltzman was known here. The second Duncan bought. The Scotch hurt her stomach. The tenor sax was a name she had heard, though she had thought him dead: a contemporary of Charlie Parker in early bop. She listened conscientiously, conscientiously not looking at Saltzman. Her hands sweated cold. Saltzman offered a cigarette. She fumbled. Politely he lit it. The sound was dull, finally. The music said little to her, and after a while she was not listening but daydreaming about her next to last man, about getting published and getting laid and getting fed and keeping warm . . . warm with the lax flabby music and the booze, warm . . .

Duncan asked, "What's that smell?"

She felt a stab on her thigh. "Oh, shit." A hot ash had fallen from her cigarette and burnt through the dress. She brushed at it.

"What's wrong?" Saltzman looked halfway interested.

"Nothing, nothing really." Her face heated.

The waitress brought another round, and, after a pause, Duncan again paid. Fixing her eyes on Saltzman's mustard beard she willed him to notice her, to speak. At last when the set finished, he did.

He asked gently, "What do you do with yourself?"

Hadn't Duncan explained? "For a job you mean? I was teaching, and then—"

"Is that how you know each other, from the College?"

They nodded and he leaned back as if his curiosity were satisfied. Quickly she added the important part. "But that's just what I do to support it, you know. I mean, I write poems."

His face shrank. *"Oh."*

His friend said cheerfully, "Everybody's doing it, doing it, doing it. They think it's poetry, but it's snot."

Her words lay on the table like a fat turd. For a moment she hated him. Did he think he would be the last poet? Duncan, the bastard, had said nothing. Produced her as random female.

Saltzman turned to him. "That workshop, how about it? I expected to hear by now. Is it coming off?"

The friend was staring at Duncan with shrewd assessment. Duncan furrowed his brow. "Arrangements take time. Departments of English move exceedingly slowly and grind exceedingly fine. I'm pushing for it, every chance I get."

"Eh." The friend's mouth sagged. He shrugged his disbelief.

"I have to know soon. Other things depend on it."

"Like he has to pay the rent," his friend smirked. "Poets pay rent too. Ask the little lady."

"I'm trying to get a decision," Duncan said. "I'm trying to put it through. But you know how encrusted with tradition—"

"Out on the West Coast I had twelve readings in two weeks, including a couple of lectures."

"Kids were standing up outside wanting to hear him," the friend said. "Crowds of college kids."

"By the way, Saturday the seventeenth we're having a sort of pre-holiday thing. Wassail bowl and all, right, Rhoda? Most of the department will be there and the boys from the Press, and we'd sure like to see you. And your friend too," he added weakly, but the tone of the invitation was confident.

Saltzman's old tomcat eyes went opaque. Dunc was putting it on the line. Even if Saltzman went, he wouldn't know if Duncan could really get him the workshop or wanted to. Cf. her vague feeling that Duncan could haved saved her job. "Sounds fine," said Saltzman. "We'll have to see. I'm spending the holidays in New York, and I don't know when I'm leaving."

The friend did not reply. Rattling the ice in her glass Rhoda came alive to ask, "Don't think I caught your name?"

"Charlie Roach," he said, inclining his head.

"He's one of the West Side Roaches," Saltzman said and caught Maud's gaze as she smiled. She had given up. She pitied him with his grizzled beard and still needing Duncan.

Rhoda was being social. "What do you do?" her voice slurred from the rapid drinking.

Charlie grinned. His teeth were stained and worn down in his ruddy face. *"Any*thing, Ma'am."

"Charlie's a true man of the golden rule, though he likes to operate a little ahead of the beat."

Rhoda was flustered, as designed, but Duncan was enjoying the show. They couldn't shock him if they slit their gullets on his tweeds. Saltzman lolled back, withdrawn. She remembered the poems in her purse and bowed her head, fingering the stiff edges of the cigarette burn.

They were leaving. As they passed the bar people here and there slapped Saltzman's shoulder. On the sidewalk he halted, turned. For a moment he stared at her and she stared back. His eyes, ice green, were glacial crevasses, his mouth curled in a perhaps amused smile. The eyes said he was bored sick with women wanting to fuck his name, with men wanting to suck his talent: he'd been used and used like an old toothpaste tube, he was well chewed. She looked back posturing, can't you see my ineffable Name, I'm as real as you when you only wanted a young girl to chew on tonight: your mistake, Willy, I'm good and you won't get into my biography for saving me, so there!

Following Duncan and Rhoda to the car she said hopefully, "My, I'm hungry," but nobody answered. In the back seat she huddled into Sandy's coat. The first time she wore it she had found old kleenexes in the pocket and unable to have preserved Sandy, preserved them. Then she caught a cold.

Two days ago she had brooded over slitting her wrists: she felt ashamed. There were years, years yet of inventive tortures and deprivations, of hollow victories and bloody defeats. She no longer felt sorry for Saltzman. She would wear the same face. The worst that could happen then might be to meet a kid who had eaten her books and survived.

As for Duncan she could no longer afford his lasagna: she perceived he was her natural predator. The system supported him, and he supported the system. In any attempt to make a deal, he was more powerful than she and he would prevail.

ROSELLEN BROWN

A LETTER TO ISMAEL IN THE GRAVE

Somebody once told me I didn't have welfare mothers' eyes.

I. I. I. I. I. Like white is supposed to be made up of all the colors, I is made up of all the words you can possibly say all running together in a circle very fast. It is red and shiny and purple and sweet. A mouthful of I-berries. Here, have some. I want to put it on the mailbox. Use it for my signature. Frame it and hang it on the wall all gold. Put it between my legs in bed at night. Sing it out in church. Show it around like a fat new baby. It's the best baby we never had, the one I made myself, after the children had gone to bed, just before you died.

You know what your sister said to me, don't you. She says it with her pointy finger. Back to the ashes, Cinderella. Now be a dead man's wife the way you were a lost man's widow.

When I was a kid I once walked across the river on the third rail, right next to the BMT. While I was at it in those days making my mama and grandmama jump like fleas, I married you. But I couldn't do that once, like walking the rail, I had to do it and keep doing it for thirteen years. So I fell in the river, my feet in flames.

Does someone always have to get blamed in this world?

The headline was 2 MORE ADDICT DEATHS IN CITY THIS WEEKEND.

What I read was WIFE SAYS SHE DIDN'T KNOW; SAYS SHE STOPPED KNOWING ANYTHING A LONG TIME AGO. And who gets blamed for that?

You know my friend Nilda. Her husband takes a shot every single day of his life for diabetes, very carefully, so he won't go blind or something, or go crazy. How can it be that another man could use his veins for filthy highways—for alleys, that's what, dark dirty alleys. So they could find you collapsed in the thick black of one of your own ruined veins.

Merciful, merciful. That you died before you had to hock your children's eyes and little toes. Before your pig of a liver killed you instead. Before I sold myself out from under you and cheap, to get money for passage. I am not beautiful, no sir, I know that, but I do not have welfare mothers' eyes. In spite of you.

All right, I said to him. But you know I've got tattoos. Those shadows, those stripes of the El laying over me all these years since you (he, Ismael, my husband!) moved me here. I swear we've got the taste of all that darkness in our soup. You have to look pretty hard even in Brooklyn to find an El that they haven't taken down for scrap iron and firewood but you worked hard on it and found us one. You couldn't get sunstroke over here if they gave you a million for trying. One time I saw the slats across my friend Rita's shoulders when she was standing down there on the stoop. They looked like those fox furs I used to stare at when I was a kid, the whole fox with the flat shiny eyes I always thought were real, and the long dark stringy tails. Didn't you used to wonder if it hurt them, and look in those live eyes, to be dragged around on some rich old lady's back?

He was looking at me the other day when I thought I was alone, sitting in the kitchen trying to think. And he said he never saw a woman who kept right on existing when her man wasn't with her. I guess I've had a lot of practice from you, with me and never with me all the same time. But Jesus, to be that way! What are we, frogs who need a swamp to croak about?

The kind of thing I've been so busy thinking is,
Whose fault were you?   But
Whose fault was the you whose fault you were? There's
a girl on the front of the Sun-Maid raisin box holding
a box of raisins with a girl on it, holding a box of
raisins with a girl on it holding

Something new, I heard them talking on TV about what's called crimes without victims? Do you think there could be something like victims without crimes? That's what we all could be, even the kids—victims' victims. Don't laugh.

It had nothing to do with heroes or heroines. But two people live in a room small enough so their shoulders touch when they pass—picture it—and don't know each other's names. One day one of them asks "What's your name?" and it turns out they have the same name. By accident. "Well," one of them says, "maybe we have something in common. What do you like best in the world?" She looks at him coyly and says, "You." She smiles because she thinks that's the right answer. "And what do you like best?" He thinks for a minute and says, "Me." So they fall together. It's a tight circle they can both fit into if they get down on all fours and crawl.

Poor Ismael. When you closed your gorgeous eyes that I envied, there must have been nothing behind them to look at. Just dark: your own closed eyes reflected and reflected.

You said I made the children a wall between us, you even made it seem that was all I had them for. But a wall is something to lean on when you have to lean, and anyway, what holds up a house, a roof overhead, if it isn't walls.

I asked you to leave. I threw you out. I left you. But I've heard about a kind of snake—this is a moreno belief, I think—that kills you and when it thinks you're dead it sticks its tail up in your nostrils to make sure you aren't breathing. If you are, it kills you again. What you used for a tail and where you went looking to see if I was still alive—I shouldn't have lay down dead for you so often.

If I ever loved you, even for a minute, then you were my fault too. I put a check mark next to you and it wouldn't rub off. I said sure. I laughed. I said I'm behind you here, give me your footprints—even for a minute. I said we fit.

What did you say to me?

So it's going on. I think of myself, I shine up the me with powder and pink lips and what do I see but a roach climbing like a little trooper up from the baseboard, and what do I think of? Me is like a genie that goes in and out of my toilet water bottle but you are always somewhere around without being called. I paid money I didn't even have to get you a better place in the ground than you ever got me up here, and a woman to say the rosary a full three days, and you're still smoke around my shoulders. I looked at this fat roach that never got sick eating the paint off the walls because there's better things to pick at, and thought how that was you lying next to me in bed—that bed the man from welfare used to say was too big for one and leer at me—and that is still you lying in darker dark and a roach might be taking away your fingers right now for all I know. For all you know.

I know something you don't know.

The priest keeps saying, spreading out his big sweaty hands to calm me down, Now Ismael knows the last great secret, he is luckier than we are. Then he goes and names all the saints whose faces you're getting to see whether you want to or not. But I saw you dying and it was like watching you do something very very private when you didn't see me looking.

It wasn't merciful, I lied, something just got sucked away out of your eyes and when it was gone your cheeks began to collapse fast. But it was more of you than you ever showed me, dressed or naked, cold or hot, sick or sober. It was more.

Now how do I get out from under you. That's what I mean, I'm like one of those women a man died while he was inside of. Had a heart attack or something, you've heard about that. No matter where they take his body, she must always see his shoulders hunkering over her with his eyes wide on her face. I know it. And she thinks it's her fault too, a little bit, somehow a shadow of the fault, a sniff, a turn, an ooze of the fault.

The night he came home with me the first time and the last, Rosa who is your daughter no matter who's in my bed, came running into the bedroom crying Daddy is a ghost and he's scaring me. He tried to comfort her but she didn't even know who he was sitting there wrapped up in a sheet, and it took me an hour to get her back to bed. Then all he wanted to do was forget we ever saw each other, and he got dressed and went home. And I was glad. If you didn't get Rosa up out of her bed to come running in there on me just in the nick of time, then I think I did, with some strong part of my brain that I can't see.

I was planning another getaway when you escaped. Rosa was at my mother's and Chico was in his first week of sleep-away camp, and I was going out and get a job, I thought something on a boat going somewhere out of Brooklyn, I don't know, but I was standing right at the threshold, in a way. Singing, singing the whole day how you weren't going to lock me up from myself the way you locked me up from you. Then they came and told me they found you and these little sunbursts of color kept popping in front of my eyes just like when I drink, dark with rainbow colors. They had to lead me. They told me as though it was no secret how you'd been robbing me and telling me stories and laughing at me and shooting your children's groceries up in your arm and my breasts turned to clean round skulls that you had kissed in the morning. Somebody, Julio, said he was surprised I cared so much, I looked so weak choking on my own blood, and he took me to the hospital to breathe in the dead air you breathed out, and I said I don't like to be made a damn fool of, that's all. And there you were turned inside out in your skin like one of your own empty pockets and who was the damn fool then? Julio, the last time I saw him maybe a month ago, ran his hand down my behind with his finger pointing like an arrow, and I thought for a second that I might be free of you. I will tell you without shame I'd like to have made a bow bent for your dear friend Julio's arrow. But after he took me to your sweaty bed and showed you to me stretched out hot with your brain dissolving right before my eyes, I told him to go away. He shames me with myself.

They took you to the morgue and I had to go and check you out like some lost package. I was right there when you died and the doctor knew who I was and you didn't have to die in the street but maybe I do have welfare mothers' eyes. So I traded them down at that place, the morgue: They gave me what was left of you and I gave them my feet and they locked them in a vault.

Now you see a widow is a dry well. You always hear
the opposite. But I'll have them too, won't I? Heart's
beetles. Six fat maggots feasting on my tongue that knew
your tongue. I. I. I the stillborn.

Ismael, I wish you were alive, I wish, I wish, so I could hate you and
get on with it.

MARGARET DRABBLE

A DAY IN THE LIFE OF A
SMILING WOMAN

There was once this woman. She was in her thirties. She was quite
famous, in a way. She hadn't really meant to be famous: it had just
happened to her, without very much effort on her part. Sometimes
she thought about it, a little bewildered, and said to herself, This is
me, Jenny Jamieson, and everybody knows it's me.

Her husband was quite famous, too, but only to people who knew
what he was doing. He was famous in his own world. He was the
editor of a weekly, and so he had quite a pull with certain kinds of
people. It was through his pull, really, that Jenny had gotten her job.
She was getting bored, the little child was at nursery school and the
big ones at big school, so he had looked about for her and asked a few
friends and found her a nice little job at a television station. But he

hadn't quite bargained for how she would catch on. Everybody had always thought Jenny was pretty—in fact, she'd been a very recognizable type for years, had Jenny: pretty, a little restless, driven into the odd moment of malice by boredom, loving her children, cooking dinners, flirting a little (or possibly more) with her husband's friends and old lovers. She deserved a little job. But when she got going, when she got on the screen, she was transformed. She became, very quickly, beautiful. It took a few weeks, while she experimented with hairstyles and clothes and facial expressions. And suddenly, she was a beauty, and total strangers talked of her with yearning. And that wasn't all, either. She was also extremely efficient. Now, she always had been efficient; she'd always been able to get all the courses of a four-course meal onto the table, perfectly cooked, at the right moment. She was never late to collect children from school, she never forgot their dinner money or their swimming things, she never ran out of sugar or lavatory paper or cellotape. So people shouldn't have been surprised at the way she settled down to work.

She was never late. She never forgot appointments. She never forgot her briefing. She began quietly, interviewing people about cultural events in a spot in an arts program, and she always managed to say the right things to everyone; she never offended and yet never made people dull. She was intelligent and quick, she had sympathy for everyone she talked to, and all the time she looked so splendid, sitting there shining and twinkling. Everyone admired her, nobody disliked her. In no time at all, she had her own program, and she was able to do whatever she fancied on it. She used to invite the strangest people to be interviewed, and she would chat to them, seriously, earnestly, cheerfully. She told everybody that she loved her job, that she was so lucky, that it fitted on so well with the children and her husband, that she didn't have to be out too much. It's a perfect compromise, she would say, smiling. She didn't take herself very seriously—it's just an entertainment, she would say. I've been lucky, she would say. All I do is have the chats I'd love to have at home, and I get paid to do it. Lovely!

Her husband did not like this state of affairs at all. He became extremely bad-tempered, never came home if he could avoid it and yet would never commit himself to being out, because he did not want to make Jenny's life any easier. He wanted to make it as difficult as possible. So he would arrive unexpectedly and depart unexpectedly. He stopped bringing his friends home. He made endless unpleasant remarks and innuendoes about Jenny's colleagues in the television world, as though he had forgotten that he had introduced her to them in the first place. Sometimes he would wake up in the middle of the night and hit her. He would accuse her of neglecting him and the children. She was not quite sure how this had all happened. It didn't seem to have much to do with her, and yet she supposed it must be her fault. At night, when it was dark, she used to think it was her fault, but in the morning she would get up and go on smiling.

Then, one night, she came back from work, as she usually did on Wednesday evenings, late, tired. She noticed, as she parked the car outside the house, that the downstairs lights were still on, and she was sorry, because she did not feel like talking. She was too tired. She would have quite liked to talk about her program, because it had been interesting—she had been talking to a South African banned politician about the problems of political education—but her husband never watched the program these days. She found her key, opened the front door. Her head ached. She was upset, she had to admit it, about South Africa. Sometimes she thought she ought to go and do something about these things that upset her. But what? She pushed open the living-room door, and there was her husband, lying on the settee. He was listening to a record and reading.

She smiled. "Hello," she said.

He did not answer. She took off her coat and hung it over the back of a chair. She was going to make herself a milk drink, as she usually did, and go straight to bed. But just for the moment, she was too tired to move. She had had a long day, so she stood there, resting, thinking of the walk to the kitchen and how comfortable it would be to get into bed. She was just about to ask her husband if he would like a drink too—though he never did, he didn't like milk and coffee kept him awake—when a strange thing happened. Her husband put down his book and looked up at her, with an expression of real hatred, and said, "I suppose you're standing there waiting for me to offer to make you a drink, aren't you?"

Now, the truth was that he had hardly ever made her a drink, in the evening after work, so she could not possibly have been expecting such a thing. He had done so perhaps three times in the last six months. The thought of his offering to get up and make her a drink had never crossed her mind. So she answered, politely. "No, I was just going to ask you if you would like one." And then an even stranger thing happened. For no sooner were the words out of her mouth than a rage so violent possessed her, as though an electric current had been driven through her, that she began to shake and scream. She screamed at him for some time, and he lay there morosely, watching her, as though satisfied that he had by accident pressed the right button.

Then she calmed down and went and made her drink and went to bed. But as she lay down, she felt as though she had had some kind of shock treatment, that she had suffered brain damage and that she would never be the same again. Let us not exaggerate. This was not the first time that this kind of thing had nearly happened to her. But this time it had happened, and the difference between its nearly happening and its happening was enormous. She was a different woman. She went to bed a different woman.

In the morning, she woke up, as usual, at about half-past seven, and thought of the day ahead. Every day, she got up regularly at a quarter to eight, and gave the children their breakfast. Various people, including her husband, suggested from time to time that she should engage somebody to help her with these things, but she always said that she preferred to do them herself, she liked to be with the children and she did not like other people to see her at that hour in the morning. Also, she would say, smiling disbelievingly, I'm afraid I might get lazy. If I give myself half an excuse, I might get lazy and stay in bed.

On this particular morning, it did cross her mind that she might stay in bed all day. I really do not see the point of carrying on, she thought, as she lay there and remembered what had happened to her the night before. I cannot possibly win, she thought. Whatever I do, I will lose, that is certain. I might as well stay in bed.

But no, she thought, it is more honorable to fight to the death. So she got out of bed.

She had not often thought in these terms before. Rather, she used to say to herself, If death were announced, I would continue, like a saint, to sweep the floor. She had not thought, much, of winning or losing or battlefields.

She had her bath, as she always did, and while she was in the bath her eldest child brought her the post and the papers and opened her letters for her. She read the *Times* while she got dressed and looked at the *Guardian* while she brushed her hair. Then, before going down to breakfast, she read the lists of things to be done that lay by her bedside table. There were several lists, old and new, and it was never safe to read the newest one only. Some of the words on the lists were about shopping: haricot beans, it said at one point; Polish sausage, at another; then vitamin pills; shoelaces for Mark; raw carrots (?); Clive Jenkins; look up octroi. It would be hard to tell whether these notes were a sign of extreme organization or of panic. She could not tell herself. Carried over from list to list was a message that said *Hospital Thursday.* This seemed to indicate either that she was so worried about going to the hospital that she kept repeating the message to herself, neurotically, night after night, or that she was so little aware of it that she thought she might forget. But today was the day, so she would not forget.

She went downstairs and made breakfast. Two children wanted bacon sandwiches, and one said she would eat only a slice of leftover melon. She made herself a cup of coffee, and while they ate, she emptied the dishwasher and started to restack it, and took the dry clothes out of the airing cupboard and sorted them into piles to put away in drawers. Then she encouraged the children to put on their coats and shoes, and took them out, and put them in the car and drove them to school. They were all, by now, at the same school, which made life easier, as she would cheerfully remark. She remembered to remind them, as they ran off, that she would not be there to collect them, as she had an appointment, but that Faith would collect them and give them tea and supper. Then she went home and remembered to put a pound note in an envelope in the cupboard for Faith, in case she left before she herself got home in the evening. She would have done this, if her husband were home, but as usual he had not said whether he would be home or not, so she had to provide for every possibility, and one of these was that Faith would want to find a pound note in the cupboard.

Then she made the beds, and put the dry washing away, and stacked the breakfast things and ran down to the shops (which were luckily near) to buy tea and supper for the children, because although Faith was perfectly capable of doing this in theory, in practice she always did something silly, and anyway the women in the shops always shortchanged her with Jenny's money because she wasn't English, and Jenny did not consider herself quite rich enough to be shortchanged every day, though sometimes she let it go. Then, when these things were done (it was now half-past nine), she went up to her bedroom to change, because she couldn't possibly spend the whole day in the jersey and skirt she was wearing, because she had to go and give the prizes at a School Speech Day that evening and wouldn't have time to come home to change in between all the other things she had to do. She was due at a committee meeting at ten-thirty; she would make it all right, but only if she made her mind up quickly about what to wear.

She had quite a lot of clothes, as her job demanded that she should, but none of them looked very good this morning. They had buttons missing, or needed cleaning, or were too avant-garde for a Speech Day. She could not find anything suitable. Racked by indecision, sweat standing up in soft beads on her upper lip and running down her arms and thighs, she stood there in front of the wardrobe and thought, Is this it? Is this where I stop?

But no, because she finally decided that her long grey dress, although slightly too smart, would please the children at the school, if not the headmistress, and, after all, they would expect her to look a little colorful or they would not have invited her. So she put it on. It was a little too smart for a committee meeting, too, but the committee wouldn't mind. She put it on, and then her boots, so she wouldn't have to change her stockings, which had holes. She did not wear tights. She considered them unhygienic. And then she got her briefcase, and put in it her minutes for the meeting, and some old notes for her speech, and her appointment card for the hospital, and the correspondence with the headmistress of the school, and a book by the man she was supposed to meet for lunch. And then, thinking that she had gotten everything, she said goodbye to her husband, who had watched some of her preparations from bed and some from his desk, which stood in the bedroom. And off she went toward the bus stop.

She did not take her car into town. She did not like driving in London. How very sensible you are, people would say, and Jenny Jamieson would say yes, it is sensible, and she would chat about the antisocial inconveniences of driving in the West End, and from time to time, she would think, If they knew how very very frightened I am of the traffic, would they continue to think me sensible?

She arrived at the committee meeting in good time, as usual, and took her place, but as she nodded and smiled at her fellow committee members, she was obliged to recognize that something rather unpleasant had happened, connected no doubt with the shock she had sustained the evening before. The unpleasant thing was that she did not like the look of these people any more. She had never liked them very much, that was not why she had attended the meeting: she attended because she considered it her duty. It was a committee that had been set up to enquire into the reorganization of training schemes for aspiring television producers, directors, and interviewers, and it also considered applications and suggestions from some such aspirants. Jenny considered she ought to sit on this committee, because her own entry into the world they desired had been so irregular, and she thought that she, a lucky person, ought to try to be fair to those people who had not had her contacts. Not everybody, after all, had the good fortune of being married to Fred Jamieson. But her colleagues on the committee did not seem to have been moved by such motives.

The longer she knew them, the more convinced she had become

that they were simply there in order to give an appearance of respectability and democracy to a system that functioned perfectly well, that continued to function and which they had no intention of altering. It was a system of nepotism, as she knew from her own experience. Whatever polite recommendations they might make, younger sons and friends of friends and clever young people from fashionable universities would continue to be favored. She had accepted this, in a way, and had thought her presence useful, even if only because she occasionally managed to make out a case for some course of action or some individual who would otherwise have been considered negligible. She had understood why the others behaved as they did: most of them were older than herself, they had been brought up in a world of patronage, they had done well on it, they were kind, well-meaning, urbane, amusing, cynical, rather timid people, they could not be expected to rock any boat, let alone the one in which they were sitting. She had respected these things in them, she had understood. And now, suddenly, looking round the polished table at their faces—at thin grey beaky Maurice, at tiny old James Hanney, at brisk young smoothy Chris Bailey, at two-faced Tom (son of one of the powers), at all the rest of them—she found that she disliked them fairly intensely.

This is odd, she said to herself, looking down at her minutes. This is very odd.

And she thought, What has happened to me is that some little bit of mechanism in me has broken. There used to be, till yesterday, a little knob that one twisted until these people came into focus as nice, harmless, well-meaning people. And it's broken, it won't twist any more.

She tried and tried, she fiddled and fiddled inside her head to make it work, but it wouldn't work. They stayed as they were, perfectly clear, not a bit blurred by her inability to reduce them to their usual shapes. Horrible, they were.

The mechanism had broken because it had been expected to do too much work. She had been straining it for years.

She didn't think she could bear the look of things without it.

She kept very quiet during the meeting, because she did not know how to express herself in this new situation. She could hardly remember the kind of things that she used to say, that she would have said if she hadn't been so filled with horror and disgust. Once or twice a diplomatic phrase occurred to her, she realized how she could have thrown in a small spanner or suggested a different approach, but it didn't seem worth bothering. And what frightened her most was that she had always known, intellectually, that it wasn't worth bothering, that her contributions were negligible; and yet she had continued to make them, because she *felt* that it was worth doing, she *felt* that she should. And now she didn't feel it. So it was simply herself that she had been indulging all this time. So there was no point in appealing any more to what she ought to do. It had never been a question of that. The actual situation, unillumined by her own good will and her own desire to make the best of things, was beyond hope.

Making the best of things, she thought, as the meeting ended, is a terrible thing to do. They must become worse before they become better, as Karl Marx said.

She did not smile very much as she left the meeting. She put on a preoccupied look instead, which absolved her from the obligation.

She was due for lunch, at one, in a French restaurant in Soho. She was to entertain a clergyman, due for interview. He had outspoken views on violence in Africa and the need for the churches to offer their support. She was hoping for conviction from him, for she herself veered toward pacifism, weakly. She was not looking forward to the lunch. There had been a day when lunches had been her delight: newly released from the burden of cooking unwanted meals for infants, and herself brooding morosely over a boiled egg or a piece of cheese, she had embarked on large meals and wine and shellfish and cigarettes and coffee and chat, with great pleasure. But the pleasure had faded, and now she feared to fall asleep in the afternoons. She was so tired, these days.

Her secretary had booked the table. The clergyman, said her secretary, had seemed delighted at the prospect of lunch. And as Jenny's program paid its interviewees badly, in her now sophisticated view, lunch was considered a justifiable expense. She looked at her watch, as she got out of the taxi. Five to one, it was. She was due at the hospital at three, she must make sure she was not late, Africa or no Africa.

She was drinking a glass of tonic when the clergyman arrived. She always ordered tonic if she got there first, because it looked like gin and didn't put other people off drinking. Other people did hate to be discouraged from drinking, she had found. The clergyman, deceived, ordered a Campari. He was expecting her to twinkle and glitter and glow like something on a Christmas tree: she could see the expectation in his eyes, as he looked at her over the menu. And she thought, Dare I disappoint him? And then she thought, sickened, as she decided on a salad: I treat people like children, and I treat my children like adults.

She thought of her children, with unaccountable yearning. The yearning was mixed, vaguely mixed, with the thought of the hospital. Jenny Jamieson loved her children with a grand passion. Sometimes, looking at them, she thought she would faint with love.

The clergyman ordered soup and *poulet grandmère*. She joined him with the *poulet*. They talked about Mozambique and Angola and Rhodesia and the leadership of the Zulus. They talked about the World Council of Churches. She was able to watch him enjoy the familiar shock of the thoroughness with which she had done her homework. She had a good memory for dates and facts and had found it extremely useful: it commanded instant respect. She knew that he knew more of the realities than she did—he had been there, after all, he had lived with them—but he was not as good at dates. She had been a good examinee and was now a good examiner.

But she did not like the clergyman. She had wanted to like him, as he had wanted to like her. But they did not like each other. She did not like him, really, because he had agreed to eat lunch with her and appear on her program. She thought of Groucho Marx this time, not Karl, and his remark that he did not want to belong to any club that admitted him as a member. What were they doing there, both of them, sitting eating an expensive meal, when an agreement had just been made that decided that Africans in Rhodesia could not vote until they had £900 income a year? The average income for an

African in Rhodesia was £156 p.a., or so she had read in her morning's paper.

It occurred to her that the clergyman did not like her for much the same reason. It was not possible for them to like each other, sitting in such a place.

The allowances we have to make, she thought, are just too much for us.

In another mood she might have essayed an ironic hint, a smile, to indicate that she had recognized that this was so, to do him the credit of thinking that he too might have known it. But why should they be let off?

She continued to think, however, that she might feel differently about the whole matter on Wednesday week, when the clergyman was to appear on her program. So she asked questions and made notes of answers, as they ate their chicken and declined pudding and drank black coffee. Then the clergyman had to go, and she had just time to arrive comfortably, by taxi, at the hospital.

She was rather surprised to find herself at the hospital, as she had been rather surprised to find herself at her doctor's the month before. She was an exceptionally healthy woman, was Jenny Jamieson, and so afraid of hypochondria (an affliction she truly despised) that she never allowed herself to think about her health. She ignored her body. It was not a subject that could be contemplated with much pleasure, for although beautiful now, momentarily, she expected daily the decay of beauty and did not allow herself to dwell too much on pleasure or on fear. She was a sensible woman. Probably you begin to see by now how sensible she was. But nevertheless, although sensible, on this occasion, she had allowed a splendid ignorance to go on a little too long. For several months now, she had been bleeding when she ought not to have been and had been too busy even to worry about it. Occasionally, she would say to herself, Oh, God (wiping the sheets on the bed, throwing away another pair of paper knickers), oh, God, I must do something about that. And then the phone would ring, or a child would call, or the post would arrive, or it would be time to go to the studio, and she would forget. So she didn't get round to going to the doctor until one morning, when the company rang her up and said that, unexpectedly, they wouldn't be wanting her after all, as her guest had been held up by an air strike in Florida. So she had a morning off, and instead of sitting down with the paper and a cup of coffee to enjoy it, she instantly, and, as it seemed, entirely arbitrarily, began to worry about the bleeding, and went up to the doctor's and sat in his surgery waiting to see him for an hour and a half. She rather thought (being a healthy person) that he would say not to be so silly, when she described her symptoms. She expected him to say that it was nothing at all. But he didn't. Instead, he listened gravely and attentively, and didn't smile once (though she smiled enough for two) and told her she ought to go and see a gynecologist. "Oh, all right," she said. And so here she found herself, in a gynecological hospital, waiting patiently for her turn.

She waited for hours. Thank God she had known it would take hours. She kept thinking how demoralizing it would have been, if one hadn't known. Luckily one was not as young and nervous as one used to be.

The surgeon was a short, nice old man. He dug around inside her with his fingers until she cried out. Does that hurt, he said. No, no, she said. Because it did not hurt. It frightened her, it did not hurt her.

She was still expecting him to smile, as she sat up on the white paper sheet in her beige petticoat, and to tell her that there was nothing there.

And he did smile. But what he said was, "You'd better come in for a little operation."

She didn't listen very attentively to his answers to her sensible questions, though she forced herself (as though on the screen) to ask them all. She asked about malignant growths, and cervical smears, and polyps and ulcers, but she wasn't listening. She remembered, faintly, a dreadful interview with a cabinet minister, when she had been so crumpled up with bellyache that she had hardly been able to hear a word the man was saying. The surgeon seemed to be trying to reassure her: he patted her on the knee. He did not recognize her:

probably he was too busy carving women up to watch the television. She had no illusions about the extent of her notoriety. And anyway, women in their petticoats look much the same. She loved him, for patting her knee through the hospital sheet.

"You go to the appointments lady, my dear," he said. "See when they can fit you in." There would be a bed free in three weeks' time.

I know what beauty is, she thought, as she walked through the front door of the hospital, dreading already her return: beauty is the love that shone through my face. And it is dying, it has been murdered, and they will see nothing but their own ugliness. Beauty is love, she thought.

She was so dazed by her encounter with the surgeon that she wandered, idly, for half an hour or so. She walked up and down the streets off Oxford Street, looking in pornographic bookshop windows.

She was terrified. She was ill, she was dying. She was looking her last on the *Loves of Lesbos*, the *ABC of Flagellation*. I have wasted my life, she thought. Oh, God, she thought, direct me, please.

On the train, she sat down quietly and began to work out the implications of death. Her life, luckily, she had heavily insured, some years before. It had seemed a good idea at the time, and she had never regretted it. Her husband, though competent in some ways, was feckless: he was also much hated, as editors often are, and if ever he lost his power to control others, others would not waste time in trying to ruin him. She had thought to herself, some years ago, as soon as she began to earn good money, I should insure myself, for the children's sake. Well, she had done it, she had not merely thought about it, she had done it. That was the kind of woman she was. So she need not worry about their material future.

But what of their need for her?

She loved them. She had made herself indispensable. That had been her aim.

Would they weep for her?

The rain fell, outside, on the dark countryside. Two men, commuters, were playing cards, as they did every night. She envied their will to brighten their lot. Inside, she was weeping away, she was weeping blood. Whatever should she say to the girls, at the other end of this journey?

A friend of hers, recently, had killed herself. Jenny, with mechanical kindness, had comforted husband and mistress and child, in so much as it was in her to do so. It was the woman who had been her friend, after all, and she was dead. The child did not seem to notice much. So much sympathy had been lavished upon the survivors. But the woman, Jenny's friend, was dead forever. She was beyond sympathy and love and fear. She was no more. What rage must have possessed her, at the moment of extinction, to know what tenderness would accrue to others from her death, while she lay rotting.

Jenny had a vision of herself dead, and her survivors basking in the warm sun of condolence. So much pleasanter for them than her presence, it would be. They did not much care for her presence, these days.

Though that, of course, was not true of the children. No, they would grieve for her, if she died, as she would, forever, for them, if they were to die.

And as she sat there, she knew that this was it, this was the reckoning. She would have to think about those things that she so much ignored. She would have to contemplate, now, here, her own not-being: Would she die under the knife, would she expire in the hands of an incompetent anesthetist, would she fade slowly from malignant growths, the months running down into weeks, the weeks into days? She had heard recently of a friend's friend who had died at home: in the morning she had had breakfast, had played cards with her child, had chatted to her friend. Then she had fallen, as it seemed, asleep. But she had been dead, there in her bed, and no gentle shaking, no offers of the already-prepared lunch, had been able to wake her. What a mystery, how devious was death, to creep so wickedly in so many quiet ways. Death was certain: her luck had run out. Death sat with her there in the carriage, but what questions could she put to this unwanted guest? She must decide, here, on the five fifty-eight, about the existence of God, and the power of human love, and the nature of chance.

She had not neglected these subjects entirely. But she had postponed judgment. Now she would have to decide. Time had run out.

She had always, until this moment, politely supposed that God must exist. At least, she had given him the benefit of the doubt—as she had given it to Fred Jamieson. But it did strike her now, again with a sudden electric sense of shock, that her own premature and sudden death would disprove the existence of God entirely, and that her faith in him had rested only on her belief that he would fulfill his obligations as she would fulfill hers. And if he failed (as the very existence of the hospital suggested he might), then he could not exist at all. How could a God exist who would be so careless of his contracts as to allow her to die and break her own contracts to her own infants?

Her children would be ruined by her death. No corrupt adult reassurances, no promises of treats, would buy them off. Any confidence in fate would be ruined by her removal. She had loved them so, and it was her love that would undo them. Her friend who had killed herself had not loved her child, so the child had survived. It was her own love that would undo them.

The apathy of God, the random blows of fate and the force for good and ill of human love: these things, combined, constituted a world so bitter, so dark, so tragic, that she felt her heart weep and die like her body.

They would cry for her and there would be no comfort. She would be dead and gone and powerless, and thus they would know the dreadful truth.

She was parting herself from God, she was leaving and turning her face from him. Only in leaving him did she realize how much she would have liked him to be there: as she would have liked her husband to like her. But it was not to be. God was too weak, too feeble, she had looked after him too nicely for too long. She had felt sorry for him because of his nonexistence. If I give him a chance to behave better, she had thought to herself for years, vaguely, maternally, he might learn how to do it: he might learn better from me and show his face to me.

But he couldn't show her his face because he didn't have one. That was why she hadn't seen it so far. She felt sorry for him, as one for a friend caught out making an empty boast. She didn't want to question him too closely about his reasons for having lied to so many for so long: she didn't want to make a fool of him. She was very careful, was Jenny Jamieson: she never made a fool of people on the box, and she was very delicate about doing it even in her own head. She always regretted it when people insisted on condemning themselves out of their own mouths, and she would do her best to prevent them. So now, too, she thought (or could imagine) that she would soon find some means of concealing from God her own violent and utter loss of faith in him: she would find some way of humoring him along. There was no point in getting angry about the matter: he was too weak to withstand anger.

The train stopped at a station, started again, continued on its way.

What grieved her most was the thought that her children would never know about the intensity of her love, the depth of her concern. It was impossible to convey to them the nature of her emotion. To a lover, one could explain such things: lovers, ripped asunder by death, at least know that the other, on the point of death, had thought of the terms of love. For a lover, death need not be a rejection and an abandoning. But for a child, it could not be anything else: no child could know how much he was loved, his mind could never encompass the massive adult passion.

She thought, I will write them a letter. In this letter, I will explain how much I loved them, and how sorry I was to abandon and forsake them, and I will give the letter to my solicitor, and he will lock it away in a safe and give them each their copy when they are eighteen.

But she knew that she would not write such a letter. For the writing of it would seal her own death warrant and date it, and it was as yet undated. She could not afford to run a risk of making certain what was at the moment at least open to hope. So she would die, in three weeks' time, in a year's time, and the letter would be unwritten and they would never know. She died and left us, they would say, because she didn't care enough for us, she didn't care enough to live.

She imagined their faces, their nightmares, their sick and endless deforming resentments, their lonely wakenings, their empty arms, their boarding schools, their substitute consolations.

And this was the price of love.

It did not seem tolerable, it did not seem possible.

She would go out like a light, she would be switched off forever. There would be nothing to grieve with, no ghost to hover anxiously over their heads. She would be forced to default, coerced by death into breaking her contract. She had contracted herself to her children, for the period of their infancy: she would have to break the contract and she would have no excuse.

The bitterness of it filled her and possessed her, but she was beginning to breathe again, because she knew, now, what it was that she feared. She had faced it, and it was nearly time to get off the train; she could think about it again later. She would store it away, for future consideration. And meanwhile, she would have to think of something to say to the girls. She opened her bag, and took out an old envelope and began to scribble herself some notes for a speech.

The headmistress met her on the station. She had been met by many such people, on many such stations, and had always, at the time, thought to herself how nice they were, these people. It was only afterward, in retrospect, that she would come to admit to herself that some of them were quite frightful. She wondered, now, as she walked up to the waiting woman in her fur coat, if one of the consequences of her last day of life would be that the dislike would always, now, set in instantly, that the judgment would always, now, be made at once, because there was so little time left for other ways of doing things. The thought crossed her mind, in the instant as she approached, paused, checked that it was the right person with the right look of recognition, and extended her cold hand: and it was so—she knew at once that she did not like this woman at all, that she could have no time for her at all. Afterward, she thought, if I had not conceived such a motion, it would not have been so: as part of her was to believe, despite the evidence, for the rest of her life, that if she had not gone to the doctor that morning, the thing inside her would not have existed at all. She should never have condoned its existence.

As they drove back to the school, the headmistress in the fur coat talked about town councilors and local education authority people and how one had to give them sherry. She then started to complain bitterly about the fact that her school had been turned into a comprehensive. As Jenny Jamieson had accepted the invitation because the school was a comprehensive, she was not well inclined toward this line of conversation. Nor did she think much of Miss Trueman's reasons for despising town councilors and aldermen, nor of her tact in uttering them. She had often received surprises of the same kind and could never decide whether those who spoke to her in such a vein simply mistook her own moderately fashionable and public political views and prejudices—or whether they were utterly indifferent to them and would have uttered them stubbornly, tactlessly, regardless of the nature of the audience.

So she did not have much to say in reply to the small talk of the headmistress, Miss Trueman. However, upon arriving at the school, she managed to make the usual obligatory remarks about the charm of its location, the modernity of its buildings, its handsome array of Speech Day flowers.

They were to have sherry before the ceremony. Jenny Jamieson went to the headmistress's lavatory and discovered to her alarm that she was losing rather a lot of blood: doubtless the surgeon had prodded whatever was producing the blood rather hard and had disturbed it considerably. She had nothing to stop it with: she had not brought anything, had not thought of it. She disliked the headmistress too much to ask her if she had any Tampax. Anyway, she thought, she is probably too old to need such things, this woman. She had a moment of panic, standing there in the centrally heated lavatory. But she decided to ignore the blood. After all, she said to herself, it takes an awful lot of blood to show. One can feel quite soaked sometimes and when one looks at one's clothes it hasn't even got through one layer, let alone to the surface.

Nevertheless, she declined a glass of sherry. She was not feeling too well, and the room was far too hot. She had a glass of water instead, as there were no soft drinks. So much for gracious living, she thought, as she watched Miss Trueman deftly condescending to the town councilors and the staff, and endured a succession of people who said how wise she was not to drink before speaking and how glad they were that they didn't have to speak themselves. She felt rather dizzy and was extremely aware of the place where the surgeon had poked her.

There were some tropical fish in a tank on a bookshelf. They had some babies, protected by an inner glass tank. They would have eaten their own babies otherwise, the mothers. She commented on the fish and admired them, for want of better things to say, and a woman to whom she had been introduced started to tell a story about her own children's goldfish and how they kept dying.

Jenny Jamieson did not like this conversation because her own fish had died the year before, and she had been extremely unhappy on the day of their death, when they had floated around keeling over, the two of them, at a sad angle, as though they had lost their sense of watery balance. She had disliked the sense of death in the room, but had been unable to save or kill them and had not moved them out of the room because it would have seemed to her to be graceless, heartless, to make them die in a strange place. Let them die here, she had thought, and had endured their passing. Then she had gently buried them at the end of the garden under the lower branches of the cotoneaster.

But what was this woman saying to her now, interrupting her own memories of funeral? She was saying, in a harsh and brutal nasal voice, laughing as she said it, "And I told the kids I'd buried them. I'd buried them in the garden, I said, but of course I hadn't. I'd put them in the obvious place. . . ." And one or two other people laughed, but Jenny had missed her cue, she didn't know what the other woman was saying. She knew her face had looked momentarily blank and baffled, and she started to speak, to say that where else should one bury them but in the garden, when the other woman said, heartily, "*You* know, I flushed them away, well, I mean to say, wouldn't you?" and Jenny worked out that this woman had actually put her children's goldfish down the lavatory and then said that she had buried them in the garden. She did not know which was more unnatural, the woman's insensitivity, or her own sensitivity, which made her so slow to recognize the meaning of words, the end of life, the obvious places to put dead bodies. She had flushed their little gold bodies down into the sewers, and what was wrong with that? Jenny Jamieson shivered and trembled: heaps of corpses filled her vision. She had buried her fish gently, reluctantly, sorrowfully: they had been in her charge and they had died. Her solicitude had been more than godly, for God left dead dogs on beaches and crushed rabbits on the brows of roads. Gold spectacles, gold fillings, mounds of pilfering and salvage. But flesh is not for salvage: it is not even flotsam or jetsam. It is waste.

And now it was time to go into the School Hall, and there was the platform, and the school orchestra, and the serried ranks of parents and children, and the returning sixth formers who had left the year before, all dolled up, free of Miss Trueman's surveillance, all come back to give the old thing a slap in the eye. And there were the prizes, dozens and dozens of them, all to be handed out with a cheerful smile; she would smile till the muscles of her face grew rigid and stiff. And here was a child presenting her with a bouquet; it smelled sickly, of cemeteries and death; it was already decaying through its cellophane in the intense and human heat. And now the headmistress was about to deliver her report.

Jenny Jamieson sat back on her chair. There was no need to listen to the report. She thought again of the surgeon's fingers and the white hospital sheet. She thought of the goldfish, wavering and keeling over, slowly gasping, unprotesting, dying in silence, rejected by their element, floating hopelessly upward. She was losing a lot of blood now; she could feel it seeping from her. Her knickers were quite wet. She was glad that she had put on her grey dress: it was of a thick material, though unfortunately it was pale enough to show, if marked. But it would absorb a good deal before it marked.

Miss Trueman talked of the difficulty of adapting to new ways, and the problems of the less gifted, and the marvelous way the school had coped with the upheavals of the last few years, and how it was not a happy unity, where each could find her place, with work fitting to her talents—"for we all have talents," said Miss Trueman, "though we may not all take our A Levels."

The school was rigidly streamed and had managed to segregate all its new nonacademic intake very thoroughly.

"Our A-Level results," said Miss Trueman, "are still as high as ever, we are proud to say."

Jenny Jamieson thought, I will never let anyone inside me again. Too often, now, I have politely opened my legs. It shall not happen again. Too many meals I have politely cooked, too many times have I apologized.

"Unfortunately," said Miss Trueman, "Mrs. Hyams has had to retire this year through ill health, but I am sure we all join in sending her our very good wishes. . . ."

Jenny Jamieson looked at the mothers and fathers, and at the girls. Blank and bored and docile they looked. They sat in rows, very quietly, and let Miss Trueman (Harrogate and Somerville) look down upon them.

She thought, again, of her own children, and the bland confidence with which she had assumed that she herself would one day sit in such a hall, as a parent, and listen to others make dull and foolish speeches and hand out prizes to her own three. How much she had expected of life. She had expected to see them grow up, to see their long legs and their adult faces and their children. It was impossible that an accident, like death, could separate them from her. And yet it was possible: such things happened, daily.

She felt her spirit tremble, as it prepared to launch itself across this dizzy gulf: had it the power? Would its wings carry it to the other shore or would she fall, here, now, forever, into the darkness?

And she thought to herself: those who do not love, die, and they are forgotten, and it is of no account. But those who love as I have loved cannot perish. The body may perish, but my love could not cease to exist: it does not need me, I am dispensable, I may drop away in that hospital like an old husk, but I am not needed, the years I put in are enough (Freud would say, Klein would say, those mighty saints and heralds)—it is enough, I am released from existence, I am freed, for my love is stronger than the grave.

Her spirit, breathless, reached the other side. With immense excitement, with discovery, with revelation, she said to herself: My love is stronger than the grave.

Later she was to say to herself, All revelations are banal. But even so, it is as hard to receive them as it is to gaze at the sun, which is, after all, a commonplace and daily sight.

Still later she was to say to herself, That was the moment at which it was decided that I should not die, for that was the moment at which I accepted death.

But at the time, she sat there neatly, listening to Miss Trueman, who was by now reciting her own biography: "How fortunate we are," she was saying, "to have with us this evening Mrs. Jamieson, who is so well known to all of us. How privileged we are," said Miss Trueman, with a most subtle and magnificent note of superiority in her privileged tones, "to have with us a woman who has distinguished herself. . . ."

Some of us, of course, thought Jenny Jamieson, are so constructed that we have to end up smiling. She thought this then, even while she was still trembling with the intensity of her conviction. She was quick.

And she rose to her feet and smiled and began her speech on cue. And whether it was a shame or a dignity, she could not tell, she did it well, this kind of thing. But, as has been said already, she did most things well. Even her spiritual crises she endured well. And came up smiling. And stood there smiling, speaking of new opportunities for girls these days and how important it was to think in terms of having careers as well as husbands, "for the two, these days," said Jenny Jamieson, smiling confidently (shining, confident, a beautiful example), "for the two these days, can be so easily combined. We are so fortunate these days," said Jenny Jamieson, "and we must take every advantage of our opportunities."

It would be hard to say what she herself thought of this ending. The force of her nature was very strong. She could not act without conviction. So she manufactured conviction. That is one way of looking at it. There are other ways.

What is true is that while she was standing there, and smiling, and speaking with such good cheer about the future of womankind, blood was seeping out of her, and trickling down her thigh, under her stocking and into her boot. There was an awful lot of it. Thank God, she said to herself, as she spoke to others of other things, thank God I put a long skirt and boots on, so it doesn't show.

For twenty minutes, she spoke and bled.

Looking back, she was to think of this day as both a joke and a victory, but at whose expense, and over whom, she could not have said.

GAIL GODWIN

A SORROWFUL WOMAN

Once upon a time there was a wife and mother one too many times.

One winter evening she looked at them: the husband durable, receptive, gentle: the child a tender golden three. The sight of them made her so sad and sick she did not want to see them ever again.

She told the husband these thoughts. He was attuned to her; he understood such things. He said he understood. What would she like him to do? "If you could put the boy to bed and read him the story about the monkey who ate too many bananas, I would be grateful." "Of course," he said. "Why, that's a pleasure." And he sent her off to bed.   •

The next night it happened again. Putting the warm dishes away in the cupboard, she turned and saw the child's grey eyes approving her movements. In the next room was the man, his chin sunk in the open collar of his favorite wool shirt. He was dozing after her good supper. The shirt was the grey of the child's trusting gaze. She began yelping without tears, retching in between. The man woke in alarm and carried her in his arms to bed. The boy followed them up the stairs, saying, "It's all right, Mommy," but this made her scream. "Mommy is sick," the father said, "go and wait for me in your room."

The husband undressed her, abandoning her only long enough to root beneath the eiderdown for her flannel gown. She stood naked except for her bra, which hung by one strap down the side of her body; she had not the impetus to shrug it off. She looked down at the right nipple, shriveled with chill, and thought, How absurd, a vertical bra. "If only there were instant sleep," she said, hicupping, and the husband bundled her into the gown and went out and came back with a sleeping draft guaranteed swift. She was to drink a little glass of cognac followed by a big glass of dark liquid and afterwards there was just time to say Thank you and could you get him a clean pair of pajamas out of the laundry, it came back today.

The next day was Sunday and the husband brought her breakfast in bed and let her sleep until it grew dark again. He took the child for a walk, and when they returned, red-cheeked and boisterous, the father made supper. She heard them laughing in the kitchen. He brought her up a tray of buttered toast, celery sticks, and black bean soup. "I am the luckiest woman," she said, crying real tears. "Nonsense," he said. "You need a rest from us," and went to prepare the sleeping draft, find the child's pajamas, select the story for the night.

She got up on Monday and moved about the house till noon. The boy, delighted to have her back, pretended he was a vicious tiger and followed her from room to room, growling and scratching. Whenever she came close, he would growl and scratch at her. One of his sharp little claws ripped her flesh, just above the wrist, and together they paused to watch a thin red line materialize on the inside of her pale arm and spill over in little beads. "Go away," she said. She got herself upstairs and locked the door. She called the husband's office and said, "I've locked myself away from him. I'm afraid." The husband told her in his richest voice to lie down, take it easy, and he was already on the phone to call one of the baby-sitters they often employed. Shortly after, she heard the girl let herself in, heard the girl coaxing the frightened child to come and play.

After supper several nights later, she hit the child. She had known she was going to do it when the father would see. "I'm sorry," she said, collapsing on the floor. The weeping child had run to hide. "What has happened to me, I'm not myself anymore." The man picked her tenderly from the floor and looked at her with much concern. "Would it help if we got, you know, a girl in? We could fix the room downstairs. I want you to feel freer," he said, understanding these things. "We have the money for a girl. I want you to think about it."

And now the sleeping draft was a nightly thing, she did not have to ask. He went down to the kitchen to mix it, he set it nightly beside her bed. The little glass and the big one, amber and deep rich brown, the flannel gown and the eiderdown.

The man put out the word and found the perfect girl. She was young, dynamic, and not pretty. "Don't bother with the room, I'll fix it up myself." Laughing, she employed her thousand energies. She painted the room white, fed the child lunch, read edifying books, raced the boy to the mailbox, hung her own watercolors on the fresh-painted walls, made spinach soufflé, cleaned a spot from the mother's coat, made them all laugh, danced in stocking feet to music in the white room after reading the child to sleep. She knitted dresses for herself and played chess with the husband. She washed and set the mother's soft ash-blonde hair and gave her neck rubs, offered to.

The woman now spent her winter afternoons in the big bedroom. She made a fire in the hearth and put on slacks and an old sweater she had loved at school, and sat in the big chair and stared out the window at snow-ridden branches, or went away into novels about other people moving through other winters.

The girl brought the child in twice a day, once in the later afternoon when he would tell of his day, all of it tumbling out quickly because there was not much time, and before he went to bed. Often now, the man took his wife to dinner. He made a courtship ceremony of it, inviting her beforehand so she could get used to the idea.

They dressed and were beautiful together again and went out into the frosty night. Over candlelight he would say, "I think you are better, you know." "Perhaps I am," she would murmur. "You look . . . like a cloistered queen," he said once, his voice breaking curiously.

One afternoon the girl brought the child into the bedroom. "We've been out playing in the park. He found something he wants to give you, a surprise." The little boy approached her, smiling mysteriously. He placed his cupped hands in hers and left a live dry thing that spat brown juice in her palm and leapt away. She screamed and wrung her hands to be rid of the brown juice. "Oh, it was only a grasshopper," said the girl. Nimbly she crept to the edge of a curtain, did a quick knee bend and reclaimed the creature, led the boy competently from the room.

"The girl upsets me," said the woman to her husband. He sat frowning on the side of the bed he had not entered for so long. "I'm sorry, but there it is." The husband stroked his creased brow and said he was sorry too. He really did not know what they would do without that treasure of a girl. "Why don't you stay here with me in bed," the woman said.

Next morning she fired the girl who cried and said, "I loved the little boy, what will become of him now?" But the mother turned away her face and the girl took down the watercolors from the walls, sheathed the records she had danced to, and went away.

"I don't know what we'll do. It's all my fault, I know. I'm such a burden, I know that."

"Let me think. I'll think of something." (Still understanding these things.)

"I know you will. You always do," she said.

With great care he rearranged his life. He got up hours early, did the shopping, cooked the breakfast, took the boy to nursery school. "We will manage," he said, "until you're better, however long that is." He did his work, collected the boy from the school, came home and made the supper, washed the dishes, got the child to bed. He managed everything. One evening, just as she was on the verge of swallowing her draft, there was a timid knock on her door. The little boy came in wearing his pajamas. "Daddy has fallen asleep on my bed and I can't get in. There's no room."

Very sedately she left her bed and went to the child's room. Things were much changed. Books were rearranged, toys. He'd done some new drawings. She came as a visitor to her son's room, wakened the father, and helped him to bed. "Ah, he shouldn't have bothered you," said the man, leaning on his wife. "I've told him not to." He dropped into his own bed and fell asleep with a moan. Meticulously she undressed him. She folded and hung his clothes. She covered his body with the bedclothes. She flicked off the light that shone in his face.

The next day she moved her things into the girl's white room. She put her hairbrush on the dresser; she put a note pad and pen beside the bed. She stocked the little room with cigarettes, books, bread, and cheese. She didn't need much.

At first the husband was dismayed. But he was receptive to her needs. He understood these things. "Perhaps the best thing is for you to follow it through," he said. "I want to be big enough to contain whatever you must do."

All day long she stayed in the white room. She was a young queen, a virgin in a tower; she was the previous inhabitant, the girl with all the energies. She tried these personalities on like costumes, then discarded them. The room had a new view of streets she'd never seen that way before. The sun hit the room in late afternoon and she took to brushing her hair in the sun. One day she decided to write a poem. "Perhaps a sonnet." She took up her pen and pad and began working from words that had lately lain in her mind. She had choices for the sonnet, ABAB or ABBA for a start. She pondered these possibilities until she tottered into a larger choice: she did not have to write a sonnet. Her poem could be six, eight, ten, thirteen lines, it could be any number of lines, and it did not even have to rhyme.

She put down the pen on top of the pad.

In the evenings, very briefly, she saw the two of them. They knocked on her door, a big knock and a little, and she would call Come in, and the husband would smile though he looked a bit tired, yet somehow this tiredness suited him. He would put her sleeping draft on the bedside table and say, "The boy and I have done all right today," and the child would kiss her. One night she tasted for the first time the power of his baby spit.

"I don't think I can see him anymore," she whispered sadly to the man. And the husband turned away, but recovered admirably and said, "Of course, I see."

So the husband came alone. "I have explained to the boy," he said. "And we are doing fine. We are managing." He squeezed his wife's pale arm and put the two glasses on her table. After he had gone, she sat looking at the arm.

"I'm afraid it's come to that," she said. "Just push the notes under the door; I'll read them. And don't forget to leave the draft outside."

The man sat for a long time with his head in his hands. Then he rose and went away from her. She heard him in the kitchen where he mixed the draft in batches now to last a week at a time, storing it in a corner of the cupboard. She heard him come back, leave the big glass and the little one outside on the floor.

Outside her window the snow was melting from the branches, there were more people on the streets. She brushed her hair a lot and seldom read anymore. She sat in her window and brushed her hair for hours, and saw a boy fall off his new bicycle again and again, a dog chasing a squirrel, an old woman peek slyly over her shoulder and then extract a parcel from a garbage can.

In the evening she read the notes they slipped under her door. The child could not write, so he drew and sometimes painted his. The notes were painstaking at first: the man and boy offering the final strength of their day to her. But sometimes, when they seemed to have had a bad day, there were only hurried scrawls.

One night, when the husband's note had been extremely short, loving but short, and there had been nothing from the boy, she stole out of her room as she often did to get more supplies, but crept upstairs instead and stood outside their doors, listening to the regular breathing of the man and boy asleep. She hurried back to her room and drank the draft.

She woke earlier now. It was spring, there were birds. She listened for sounds of the man and the boy eating breakfast; she listened for the roar of the motor when they drove away. One beautiful noon, she went out to look at her kitchen in the daylight. Things were changed. He had bought some new dish towels. Had the old ones worn out? The canisters seemed closer to the sink. She inspected the cupboard and saw new things among the old. She got out flour, baking powder, salt, milk (he bought a different brand of butter), and baked a loaf of bread and left it cooling on the table.

The force of the two joyful notes slipped under her door that evening pressed her into the corner of the little room; she hardly had space to breathe. As soon as possible, she drank the draft.

Now the days were too short. She was always busy. She woke with the first bird. Worked till the sun set. No time for hair brushing. Her fingers raced the hours.

Finally, in the nick of time, it was finished one late afternoon. Her veins pumped and her forehead sparkled. She went to the cupboard, took what was hers, closed herself into the little white room, and brushed her hair for a while.

The man and boy came home and found: five loaves of warm bread, a roast stuffed turkey, a glazed ham, three pies of different fillings, eight molds of the boy's favorite custard, two weeks' supply of fresh-laundered sheets and shirts and towels, two hand-knitted sweaters (both of the same grey color), a sheath of marvelous water-color beasts accompanied by mad and fanciful stories nobody could ever make up again, and a tablet full of love sonnets addressed to the man. The house smelled redolently of renewal and spring. The man ran to the little room, could not contain himself to knock, flung back the door.

"Look, Mommy is sleeping," said the boy. "She's tired from doing all our things again." He dawdled in a stream of the last sun for that day and watched his father roll tenderly back her eyelids, lay his ear softly to her breast, test the delicate bones of her wrist. The father put down his face into her fresh-washed hair.

"Can we eat the turkey for supper?" the boy asked.

ANN BEATTIE

DOWNHILL

Walking the dog at 7:30 A.M., I sit on the wet grass by the side of the road, directly across from the beaver pond and diagonally across from the graveyard. In back of me is a grapevine that I snitch from. The grapes are bitter. The dog lifts a leg on a gravestone, rolls in dead squirrel in the road, comes to my side, finally—thank God none of the commuters ran over him—and licks my wrist. The wet wrist feels awful. I rub it along his back, passing it off as a stroke. I do it several times. "Please don't leave me," I say to the dog, who cocks his head and settles in the space between my legs on the grass.

My mother writes Jon this letter:

"Oh, Jon, we are so happy that September marks the beginning of your last year in law school. My husband said to me Saturday (we were at the Turkish restaurant we took you and Maria to when she was recuperating—the one you both liked so much) that now when he gets mad he can say, 'I'll sue!' and mean it. It has been uphill for so long, and now it will be downhill."

Curiously, that week an old friend of Jon's sent us a toy—a small bent-kneed skier who, when placed at the top of a slanting board, would glide to the bottom. I tried to foul up the toy every which way, I even tried making it ski on sandpaper, and it still worked. I tacked the sandpaper to a board, and down it went. The friend had bought it in Switzerland, where he and his wife were vacationing. So said the note in the package that was addressed to Jon, which I tore open because of the unfamiliar handwriting, thinking it might be evidence.

Why do I think Jon is unfaithful? Because it would be logical for him to be unfaithful. Some days I don't even comb my hair. He must leave the house and see women with their hair clean and brushed back from their faces, and he must desire them and then tell them. It is only logical that if he admires the beauty of all the women with neatly arranged hair one of them will want him to mess it up. It is only logical that she will invite him home. That smile, that suggestion from a woman would lure him as surely as a spring rain makes the earthworms twist out of the ground. It is even hard to blame him; he has a lawyer's logical mind. He remembers things. He would not forget to comb his hair. He would certainly not hack his hair off with manicuring scissors. If he cut his own hair, he would do it neatly, with the correct scissors.

"What have you done?" Jon whispered. Illogical, too, for me to have cut it in the living room—to leave the clumps of curls fallen on the rug. "What have you done?" His hands on my head, feeling my bones, the bones in my skull, looking into my eyes. "You've cut off your hair," he said. He will be such a good lawyer. He understands everything.

The dog enjoys a fire. I cook beef bones for him, and when he is tired of pawing and chewing I light a fire, throwing in several gift pinecones that send off green and blue and orange sparks, and I brush him with Jon's French hairbrush until his coat glows in the firelight. The first few nights I lit the fire and brushed him, I washed the brush afterward, so Jon wouldn't find out. The doctors would tell me that was unreasonable: Jon said he would be gone a week. A logical woman, I no longer bother with washing the brush.

I have a Scotch-and-milk before bed. The fire is still roaring, so I bring my pillow to the hearth and stretch out on the bricks. My eyelids get very warm and damp—the way they always did when I cried all the time, which I don't do anymore. After all, this is the fifth night. As the doctors say, one must be adaptable. The dog tires of all the attention and chooses to sleep under the desk in the study. I have to call him twice—the second time firmly—before he comes back to settle in the living room. And when my eyes have been closed for five minutes he walks quietly away, back to the kneehole in the desk. At one time, Jon decided the desk was not big enough. He bought a door and two filing cabinets and made a new desk. The dog, a lover of small, cramped spaces, wandered unhappily from corner to corner, no longer able to settle anywhere. Jon brought the old desk back. A very kind man.

Like Columbus's crew, I begin to panic. It has been so long since I've seen Jon. Without him to check on me, I could wander alone in the house and then disappear forever—just vanish while rounding a corner, or by slipping down, down into the bathwater, or up into the draft the fire creates. Couldn't that pull me with it—couldn't I go, with the cold air, up the chimney, arms outstretched, with my cupped hands making a parasol? Or while sitting in Jon's chair I might become smaller—become a speck, an ash. The dog would sniff and sniff, and then jump into the chair and settle down upon me and close his eyes.

To calm myself, I make tea. Earl Grey, an imported tea. Imported means coming to; exported means going away. I feel in my bones (my shinbones) that Jon will not come home. But perhaps I am just cold, since the fire is not yet lit. I sip the Earl Grey tea—results will be conclusive.

He said he was going to his brother's house for a week. He said that after caring for me he, also, had to recuperate. I have no hold on him. Even our marriage is common-law—if four years and four months make it common-law. He said he was going to his brother's. But how do I know where he's calling from? And why has he written no letters? In his absence, I talk to the dog, I pretend that I am Jon, that I am logical and reassuring. I tell the dog that Jon needed this rest and will soon be back. The dog grows anxious, sniffs Jon's clothes closet, and hangs close to the security of the kneehole. It *has* been a long time.

Celebrated my birthday in solitude. Took the phone off the hook so I wouldn't have to "put Jon on" when my parents called. Does the dog know that today is a special day? No day is special without beef bones, but I have forgotten to buy them to create a celebration. I go to the kneehole and stroke his neck in sorrow.

It occurs to me that this is a story of a woman whose man went away. Billie Holiday could have done a lot with it.

I put on a blue dress and go out to a job interview. I order a half cord of wood; there will be money when the man delivers it on Saturday. I splurge on canned horsemeat for the dog. "You'll never leave, will you?" I say as the dog eats, stabbing his mouth into the bowl of food. I think, giddily, that a dog is better than a hog. Hogs are only raised for slaughter; dogs are raised to love. Although I know this is true, I would be hesitant to voice this observation. The doctor (glasses sliding down nose, lower lip pressed to the upper) would say, "Might not *some* people love hogs?"

I dream that Jon has come back, that we do an exotic dance in the living room. Is it, perhaps, the tango? As he leads he tilts me back, and suddenly I can't feel the weight of his arms anymore. My body is very heavy and my neck stretches farther and farther back until my body seems to stretch out of the room, passing painlessly through the floor into blackness.

Once when the electricity went off Jon went to the kitchen to get candles, and I crawled under the bed, loving the darkness and wanting to stay in it. The dog came and curled beside me, at the side of the bed. Jon came back quickly, his hand cupped in front of the white candle. "Maria?" he said. "Maria?" When he left the room again, I slid forward a little to peek and saw him walking down the hallway. He walked so quickly that the candle blew out. He stopped to relight it and called my name louder—so loudly that he frightened me. I wanted to answer, to call out that I was under the bed, but his voice frightened me. I stayed there, shivering, thinking him as terrible as the Gestapo, praying that the lights wouldn't come on so he would find me. Even hiding and not answering was better than that. I put my hands together and blew into them, because I wanted to scream. When the lights came back on and he found me, he pulled me out by my hands, and the scream my hands had blocked came out.

After the hot grape jelly is poured equally into a dozen glasses, the fun begins. Melted wax is dropped in to seal them. As the white wax drips, I think, If there were anything down in there but jelly it would be smothered. I had laid in no cheesecloth, so I pulled a pair of lacy white underpants over a big yellow bowl, poured the jelly mixture through that.

In the morning Jon is back. He walks through the house to see if anything is amiss. Our clothes are still in the closets; all unnecessary lights have been turned off. He goes into the kitchen and then is annoyed because I have not gone grocery shopping. He has some toast with the grape jelly. He spoons more jelly from the glass to his mouth when the bread is gone.

"Talk to me, Maria. Don't shut me out," he says, licking the jelly from his upper lip. He is like a child, but one who orders me to do and feel things.

"Feel this arm," he says. It is tight from his chopping wood at his brother's camp.

I met his brother once. Jon and his brother are twins, but very dissimilar. His brother is always tan—wide and short, with broad shoulders. Asleep, he looks like the logs that he chops. When Jon and I were first dating we went to his brother's camp, and the three of us slept in a tent because the house was not yet built. Jon's brother snored all night. "I hate it here," I whispered to Jon, shivering against him. He tried to soothe me, but he wouldn't make love to me there. "I hate your brother," I said, in a normal tone of voice, because his brother was snoring so loudly he'd never hear me. Jon put his hand over my mouth. "Sh-h-h," he said. "Please." Naturally, Jon did not invite me on this trip to see him. I explain all this to the dog now, and he is hypnotized. He closes his eyes and listens to the drone of my voice. He appreciates my hand stroking in tempo with my sentences. Jon pushes the jelly away and stares at me. "Stop talking about something that happened years ago," he says, and stalks out of the room.

The wood arrives. The firewood man has a limp; he's missing a toe. I asked, and he told me. He's a good woodman—the toe was lost canoeing. Jon helps him stack the logs in the shed. I peek in and see that there was already a lot more wood than I thought.

Jon comes into the house when the man leaves. His face is heavy and ugly.

"Why did you order more?" Jon says.

"To keep warm. I have to keep warm."

I fix a beef stew for dinner, but feed it to the dog. He is transfixed; the steam warns him it is too hot to eat, yet the smell is delicious. He laps tentatively at the rim of the bowl, like an epicure sucking in a single egg of caviar. Finally, he eats it all. And then there is the bone, which he carries quickly to his private place under the desk. Jon is furious; I have prepared something for the dog but not for us.

"This has got to stop," he whispers in my face, his hand tight around my wrist.

The dog and I climb to the top of the hill and watch the commuters going to work in their cars. I sit on a little canvas stool—the kind fishermen use—instead of the muddy ground. It is September

—mud everywhere. The sun is setting. Wide white clouds hang in the air, seem to cluster over this very hilltop. And then Jon's face is glowing in the clouds—not a vision, the real Jon. He is on the hilltop, clouds rolling over his head, saying to me that we have reached the end. Mutiny on the Santa Maria! But I only sit and wait, staring straight ahead. How curious that this is the end. He sits in the mud, calls the dog to him. Did he really just say that to me? I repeat it: "We have reached the end."

"I know," he says.

The dog walks into the room. Jon is at the desk. The kneehole is occupied, so the dog curls in the corner. He did not always circle before lying down. Habits are acquired, however late. Like the furniture, the plants, the cats left to us by the dead, they take us in. We think we are taking them in, but they take us in, demand attention.

I demand attention from Jon, at his desk at work, his legs now up in the lotus position on his chair to offer the dog his fine resting place.

"Jon, Jon!" I say, and dance across the room. I posture and prance. What a good lawyer he will be; he shows polite interest.

"I'll set us on fire," I say.

That is going too far. He shakes his head to deny what I have said. He leads me by my wrist to bed, pulls the covers up tightly. If I were a foot lower down in the bed I would smother if he kept his hands on those covers. Like grape jelly.

"Will there be eggs and bacon and grape jelly on toast for breakfast?" I ask.

There will be. He cooks for us now.

I am so surprised. When he brings the breakfast tray I find out that *today* is my birthday. There are snapdragons and roses. He kisses my hands, lowers the tray gently to my lap. The tea steams. The phone rings. I have been hired for the job. His hand covers the mouthpiece. Did I go for a job? He tells them there was a mistake, and hangs up and walks away, as if from something dirty. He walks out of the room and I am left with the hot tea. Tea is boiled so it can cool. Jon leaves so he can come back. Certain of this, I call and they both come—Jon and dog—to settle down with me. We have come to the end, yet we are safe. I move to the center of the bed to make room for Jon; tea sloshes from the cup. His hand goes out to steady it. There's no harm done—the saucer contains it. He smiles, approvingly, and as he sits down his hand slides across the sheet like a rudder through still waters.

GLENDA ADAMS

RECLAMATION

This is the story of a body, my body, and of the many efforts that have been made to separate us.

THE THROAT

The throat is white. Blue-white. Grey-white. Across the throat is a white scar, once pink, and before that red. When the head is thrown back, in pain or terror, the throat is stretched tight and the scream can be seen as it forms.

Men are drawn to this scar. Some wait for weeks or months before asking why. Others ask immediately. I try to please them and give each the story he wishes to hear. To one, who asked immediately, shouting above the other shouting party voices, I said: Once, when I was freckled and hopeful I fell in love. He was a French-horn player in the band of the Royal Irish Guards. He wore a red coat and black trousers and played Andalusia, Dance of the Clowns, and *Besame Mucho*. But he left my life. I failed to kill myself for I did not know where to cut.

This story pleased the party man and increased his fascination. He took me aside, away from the shouting voices, and talked to me softly about himself, his face close to mine. He told me how sad his life had been, how his misfortunes had been far greater than mine, how he was searching for love, for a woman who would understand and care for him. He held my hand. Then he stroked my forearm and traced patterns on the inside of my elbow. He squeezed my shoulder and outlined my ear and my jaw with his fingers. And finally holding his breath, he touched my throat and the scar, with his two thumbs. "Would you do the same for me?" he asked.

Another man, one who seemed to offer a refuge, advised me to wear pullovers with high turtlenecks and long sleeves in order to hide my body and my story.

Here is the real story of the scar: When I was an infant, so they tell me, my father poured a freshly brewed pot of tea on me. An accident. They removed my hot, wet clothes and explored my body to see what damage had been done. It was then, among the folds of skin under the chin, that they discovered the birthmark, small and round, the size of a penny and the color of tea with cream.

The birthmark grew with me to the size of a silver dollar. My treasure island, beneath which lay buried my voice.

"We'll have to do something about it. Remove it. It looks terrible," my mother said one year as she looked at our vacation pictures. "They can cut things out these days and it hardly leaves a mark." She held a photograph in which I stood on a narrow rock path that wound down the face of a cliff to the breaking ocean waves. My father had taken the photograph from the top of the cliff. He had called out instructions as I climbed unwillingly down the path toward the sea. I was frightened and told him I did not want to go any further, but he told me not to be silly and described to me how spectacular the photograph would be. From where I stood, between my father and the ocean, I could scarcely hear his voice. I wore wildflowers in my belt, banksia and sarsaparilla, and before he took the photograph my father called to me to hold the flowers in my hands, in front of me at my waist. He told me to turn my back to the sea and look up toward him. He told me to lift my chin and look right up at him and smile. "I can't," I said. "It makes me dizzy." I stood close to the cliff face and closed my eyes. I rested my cheek against the sandstone of the cliff.

"Don't be a baby," he called. He said he was losing his patience. "Step back a little, then look up, and smile."

To please him, and to get it over with, I stepped back to the edge of the path and turned my face to him. But I could not smile, for I was too afraid.

"What a spectacular shot," my mother said as she held the photograph. "Wonderful churning waves. But that birthmark will have to go. You'll be grateful later on, when you're thinking about boys."

And the birthmark went. They bought me a nightgown and a blue chenille dressing gown to take to the hospital, the way they bought a new bedjacket for my grandmother before she died.

"They are going to cut your throat," my brother said.

The doctor bent over me with the needle. "You'll forget it ever existed," he said. "No one will ever know. And by the time you're looking at boys, there won't even be a scar to spoil it."

"But I need my birthmark," I said.

THE VOICE

The voice became inaudible, even when it called for help or cried out in pain or made a simple request. When the voice said: "Please pass the teapot," there was silence until he, whoever he happened to be, said: "Mmmm? Did you say something?"

Another he, placing his ear before my mouth and frowning, said: "What did you say your name was?" before he drifted away.

The one who advised turtleneck sweaters said: "Stay with me and I'll take care of you."

THE HAIR, THE FACE, THE TEETH

The hair and the face were once the timid brown of the mouse.

At first the hair was long. It grew straight and was worn always in braids. I longed to let it fly free, to shake my head and feel my hair as I ran. But my mother said braids were for my own good, for no dirt or leaf or twig or louse could then find a home on me.

I brushed my hair every morning on the back verandah in the sun. My mother left me alone for fifteen minutes to brush and braid.

I brushed the hair counting the strokes, and when I had done I let my head fall back and felt the long brown hair against my back. I took the strands of hair from the brush and stood in the yard among the bushes and trees and held out my hand. The magpies came swooping and calling to fetch it for their nests. Sometimes the magpies raided my very head and plucked at the living strands.

When my brother watched the brushing, he said: "Your hair is the color of mud, and your face is a dirty mud puddle."

Once my father came onto the verandah and said: "Here, let me show you how to do it. None of those weak, halfhearted strokes." He took the brush and brushed so hard that he had to place his left hand about my neck, at the base of the throat, to brace himself for each stroke. There were red marks on my forehead and neck where he brought the brush down. Then he braided the hair, pulling it back so tight that the skin of my face felt it would split.

I cried out in pain and my mother came. "She's old enough to do that herself," she said.

"The hair should be cut off," said my father.

The next day as I stood brushing and thinking, my mother came with a towel and a pair of scissors and said it would save time in the mornings and be altogether less trouble if I had short hair.

"But I need my hair," I said.

She cut the hair short and ragged, so that it covered the forehead, the ears, the cheeks and the jawbone.

"Your head is a coconut that should be smashed open," said my brother.

"Stylish these days," said my mother, "and at least the forehead is covered, it is too broad and high, and the cheeks and jaw are covered, they are too prominent. Make the most of your good feature. Smile a lot. Without those teeth you would be nothing."

"I shall kick your teeth in," said my brother, and he often tried to.

My father said nothing. He stood and watched the cutting of the hair, his jaws clamped together.

Those brown tight braids now lie in a show box lined with tissue paper in the top drawer of my dresser.

THE HANDS AND WRISTS

The hands are older than their years. They are torn and scarred. The life line is difficult to trace. The fingertips are blunt, the nails are square. The fingers of the hands were once always folded under, out of sight, in the safety of the clenched fist.

The thumbs are double-jointed.

"All the better to string you up by," said my brother, who proved that two thumbs tied together with several strands of mere cotton thread render the body more helpless than thick ropes binding the arms and legs.

There is an indentation around the base of the ring finger, but it is the type of scar that will disappear in due course.

The wrists are smooth and white and unmarked, with veins that are a beautiful slate blue.

THE FEET

The feet faithfully followed the man who offered a refuge.

Once we picked our way through a vast and complex swamp. The aim was to get some exercise, some fresh air, to get away from people and spend a day close to nature, and to finish a roll of film.

"Stay very close," said the man, "for it is easy to get completely lost in a swamp like this. You should have worn something bright. There are patches of water and ponds hidden in the reeds. Just follow me."

I stayed very close. I marked his footsteps, my eyes lowered
watching his heels. We stopped to eat a peach and drink tea from the
flask we had brought. We ate and drank standing up, for the ground
was too wet for sitting.

"This mud is a nuisance," he said. "We must find higher, drier
ground."

We walked, without speaking, for an hour or two, and after a
while I found I did not have to concentrate so hard to follow. I was
able to note the bushes and swamp flowers that thrived in the wet.
There were small stones and masses of various browns and greens. I
watched the water bubble from the earth beneath the weight of our
feet. And soon, by narrowing my eyes, I perceived that we were
walking on the surface of the water itself. The water was brown and
it covered the brown earth in a fine film. I no longer was able to mark
his footsteps. He was walking quickly, and the water covered his
footprints. But I followed the slapping, splashing sound of his feet
and the snapping of the reeds that broke as he passed.

I contemplated my feet standing in and on the muddy water. And
as I looked I saw in the water the clouds, the sky, and a bird flying. I
saw the reeds and the swamp flowers reflected and transforming the
brown, flat opaque swamp water. I shifted my weight and the water
rippled, and the reflections changed and rippled. Even with my
head bowed and my eyes lowered in customary fear I saw the world.
And then I straightened my back and raised my eyes to look about
me.

I saw that I was alone. He had gone on and left me behind. I called,
but he did not hear or he did not answer. I listened for the splashing
of his feet, but I heard only the splashing and the cracking of the
swamp creatures.

I thought: if I had kept my mind on what I was doing and followed
him closely, I would be safe now.

But I laughed, and I kept looking about and refused to shed tears.

I found my own way home. But he was not there. And he did not
come. And I waited, while my hair grew long, wanting to show him
my new voice and my new face and my new straight back and my new

unclenched hands. Until I knew that when I stopped following him in the swamp that day it was he who had gotten lost.

My feet are firm and straight and strong and white. They have walked at the edge of the sea. They have walked around the rim of the volcano and felt the heat of the rock. And they are at ease in the soft, damp browns of the swamp. And now I often feel free enough not to smile.

JOAN MURRAY

ASYLUM

". . . and Thy gifts which we are about to receive. Amen."

Their fingers lit upon knives and forks. Shrieks of pain rose around the table, shattering the incense of the blessing which still hung in the air. Each of them rose. Hal thrust his hand into the crystal water glass and looked apologetically at his wife.

"Good God, Carol, put them down!"

She dropped the silver obediently letting it crash onto a Lenox china plate and rebound destructively onto the stemware.

The children had run for the first floor bathroom. Missy had gotten to the sink first and in her rage of pain kicked Jonathan away, forcing him to soothe his tortured fingers in the toilet. Lillian and Lou were in the kitchen, composing themselves under the steady flow of tap water.

Carol was rushed to the emergency room at St. Lawrence's. (Himself roasted to death on a gridiron.) Third-degree burns. Flesh grilled. Hands swathed. She had baked the knifes and forks for ten minutes in a preheated five-hundred-degree oven along with the pop-up biscuits.

"New house company excitement. Oversight! Scatterbrained! Numbskull! Ha ha," say Louis and Hal, his son.

Of course she could do nothing for a while. So Mother came. Then Lillian. Then a high school girl. Two dollars an hour.

But at two A.M. one night she was awakened by cries from a soaked mattress in Jonathan's room. ("Soda till bedtime. You never obey.") The next day, lunchtime, Jon opening his baggie in the cafeteria perceived that the rye bread was slightly wet or slimy, as was the ham inside. He ate half in his obedience, and threw the rest away, as it was truly disgusting.

That night: "We having fried chicken?" Hal asked, busy-beeing cutesy in the kitchen before dinner: I take such an interest in your work.

"No."

He didn't bother to ask about the soup bowl full of vegetable oil on the kitchen counter.

Twice she ironed his shirts without washing them. He wore them, never knowing. Hemming his trousers, she inadvertently cut one leg an inch shorter than the other. He wore them, never knowing. She faked orgasm one night. And the next time pretended he was Peter Falk.

Jack, who is Hal's supervisor, came to play cards one Friday night with his wife, Agnes. It was Jack who persuaded Hal that a man who was on his way to the top ought to make a sensible investment like real estate. It was Agnes who persuaded Hal to move into their development.

That night they did not miss the ace of spades and queen of hearts which were taped on the inside of the medicine cabinet. (Hope she'll notice. Prying witch: "What's your mortgage: Does your daughter go to speech therapy?" G-g-go to hell.)

"I'm so glad to hear from Hal how much you love it here. Being out of harm's way is what life is all about."

(I believe there is a termite squeezing through your two front teeth.)

"And retiring at thirty-five, Carol! A lady of leisure! And being a legal secretary you can always find work later on when your children are gone."

(Dead and buried. Hebeas corpus.)

The PTA is play school. Carol plays there with Agnes at (*1*) being significant, (*2*) lending a hand, (*3*) making a contribution. Carol does lay-put for the Parent Newsletter. A discount coupon for a lingerie shop and an ad for the Sew & Save fabric shop were printed upside down. "Eye-catching!" "New job jitters."

"You must try to save money, Carol. We have a huge mortgage over our heads. Not to mention a gorgeous gabled roof and twenty-four-hour security."

(I have saved and saved, and this is my rainy day. Rainy life.)

"Carol, you're not listening to me. Is the garden more interesting than I am?"

(This is my garden thrusting up jonquils planted by another hand. Green thumbs in milk bottles. Adultress of the milk truck, trite as it may seem. Agnes missed no trick. Not even the divorce. Agony in my garden.)

"You sure are in a dream world."

(Waking up one day we find we are the Fairy Queen enamored of an ass for a decade. Hal, I loved you once.)

"I think the kids are as crazy about this place as you are. They've got everything at their fingertips. (Scars.) And they're sure to make friends soon."

Tasha is Aggie's daughter. You can tell by her nose. She might hate Missy as Missy hates her. They are the only girls on the street.

Tasha sat in chocolate ice cream, not noticing for the wooden chair. A pity, those white pants, so nice.

"Missy's mother spilled it."

"Did Missy's mother offer you ice cream?"

"No."

Jonathan has six almost friends. But Jonathan can't afford a bike yet.

Carol spends the money on ceramic lions, tigers, leopards, a giraffe, anything she can get her hands on. They are all about a foot tall. She keeps them wrapped in newspaper in the spare closet. No one knew until the day Hal drove into Brooklyn to pick up Lillian and Lou for another dinner. Carol assembled close to thirty beasts across the foyer floor and fanning out into the living room and family room.

Lou had a good laugh. "Quite a little card. Quite a little cook. You hooked a good one, Hal!"

Lillian admired the tallest of the lions. The one with fangs a-roaring.

Hal began moving the ceramics toward the walls so his parents could enter.

After they had left he expected an explanation. That night Carol pretended he was Kurt Vonnegut, Jr.

Carol spent her days doing housework. Each week she vacuumed the living room carpet diagonally from corner to corner until a large X was visible. She waxed the kitchen floor twice a week, but never washed it. She inadvertently starched the pillowcases and put ten-watt bulbs in all the lamps.

Hal is a sport. Hal played Santa for his neighbors, and was the master of ceremonies at his sister June's wedding. Hal thrives on originality: his recipe for peanut cakes was accepted by the Parent Newsletter; his portraits of Joe Namath and Rusty Staub, copied from trading cards, are hung in Jon's room. Nonetheless, Hal was very annoyed about the lightbulbs (which he noticed). And he could not believe Carol had thought they were hundreds. "After all!"

"The trouble with you, Carol, is that you're an overprotective mother. You stay so close to the kids all day. Give them a little freedom. It will do you some good."

The next day Carol took the train to New York. She spent over two hundred dollars in Bloomingdale's, and was not home when the children returned from school. They sat on the front steps for a half hour cursing her in pig latin. Then they went to Agnes'.

Carol was not home when Hal arrived from work all eager to sniff-snuff over the cooking pots. He assumed, of course, that one of the children had been injured and Carol had rushed with them to the hospital.

When Missy called a half hour later, Hal asked, "Is it serious?"

They were all eating Chef Boy-ar-dee Beef-o-ghetti when Carol returned. She had had a splendid day, she announced, and showed them a bright, silk scarf she had bought.

"Very nice. Cheerful."

She went to the upstairs bathroom, sat on the edge of the tub and laid a hundred dollar earring in her naval. She dropped its partner in the toilet and flushed. Five minutes later she flushed again.

"I'm glad you had a nice day, honey," Hal said before shutting off the boudoir lamp. "Just don't get the Bloomingdale's habit, or this house is bye-bye, you know."

"I know."

"Promise you won't go there."

"I promise."

The next day Carol arrived home at eight-thirty P.M. She had spent nearly three hundred dollars in Altman's.

Hal was disturbed, naturally. Especially because he had to eat canned pasta again. But Agnes' question ("Is Carol seeing someone?") made him feel romantic. He, of course, knew nothing about her purchases. Carol had left the packages on the train.

When Hal was in Albany two weeks later, the bills came. Carol put them in the bottom of the freezer chest in the basement. On Tuesday night she wrote a letter to Albany suggesting "an intimate liaison" with the new governor as a way "to become acquainted with the needs and aspirations of your constituents." The next night she slept with Jack while Agnes baby-sat for Missy and Jonathan. Good old Baggie Aggie, she'll do anything for a neighbor in distress. Jack thinks Carol called him "Governor" once. "Charming English affectation. Not bad in the sack."

Agnes couldn't get much about Carol's alleged "visit to the g-y-n-"

with Carol's children standing in the doorway, but she was glad to get rid of the kids.

While he was watching his wife iron a shirt later that night, Jack commented, "Hal and Carol don't have much of a relationship. But they do have one hell of a nice house."

"She's a lucky girl."

THE GIRL

A TIME OF WATER, A TIME OF TREES

I am young and half asleep.
It is a time of water, a time of trees.

—Anne Sexton, "Three Green Windows" (1962)

ALICE MUNRO

RED DRESS—1946

My mother was making me a dress. All through the month of November I would come from school and find her in the kitchen, surrounded by cut-up red velvet and scraps of tissue-paper pattern. She worked at an old treadle machine pushed up against the window to get the light, and also to let her look out, past the stubble fields and bare vegetable garden, to see who went by on the road. There was seldom anybody to see.

The red velvet material was hard to work with, it pulled, and the style my mother had chosen was not easy either. She was not really a good sewer. She liked to make things; that is different. Whenever she could she tried to skip basting and pressing and she took no pride in the fine points of tailoring, the finishing of buttonholes and the overcasting of seams as, for instance, my aunt and my grandmother did. Unlike them she started off with an inspiration, a brave and dazzling idea; from that moment on, her pleasure ran downhill. In the first place she could never find a pattern to suit her. It was no wonder; there were no patterns made to match the ideas that blossomed in her head. She had made me, at various times when I was younger, a flowered organdy dress with a high Victorian neckline edged in scratchy lace, with a poke bonnet to match; a Scottish plaid outfit with a velvet jacket and tam; an embroidered peasant blouse worn with a full red skirt and black laced bodice. I had worn these clothes with docility, even pleasure, in the days when I was unaware of the world's opinion. Now, grown wiser, I wished for dresses like those my friend Lonnie had, bought at Beale's store.

I had to try it on. Sometimes Lonnie came home from school with me and she would sit on the couch watching. I was embarrassed by the way my mother crept around me, her knees creaking, her breath coming heavily. She muttered to herself. Around the house she wore no corset or stockings, she wore wedge-heeled shoes and ankle socks; her legs were marked with lumps of blue-green veins. I thought her squatting position shameless, even obscene; I tried to keep talking to Lonnie so that her attention would be taken away from my mother as much as possible. Lonnie wore the composed, polite, appreciative expression that was her disguise in the presence of grownups. She laughed at them and was a ferocious mimic, and they never knew.

My mother pulled me about, and pricked me with pins. She made me turn around, she made me walk away, she made me stand still. "What do you think of it, Lonnie?" she said around the pins in her mouth.

"It's beautiful," said Lonnie, in her mild, sincere way. Lonnie's own mother was dead. She lived with her father who never noticed her, and this, in my eyes, made her seem both vulnerable and privileged.

"It *will* be, if I can ever manage the fit," my mother said. "Ah, well," she said theatrically, getting to her feet with a woeful creaking and sighing, "I doubt if she appreciates it." She enraged me, talking like this to Lonnie, as if Lonnie were grown up and I were still a child. "Stand still," she said, hauling the pinned and basted dress over my head. My head was muffled in velvet, my body exposed, in an old cotton school slip. I felt like a great raw lump, clumsy and goose-pimpled. I wished I was like Lonnie, light-boned, pale and thin; she had been a Blue Baby.

"Well, nobody ever made me a dress when I was going to high school," my mother said, "I made my own, or I did without." I was afraid she was going to start again on the story of her walking seven miles to town and finding a job waiting on tables in a boardinghouse, so that she could go to high school. All the stories of my mother's life which had once interested me had begun to seem melodramatic, irrelevant, and tiresome.

"One time I had a dress given to me," she said. "It was a cream-colored cashmere wool with royal blue piping down the front and lovely mother-of-pearl buttons, I wonder whatever became of it."

When we got free Lonnie and I went upstairs to my room. It was cold, but we stayed there. We talked about the boys in our class, going up and down the rows and saying, "Do you like him? Well, do you half-like him? Do you *hate* him? Would you go out with him if he asked you?" Nobody had asked us. We were thirteen, and we had been going to high school for two months. We did questionnaires in magazines, to find out whether we had personality and whether we would be popular. We read articles on how to make up our faces to accentuate our good points and how to carry on a conversation on the first date and what to do when a boy tried to go too far. Also we read articles on frigidity of the menopause, abortion, and why husbands seek satisfaction away from home. When we were not doing schoolwork, we were occupied most of the time with the garnering, passing on, and discussing of sexual information. We had made a pact to tell each other everything. But one thing I did not tell was about this dance, the high school Christmas Dance for which my mother was making me a dress. It was that I did not want to go.

At high school I was never comfortable for a minute. I did not know about Lonnie. Before an exam, she got icy hands and palpitations, but I was close to despair at all times. When I was asked a question in class, any simple little question at all, my voice was apt to come out squeaky, or else hoarse and trembling. When I had to go to the blackboard I was sure—even at a time of the month when this could not be true—that I had blood on my skirt. My hands became slippery with sweat when they were required to work the blackboard compass. I could not hit the ball in volleyball; being called upon to perform an action in front of others made all my reflexes come undone. I hated Business Practice because you had to rule pages for an account book, using a straight pen, and when the teacher looked over my shoulder all the delicate lines wobbled and ran together. I hated Science; we perched on stools under harsh lights behind tables of unfamiliar, fragile equipment, and were taught by the principal of the school, a man with a cold, self-relishing voice—he read the Scriptures every morning—and a great talent for inflicting humiliation. I hated English because the boys played bingo at the back of the room while the teacher, a stout, gentle girl, slightly cross-eyed, read Wordsworth at the front. She threatened them, she begged them, her face red and her voice as unreliable as mine. They offered burlesqued apologies and when she started to read again they took up rapt postures, made swooning faces, crossed their eyes, flung their hands over their hearts. Sometimes she would burst into tears, there was no help for it, she had to run out into the hall. Then the boys made loud mooing noises; our hungry laughter—oh, mine too—pursued her. There was a carnival atmosphere of brutality in the room at such times, scaring weak and suspect people like me.

But what was really going on in the school was not Business Practice and Science and English, there was something else that gave life its urgency and brightness. That old building, with its rock-walled clammy basements and black cloakrooms and pictures of dead royalties and lost explorers, was full of the tension and excitement of sexual competition, and in this, in spite of daydreams of vast successes, I had premonitions of total defeat. Something had to happen, to keep me from that dance.

With December came snow, and I had an idea. Formerly I had considered falling off my bicycle and spraining my ankle and I had tried to manage this, as I rode home along the hard-frozen, deeply rutted country roads. But it was too difficult. However, my throat and bronchial tubes were supposed to be weak; why not expose them? I started getting out of bed at night and opening my window a little. I knelt down and let the wind, sometimes stinging with snow, rush in around my bared throat. I took off my pajama top. I said to myself the words "blue with cold" and as I knelt there, my eyes shut, I pictured my chest and throat turning blue, the cold, greyed blue of veins under the skin. I stayed until I could not stand it any more, and then I took a handful of snow from the windowsill and smeared it all over my chest, before I buttoned my pajamas. It would melt against the flannelette and I would be sleeping in wet clothes, which was supposed to be the worst thing of all. In the morning, the moment I woke up, I cleared my throat, testing for soreness, coughed experimentally, hopefully, touched my forehead to see if I had fever. It was no good. Every morning, including the day of the dance, I rose defeated, and in perfect health.

The day of the dance I did my hair up in steel curlers. I had never done this before, because my hair was naturally curly, but today I wanted the protection of all possible female rituals. I lay on the couch in the kitchen, reading *The Last Days of Pompeii*, and wishing I was there. My mother, never satisfied, was sewing a white lace collar on the dress; she had decided it was too grownup-looking. I watched the hours. It was one of the shortest days of the year. Above the couch, on the wallpaper, were old games of Xs and Os, old drawings and scribblings my brother and I had done when we were sick with bronchitis. I looked at them and longed to be back safe behind the boundaries of childhood.

When I took out the curlers my hair, both naturally and artificially stimulated, sprang out in an exuberant glossy bush. I wet it, I combed it, beat it with the brush, and tugged it down along my cheeks. I applied face powder, which stood out chalkily on my hot face. My mother got out her Ashes of Roses Cologne, which she never used, and let me splash it over my arms. Then she zipped up the dress and turned me around to the mirror. The dress was princess style, very tight in the midriff. I saw how my breasts, in their new stiff brassiere, jutted out surprisingly, with mature authority, under the childish frills of the collar.

"Well I wish I could take a picture," my mother said. "I am really, genuinely proud of that fit. And you might say thank you for it."

"Thank you," I said.

The first thing Lonnie said when I opened the door to her was, "Jesus, what did you do to your hair?"

"I did it up."

"You look like a Zulu. Oh, don't worry. Get me a comb and I'll do the front in a roll. It'll look all right. It'll even make you look older."

I sat in front of the mirror and Lonnie stood behind me, fixing my hair. My mother seemed unable to leave us. I wished she would. She watched the roll take shape and said, "You're a wonder, Lonnie. You should take up hairdressing."

"That's a thought," Lonnie said. She had on a pale blue crepe dress, with a peplum and bow; it was much more grownup than mine even without the collar. Her hair had come out as sleek as the girl's on the bobby-pin card. I had always thought secretly that Lonnie could not be pretty because she had crooked teeth, but now I saw that crooked teeth or not, her stylish dress and smooth hair made me look a little like a golliwog, stuffed into red velvet, wide-eyed, wild-haired, with a suggestion of delirium.

My mother followed us to the door and called out into the dark, "Au reservoir!" This was a traditional farewell of Lonnie's and mine; it sounded foolish and desolate coming from her, and I was so angry with her for using it that I did not reply. It was only Lonnie who called back cheerfully, encouragingly, "Good night!"

The gymnasium smelled of pine and cedar. Red and green bells of fluted paper hung from the basketball hoops; the high, barred windows were hidden by green boughs. Everybody in the upper grades seemed to have come in couples. Some of the Grade Twelve and Thirteen girls had brought boy friends who had already graduated, who were young businessmen around the town. These young men smoked in the gymnasium, nobody could stop them, they were free. The girls stood beside them, resting their hands casually on male sleeves, their faces bored, aloof, and beautiful. I longed to be like that. They behaved as if only they—the older ones—were really at the dance, as if the rest of us, whom they moved among and peered around, were, if not invisible, inanimate; when the first dance was announced—a Paul Jones—they moved out languidly, smiling at each other as if they had been asked to take part in some half-forgotten childish game. Holding hands and shivering, crowding up together, Lonnie and I and the other Grade Nine girls followed.

I didn't dare look at the outer circle as it passed me, for fear I should see some unmannerly hurrying-up. When the music stopped I stayed where I was, and half raising my eyes I saw a boy named Mason Williams coming reluctantly towards me. Barely touching my waist and my fingers, he began to dance with me. My legs were hollow, my arm trembled from the shoulder, I could not have spoken. This Mason Williams was one of the heroes of the school; he played basketball and hockey and walked the halls with an air of royal sullenness and barbaric contempt. To have to dance with a nonentity like me was as offensive to him as having to memorize Shakespeare. I felt this as keenly as he did, and imagined that he was exchanging looks of dismay with his friends. He steered me, stumbling, to the edge of the floor. He took his hand from my waist and dropped my arm.

"See you," he said. He walked away.

It took me a minute or two to realize what had happened and that he was not coming back. I went and stood by the wall alone. The Physical Education teacher, dancing past energetically in the arms of a Grade Ten boy, gave me an inquisitive look. She was the only teacher in the school who made use of the words social adjustment, and I was afraid that if she had seen, or if she found out, she might make some horribly public attempt to make Mason finish out the dance with me. I myself was not angry or surprised at Mason; I accepted his position, and mine, in the world of school and I saw that what he had done was the realistic thing to do. He was a Natural Hero, not a Student Council type of hero bound for success beyond the school; one of those would have danced with me courteously and patronizingly and left me feeling no better off. Still, I hoped not many people had seen. I hated people seeing. I began to bite the skin on my thumb.

When the music stopped I joined the surge of girls to the end of the gymnasium. Pretend it didn't happen, I said to myself. Pretend this is the beginning, now.

The band began to play again. There was movement in the dense crowd at our end of the floor, it thinned rapidly. Boys came over, girls went out to dance. Lonnie went. The girl on the other side of me went. Nobody asked me. I remembered a magazine article Lonnie and I had read, which said *Be gay! Let the boys see your eyes sparkle, let them hear laughter in your voice! Simple, obvious, but how many girls forget!* It was true, I had forgotten. My eyebrows were drawn together with tension, I must look scared and ugly. I took a deep breath and tried to loosen my face. I smiled. But I felt absurd, smiling at no one. And I observed that girls on the dance floor, popular girls, were not smiling; many of them had sleepy, sulky faces and never smiled at all.

Girls were still going out to the floor. Some, despairing, went with each other. But most went with boys. Fat girls, girls with pimples, a poor girl who didn't own a good dress and had to wear a skirt and sweater to the dance; they were claimed, they danced away. Why take them and not me? Why everybody else and not me? I have a red velvet dress, I did my hair in curlers, I used a deodorant and put on cologne. *Pray*, I thought, I couldn't close my eyes but I said over and over again in my mind. *Please, me, please*, and I locked my fingers behind my back in a sign more potent than crossing, the same secret sign Lonnie and I used not to be sent to the blackboard in Math.

It did not work. What I had been afraid of was true. I was going to be left. There was something mysterious the matter with me, something that could not be put right like bad breath or overlooked like pimples, and everybody knew it, and I knew it; I had known it all along. But I had not known it for sure, I had hoped to be mistaken. Certainty rose inside me like sickness. I hurried past one or two girls who were also left and went into the girls' washroom. I hid myself in a cubicle.

That was where I stayed. Between dances girls came in and went out quickly. There were plenty of cubicles; nobody noticed that I was not a temporary occupant. During the dances, I listened to the music which I liked but had no part of any more. For I was not going to try any more. I only wanted to hide in here, get out without seeing anybody, get home.

One time after the music started somebody stayed behind. She was taking a long time running the water, washing her hands, combing her hair. She was going to think it funny that I stayed in so long. I had better go out and wash my hands, and maybe while I was washing them she would leave.

It was Mary Fortune. I knew her by name, because she was an officer of the Girls' Athletic Society and she was on the Honor Roll and she was always organizing things. She had something to do with organizing this dance; she had been around to all the classrooms asking for volunteers to do the decorations. She was in Grade Eleven or Twelve.

"Nice and cool in here," she said. "I came in to get cooled off. I get so hot."

She was still combing her hair when I finished my hands. "Do you like the band?" she said.

"It's all right." I didn't really know what to say. I was surprised at her, an older girl, taking this time to talk to me.

"I don't. I can't stand it. I hate dancing when I don't like the band. Listen. They're so choppy. I'd just as soon not dance as dance to that."

I combed my hair. She leaned against a basin, watching me.

"I don't want to dance and don't particularly want to stay in here. Let's go and have a cigarette."

"Where?"

"Come on, I'll show you."

At the end of the washroom there was a door. It was unlocked and led into a dark closet full of mops and pails. She had me hold the door open, to get the washroom light, until she found the knob of another door. This door opened into darkness.

"I can't turn on the light or somebody might see," she said. "It's the janitor's room." I reflected that athletes always seemed to know more than the rest of us about the school as a building; they knew where things were kept and they were always coming out of unauthorized doors with a bold, preoccupied air. "Watch out where you're going," she said. "Over at the far end there's some stairs. They go up to a closet on the second floor. The door's locked at the top, but there's like a partition between the stairs and the room. So if we sit on the steps, even if by chance someone did come in here, they wouldn't see us."

"Wouldn't they smell smoke?" I said.

"Oh, well, Live dangerously."

There was a high window over the stairs which gave us a little light. Mary Fortune had cigarettes and matches in her purse. I had not smoked before except the cigarettes Lonnie and I made ourselves, using papers and tobacco stolen from her father; they came apart in the middle. These were much better.

"The only reason I even came tonight," Mary Fortune said, "is because I am responsible for the decorations and I wanted to see, you know, how it looked once people got in there and everything. Otherwise why bother? I'm not boy-crazy."

In the light from the high window I could see her narrow, scornful face, her dark skin pitted with acne, her teeth pushed together at the front, making her look adult and commanding.

"Most girls are. Haven't you noticed that? The greatest collection of boy-crazy girls you could imagine is right here in this school."

I was grateful for her attention, her company and her cigarette. I said I thought so too.

"Like this afternoon. This afternoon I was trying to get them to hang the bells and junk. They just get up on the ladders and fool around with boys. They don't care if it ever gets decorated. It's just an excuse. That's the only aim they have in life, fooling around with boys. As far as I'm concerned, they're idiots."

We talked about teachers, and things at school. She said she wanted to be a physical education teacher and she would have to go to college for that, but her parents did not have enough money. She said she planned to work her own way through, she wanted to be independent anyway, she would work in the cafeteria and in the summer she would do farm work, like picking tobacco. Listening to her, I felt the acute phase of my unhappiness passing. Here was someone who had suffered the same defeat as I had—I saw that— but she was full of energy and self-respect. She had thought of other things to do. She would pick tobacco.

We stayed there talking and smoking during the long pause in the music, when, outside, they were having doughnuts and coffee. When the music started again Mary said, "Look, do we have to hang around here any longer? Let's get our coats and go. We can go down to Lee's and have a hot chocolate and talk in comfort, why not?"

We felt our way across the janitor's room, carrying ashes and cigarette butts in our hands. In the closet, we stopped and listened to make sure there was nobody in the washroom. We came back into the light and threw the ashes into the toilet. We had to go out and cut across the dance floor to the cloakroom, which was beside the outside door.

A dance was just beginning. "Go round the edge of the floor," Mary said. "Nobody'll notice us."

I followed her. I didn't look at anybody. I didn't look for Lonnie. Lonnie was probably not going to be my friend any more, not as much as before anyway. She was what Mary would call boy-crazy.

I found that I was not so frightened, now that I had made up my mind to leave the dance behind. I was not waiting for anybody to choose me. I had my own plans. I did not have to smile or make signs for luck. It did not matter to me. I was on my way to have a hot chocolate, with my friend.

A boy said something to me. He was in my way. I thought he must be telling me that I had dropped something or that I couldn't go that way or that the cloakroom was locked. I didn't understand that he was asking me to dance until he said it over again. It was Raymond Bolting from our class, whom I had never talked to in my life. He thought I meant yes. He put his hand on my waist and almost without meaning to, I began to dance.

We moved to the middle of the floor. I was dancing. My legs had forgotten to tremble and my hands to sweat. I was dancing with a boy who had asked me. Nobody told him to, he didn't have to, he just asked me. Was it possible, could I believe it, was there nothing the matter with me after all?

I thought that I ought to tell him there was a mistake, that I was just leaving, I was going to have a hot chocolate with my girl friend. But I did not say anything. My face was making certain delicate adjustments, achieving with no effort at all the grave absent-minded look of these who were chosen, those who danced. This was the face that Mary Fortune saw, when she looked out of the cloakroom door, her scarf already around her head. I made a weak waving motion with the hand that lay on the boy's shoulder, indicating that I apologized, that I didn't know what had happened, and also that it was no use waiting for me. Then I turned my head away, and when I looked again she was gone.

Raymond Bolting took me home and Harold Simons took Lonnie home. We all walked together as far as Lonnie's corner. The boys were having an argument about a hockey game, which Lonnie and I could not follow. Then we separated into couples and Raymond continued with me the conversation he had been having with Harold. He did not seem to notice that he was now talking to me instead. Once or twice I said, "Well I don't know I didn't see that game," but after a while I decided just to say "H'm hmm," and that seemed to be all that was necessary.

One other thing he said was, "I didn't realize you lived such a long ways out." And he sniffled. The cold was making my nose run a little too, and I worked my fingers through the candy wrappers in my coat pocket until I found a shabby Kleenex. I didn't know whether I ought to offer it to him or not, but he sniffled so loudly that I finally said, "I just have this one Kleenex, it probably isn't even clean, it probably has ink on it. But if I was to tear it in half we'd each have something."

"Thanks," he said. "I sure could use it."

It was a good thing, I thought, that I had done that, for at my gate, when I said, "Well, good night," and after he said, "Oh, yeah. Good night," he leaned towards me and kissed me, briefly, with the air of one who knew his job when he saw it, on the corner of my mouth. Then he turned back to town, never knowing he had been my rescuer, that he had brought me from Mary Fortune's territory into the ordinary world.

I went around the house to the back door, thinking, I have been to a dance and a boy has walked me home and kissed me. It was all true. My life was .possible. I went past the kitchen window and I saw my mother. She was sitting with her feet on the open oven door, drinking tea out of a cup without a saucer. She was just sitting and waiting for me to come home and tell her everything that had happened. And I would not do it, I never would. But when I saw the waiting kitchen, and my mother in her faded, fuzzy paisley kimono, with her sleepy but doggedly expectant face, I understood what a mysterious and oppressive obligation I had to be happy, and how I had almost failed it, and would be likely to fail it, every time, and she would not know.

JOYCE CAROL OATES

WHERE ARE YOU GOING, WHERE HAVE YOU BEEN?

Her name was Connie. She was fifteen and she had a quick, nervous, giggling habit of craning her neck to glance into mirrors or checking other people's faces to make sure her own was all right. Her mother, who noticed everything and knew everything and who hadn't much reason any longer to look at her own face, always scolded Connie about it. "Stop gawking at yourself. Who are you? You think you're so pretty?" she would say. Connie would raise her eyebrows at these familiar old complaints and look right through her mother, into a shadowy vision of herself as she was right at that moment: she knew she was pretty and that was everything. Her mother had been pretty once too, if you could believe those old snapshots in the album, but now her looks were gone and that was why she was always after Connie.

"Why don't you keep your room clean like your sister? How've you got your hair fixed—what the hell stinks? Hair spray? You don't see your sister using that junk."

Her sister June was twenty-four and still lived at home. She was a secretary in the high school Connie attended, and if that wasn't bad enough—with her in the same building—she was so plain and chunky and steady that Connie had to hear her praised all the time by her mother and her mother's sisters. June did this, June did that, she saved money and helped clean the house and cooked and Connie couldn't do a thing, her mind was all filled with trashy daydreams. Their father was away at work most of the time and when he came home he wanted supper and he read the newspaper at supper and after supper he went to bed. He didn't bother talking much to them, but around his bent head Connie's mother kept picking at her until Connie wished her mother was dead and she herself was dead and it was all over. "She makes me want to throw up sometimes," she complained to her friends. She had a high, breathless, amused voice that made everything she said sound a little forced, whether it was sincere or not.

There was one good thing: June went places with girl friends of hers, girls who were just as plain and steady as she, and so when Connie wanted to do that her mother had no objections. The father of Connie's best girlfriend drove the girls the three miles to town and left them at a shopping plaza so they could walk through the stores or go to a movie, and when he came to pick them up again at eleven he never bothered to ask what they had done.

They must have been familiar sights, walking around the shopping plaza in their shorts and flat ballerina slippers that always scuffed the sidewalk, with charm bracelets jingling on their thin wrists; they would lean together to whisper and laugh secretly if someone passed who amused or interested them. Connie had long dark blond hair that drew anyone's eye to it, and she wore part of it pulled up on her head and puffed out and the rest of it she let fall down her back. She wore a pullover jersey blouse that looked one way when she was at home and another way when she was away from home. Everything about her had two sides to it, one for home and one for anywhere that was not home: her walk, which could be childlike and bobbing, or languid enough to make anyone think she was hearing music in her head; her mouth, which was pale and smirking most of the time, but bright and pink on these evenings out; her laugh, which was cynical and drawling at home—"Ha, ha, very funny,"—but high-pitched and nervous anywhere else, like the jingling of the charms on her bracelet.

Sometimes they did go shopping or to a movie, but sometimes they went across the highway, ducking fast across the busy road, to a drive-in restaurant where older kids hung out. The restaurant was shaped like a big bottle, though squatter than a real bottle, and on its cap was a revolving figure of a grinning boy holding a hamburger aloft. One night in midsummer they ran across, breathless with daring, and right away someone leaned out a car window and invited them over, but it was just a boy from high school they didn't like. It made them feel good to be able to ignore him. They went up through the maze of parked and cruising cars to the bright-lit, fly-infested restaurant, their faces pleased and expectant as if they were entering a sacred building that loomed up out of the night to give them what haven and blessing they yearned for. They sat at the counter and crossed their legs at the ankles, their thin shoulders rigid with excitement, and listened to the music that made everything so good: the music was always in the background, like music at a church service; it was something to depend upon.

A boy named Eddie came in to talk with them. He sat backwards on his stool, turning himself jerkily around in semicircles and then stopping and turning back again, and after a while he asked Connie if she would like something to eat. She said she would and so she tapped her friend's arm on her way out—her friend pulled her face up into a brave, droll look—and Connie said she would meet her at eleven, across the way. "I just hate to leave her like that," Connie said earnestly, but the boy said that she wouldn't be alone for long. So they went out to his car, and on the way Connie couldn't help but let her eyes wander over the windshields and faces all around her, her face gleaming with a joy that had nothing to do with Eddie or even this place; it might have been the music. She drew her shoulders up and sucked in her breath with the pure pleasure of being alive, and just at that moment she happened to glance at a face just a few feet from hers. It was a boy with shaggy black hair, in a convertible jalopy painted gold. He stared at her and then his lips widened into a grin. Connie slit her eyes at him and turned away, but she couldn't help glancing back and there he was, still watching her. He wagged a finger and laughed and said, "Gonna get you, baby," and Connie turned away again without Eddie noticing anything.

She spent three hours with him, at the restaurant where they ate hamburgers and drank Cokes in wax cups that were always sweating, and then down an alley a mile or so away, and when he left her off at five to eleven only the movie house was still open at the plaza. Her girl friend was there, talking with a boy. When Connie came up, the two girls smiled at each other and Connie said, "How was the movie?" and the girl said, "*You* should know." They rode off with the girl's father, sleepy and pleased, and Connie couldn't help but look back at the darkened shopping plaza with its big empty parking lot and its signs that were faded and ghostly now, and over at the drive-in restaurant where cars were still circling tirelessly. She couldn't hear the music at this distance.

Next morning June asked her how the movie was and Connie said, "So-so."

She and that girl and occasionally another girl went out several times a week, and the rest of the time Connie spent around the house—it was summer vacation—getting in her mother's way and thinking, dreaming about the boys she met. But all the boys fell back and dissolved into a single face that was not even a face but an idea, a feeling, mixed up with the urgent insistent pounding of the music and the humid night air of July. Connie's mother kept dragging her back to the daylight by finding things for her to do or saying suddenly, "What's this about the Pettinger girl?"

And Connie would say nervously, "Oh, her. That dope." She always drew thick clear lines between herself and such girls, and her mother was simple and kind enough to believe it. Her mother was so simple. Connie thought that it was maybe cruel to fool her so much. Her mother went scuffling around the house in old bedroom slippers and complained over the telephone to one sister about the other, then the other called up and the two of them complained about the third one. If June's name was mentioned her mother's tone was approving, and if Connie's name was mentioned it was disapproving. This did not really mean she disliked Connie, and actually Connie thought that her mother preferred her to June just because she was prettier, but the two of them kept up a pretense of exasperation, a sense that they were tugging and struggling over something of little value to either of them. Sometimes, over coffee, they were almost friends, but something would come up—some vexation that was like a fly buzzing suddenly around their heads—and their faces went hard with contempt.

One Sunday Connie got up at eleven—none of them bothered with church—and washed her hair so that it could dry all day long in the sun. Her parents and sister were going to a barbecue at an aunt's house and Connie said no, she wasn't interested, rolling her eyes to let her mother know just what she thought of it. "Stay home alone then," her mother said sharply. Connie sat out back in a lawn chair and watched them drive away, her father quiet and bald, hunched around so that he could back the car out, her mother with a look that was still angry and not at all softened through the windshield, and in the back seat poor old June, all dressed up as if she didn't know what a barbecue was, with all the running yelling kids and the flies. Connie sat with her eyes closed in the sun, dreaming and dazed with the warmth about her as if this were a kind of love, the caresses of love, and her mind slipped over onto thoughts of the boy she had been with the night before and how nice he had been, how sweet it always was, not the way someone like June would suppose but sweet, gentle, the way it was in movies and promised in songs; and when she opened her eyes she hardly knew where she was, the backyard ran off into weeds and a fencelike line of trees and behind it the sky was perfectly blue and still. The asbestos "ranch house" that was now three years old startled her—it looked small. She shook her head as if to get awake.

It was too hot. She went inside the house and turned on the radio to drown out the quiet. She sat on the edge of her bed, barefoot, and listened for an hour and a half to a program called XYZ Sunday Jamboree, record after record of hard, fast, shrieking songs she sang along with, interspersed by exclamations from "Bobby King": "An' look here, you girls at Napoleon's—Son and Charley want you to pay real close attention to this song coming up!"

And Connie paid close attention herself, bathed in a glow of slow-pulsed joy that seemed to rise mysteriously out of the music itself and lay languidly about the airless little room, breathed in and breathed out with each gentle rise and fall of her chest.

After a while she heard a car coming up the drive. She sat up at once, startled, because it couldn't be her father so soon. The gravel kept crunching all the way in from the road—the driveway was long—and Connie ran to the window. It was a car she didn't know. It was an open jalopy, painted a bright gold that caught the sunlight opaquely. Her heart began to pound and her fingers snatched at her hair, checking it, and she whispered, "Christ, Christ," wondering how bad she looked. The car came to a stop at the side door and the horn sounded four short taps, as if this were a signal Connie knew.

She went into the kitchen and approached the door slowly, then hung out the screen door, her bare toes curling down off the step. There were two boys in the car and now she recognized the driver: he had shaggy, shabby black hair that looked crazy as a wig and he was grinning at her.

"I ain't late, am I?" he said.

"Who the hell do you think you are?" Connie said.

"Toldja I'd be out, didn't I?"

"I don't even know who you are."

She spoke sullenly, careful to show no interest or pleasure, and he spoke in a fast, bright monotone. Connie looked past him to the other boy, taking her time. He had fair brown hair, with a lock that fell onto his forehead. His sideburns gave him a fierce, embarrassed look, but so far he hadn't even bothered to glance at her. Both boys wore sunglasses. The driver's glasses were metallic and mirrored everything in miniature.

"You wanta come for a ride?" he said.

Connie smirked and let her hair fall loose over one shoulder.

"Don'tcha like my car? New paint job," he said. "Hey."

"What?"

"You're cute."

She pretended to fidget, chasing flies away from the door.

"Don'tcha believe me, or what?" he said.

"Look, I don't even know who you are," Connie said in disgust.

"Hey, Ellie's got a radio, see. Mine broke down." He lifted his friend's arm and showed her the little transistor radio the boy was holding, and now Connie began to hear the music. It was the same program that was playing inside the house.

"Bobby King?" she said.

"I listen to him all the time. I think he's great."

"He's kind of great," Connie said reluctantly.

"Listen, that guy's *great*. He knows where the action is."

Connie blushed a little, because the glasses made it impossible for her to see just what this boy was looking at. She couldn't decide if she liked him or if he was just a jerk, and so she dawdled in the doorway and wouldn't come down or go back inside. She said, "What's all that stuff painted on your car?"

"Can'tcha read it?" He opened the door very carefully, as if he were afraid it might fall off. He slid out just as carefully, planting his feet firmly on the ground, the tiny metallic world in his glasses slowing down like gelatine hardening, and in the midst of it Connie's bright green blouse. "This here is my name, to begin with," he said. ARNOLD FRIEND was written in tarlike black letters on the side, with a drawing of a round, grinning face that reminded Connie of a pumpkin, except it wore sunglasses. "I wanta introduce myself, I'm Arnold Friend and that's my real name and I'm gonna be your friend, honey, and inside the car's Ellie Oscar, he's kinda shy." Ellie brought his transistor radio up to his shoulder and balanced it there. "Now, these numbers are a secret code, honey," Arnold Friend explained. He read off the numbers thirty-three, nineteen, seventeen and raised his eyebrows at her to see what she thought of that, but she didn't think much of it. The left rear fender had been smashed and around it was written, on the gleaming gold background: DONE BY CRAZY WOMAN DRIVER. Connie had to laugh at that. Arnold Friend was pleased at her laughter and looked up at her. "Around the other side's a lot more—you wanta come and see them?"

"No."

"Why not?"

"Why should I?"

"Don'tcha wanta see what's on the car? Don'tcha wanta go for a ride?"

"I don't know."

"Why not?"

"I got things to do."

"Like what?"

"Things."

He laughed as if she had said something funny. He slapped his thighs. He was standing in a strange way, leaning back against the car as if he were balancing himself. He wasn't tall, only an inch or so taller than she would be if she came down to him. Connie liked the way he was dressed, which was the way all of them dressed: tight faded jeans stuffed into black, scuffed boots, a belt that pulled his waist in and showed how lean he was, and a white pullover shirt that was a little soiled and showed the hard small muscles of his arms and shoulders. He looked as if he probably did hard work, lifting and carrying things. Even his neck looked muscular. And his face was a familiar face, somehow: the jaw and chin and cheeks slightly darkened because he hadn't shaved for a day or two, and the nose long and hawklike, sniffing as if she were a treat he was going to gobble up and it was all a joke.

"Connie, you ain't telling the truth. This is your day set aside for a ride with me and you know it," he said, still laughing. The way he straightened and recovered from his fit of laughing showed that it had been all fake.

"How do you know what my name is?" she said suspiciously.

"It's Connie."

"Maybe and maybe not."

"I know my Connie," he said, wagging his finger. Now she remembered him even better, back at the restaurant, and her cheeks warmed at the thought of how she had sucked in her breath just at the moment she passed him—how she must have looked to him. And he had remembered her. "Ellie and I come out here especially for you," he said. "Ellie can sit in back. How about it?"

"Where?"

"Where what?"

"Where're we going?"

He looked at her. He took off the sunglasses and she saw how pale the skin around his eyes was, like holes that were not in shadow but instead in light. His eyes were like chips of broken glass that catch the light in an amiable way. He smiled. It was as if the idea of going for a ride somewhere, to someplace, was a new idea to him.

"Just for a ride, Connie sweetheart."

"I never said my name was Connie," she said.

"But I know what it is. I know your name and all about you, lots of things," Arnold Friend said. He had not moved yet but stood still leaning back against the side of his jalopy. "I took a special interest in you, such a pretty girl, and found out all about you—like I know your parents and sister are gone somewheres and I know where and how long they're going to be gone, and I know who you were with last night, and your best girlfriend's name is Betty. Right?"

He spoke in a simple lilting voice, exactly as if he were reciting the words to a song. His smile assured her that everything was fine. In the car Ellie turned up the volume on his radio and did not bother to look around at them.

"Ellie can sit in the back seat," Arnold Friend said. He indicated his friend with a casual jerk of his chin, as if Ellie did not count and she should not bother with him.

"How'd you find out all that stuff?" Connie said.

"Listen: Betty Schultz and Tony Fitch and Jimmy Pettinger and Nancy Pettinger," he said in a chant. "Raymond Stanley and Bob Hutter—"

"Do you know all those kids?"

"I know everybody."

"Look, you're kidding. You're not from around here."

"Sure."

"But—how come we never saw you before?"

"Sure you saw me before," he said. He looked down at his boots, as if he were a little offended. "You just don't remember."

"I guess I'd remember you," Connie said.

"Yeah?" He looked up at this, beaming. He was pleased. He began to mark time with the music from Ellie's radio, tapping his fists lightly together. Connie looked away from his smile to the car, which was painted so bright it almost hurt her eyes to look at it. She looked at that name, ARNOLD FRIEND. And up at the front fender was an expression that was familiar—MAN THE FLYING SAUCERS. It was an expression kids had used the year before but didn't use this year. She looked at it for a while as if the words meant something to her that she did not yet know.

"What're you thinking about? Huh?" Arnold Friend demanded. "Not worried about your hair blowing around in the car, are you?"

"No."

"Think I maybe can't drive good?"

"How do I know?"

"You're a hard girl to handle. How come?" he said. "Don't you know I'm your friend. Didn't you see me put my sign in the air when you walked by?"

"What sign?"

"My sign." And he drew an X in the air, leaning out toward her. They were maybe ten feet apart. After his hand fell back to his side the X was still in the air, almost visible. Connie let the screen door close and stood perfectly still inside it, listening to the music from her radio and the boy's blend together. She stared at Arnold Friend. He stood there so stiffly relaxed, pretending to be relaxed, with one hand idly on the door handle as if he were keeping himself up that way and had no intention of ever moving again. She recognized most things about him, the tight jeans that showed his thighs and buttocks and the greasy leather boots and the tight shirt, and even that slippery friendly smile of his, that sleepy dreamy smile that all the boys used to get across ideas they didn't want to put into words.

She recognized all this and also the singsong way he talked, slightly mocking, kidding, but serious and a little melancholy, and she recognized the way he tapped one fist against the other in homage to the perpetual music behind him. But all these things did not come together.

She said suddenly, "Hey, how old are you?"

His smile faded. She could see then that he wasn't a kid, he was much older—thirty, maybe more. At this knowledge her heart began to pound faster.

"That's a crazy thing to ask. Can'tcha see I'm your own age?"

"Like hell you are."

"Or maybe a coupla years older. I'm eighteen."

"Eighteen?" she said doubtfully.

He grinned to reassure her and lines appeared at the corners of his mouth. His teeth were big and white. He grinned so broadly his eyes became slits and she saw how thick the lashes were, thick and black as if painted with a black tarlike material. Then, abruptly, he seemed to become embarrassed and looked over his shoulder at Ellie. "*Him*, he's crazy," he said. "Ain't he a riot? He's a nut, a real character." Ellie was still listening to the music. His sunglasses told nothing about what he was thinking. He wore a bright orange shirt unbuttoned halfway to show his chest, which was a pale, bluish chest and not muscular like Arnold Friend's. His shirt collar was turned up all around and the very tips of the collar pointed out past his chin as if they were protecting him. He was pressing the transistor radio up against his ear and sat there in a kind of daze, right in the sun.

"He's kinda strange," Connie said.

"Hey, she says you're kinda strange! Kinda strange!" Arnold Friend cried. He pounded on the car to get Ellie's attention. Ellie turned for the first time and Connie saw with shock that he wasn't a kid either—he had a fair, hairless face, cheeks reddened slightly as if the veins grew too close to the surface of his skin, the face of a forty-year-old baby. Connie felt a wave of dizziness rise in her at this sight and she stared at him as if waiting for something to change the shock of the moment, make it all right again. Ellie's lips kept shaping words, mumbling along with the words blasting in his ear.

"Maybe you two better go away," Connie said faintly.

"What? How come?" Arnold Friend cried. "We come out here to take you for a ride. It's Sunday." He had the voice of the man on the radio now. It was the same voice, Connie thought. "Don'tcha know it's Sunday all day? And honey, no matter who you were with last night, today you're with Arnold Friend and don't you forget it! Maybe you better step out here," he said, and this last was in a different voice. It was a little flatter, as if the heat was finally getting to him.

"No. I got things to do."

"Hey."

"You two better leave."

"We ain't leaving until you come with us."

"Like hell I am—"

"Connie, don't fool around with me. I mean—I mean, don't fool *around*," he said, shaking his head. He laughed incredulously. He placed his sunglasses on top of his head, carefully, as if he were indeed wearing a wig, and brought the stems down behind his ears. Connie stared at him, another wave of dizziness and fear rising in her so that for a moment he wasn't even in focus but was just a blur standing there against his gold car, and she had the idea that he had driven up the driveway all right but had come from nowhere before that and belonged nowhere and that everything about him and even about the music that was so familiar to her was only half real.

"If my father comes and sees you—"

"He ain't coming. He's at a barbecue."

"How do you know that?"

"Aunt Tillie's. Right now they're—uh—they're drinking. Sitting around," he said vaguely, squinting as if he were staring all the way to town and over to Aunt Tillie's back yard. Then the vision seemed to get clear and he nodded energetically. "Yeah. Sitting around. There's your sister in a blue dress, huh? And high heels, the poor sad bitch—nothing like you, sweetheart! And your mother's helping some fat woman with the corn, they're cleaning the corn—husking the corn—"

"What fat woman?" Connie cried.

"How do I know what fat woman, I don't know every goddamn fat woman in the world!" Arnold Friend laughed.

"Oh, that's Mrs. Hornsby. . . . Who invited her?" Connie said. She felt a little light-headed. Her breath was coming quickly.

"She's too fat. I don't like them fat. I like them the way you are, honey," he said, smiling sleepily at her. They stared at each other for a while through the screen door. He said softly, "Now, what you're going to do is this: you're going to come out that door. You're going to sit up front with me and Ellie's going to sit in the back, the hell with Ellie, right? This isn't Ellie's date. You're my date. I'm your lover, honey."

"What? You're crazy—"

"Yes, I'm your lover. You don't know what that is but you will," he said. "I know that too. I know all about you. But look: it's real nice and you couldn't ask for nobody better than me, or more polite. I always keep my word. I'll tell you how it is, I'm always nice at first, the first time. I'll hold you so tight you won't think you have to try to get away or pretend anything because you'll know you can't. And I'll come inside you where it's all secret and you'll give in to me and you'll love me—"

"Shut up! You're crazy!" Connie said. She backed away from the door. She put her hands up against her ears as if she'd heard something terrible, something not meant for her. "People don't talk like that, you're crazy," she muttered. Her heart was almost too big now for her chest and its pumping made sweat break out all over her. She looked out to see Arnold Friend pause and then take a step toward the porch, lurching. He almost fell. But, like a clever drunken man, he managed to catch his balance. He wobbled in his high boots and grabbed hold of one of the porch posts.

"Honey?" he said. "You still listening?"

"Get the hell out of here!"

"Be nice, honey. Listen."

"I'm going to call the police—"

He wobbled again and out of the side of his mouth came a fast spat curse, an aside not meant for her to hear. But even this "Christ!" sounded forced. Then he began to smile again. She watched this smile come, awkward as if he were smiling from inside a mask. His whole face was a mask, she thought wildly, tanned down to his throat but then running out as if he had plastered makeup on his face but had forgotten about his throat.

"Honey—? Listen, here's how it is. I always tell the truth and I promise you this: I ain't coming in that house after you."

"You better not! I'm going to call the police if you—if you don't—"

"Honey," he said, talking right through her voice, "honey, I'm not coming in there but you are coming out here. You know why?"

She was panting. The kitchen looked like a place she had never seen before, some room she had run inside but that wasn't good enough, wasn't going to help her. The kitchen window had never had a curtain, after three years, and there were dishes in the sink for her to do—probably—and if you ran your hand across the table you'd probably feel something sticky there.

"You listening, honey? Hey?"

"—going to call the police—"

"Soon as you touch the phone I don't need to keep my promise and can come inside. You won't want that."

She rushed forward and tried to lock the door. Her fingers were shaking. "But why lock it," Arnold Friend said gently, talking right into her face. "It's just a screen door. It's just nothing." One of his boots was at a strange angle, as if his foot wasn't in it. It pointed out to the left, bent at the ankle. "I mean, anybody can break through a screen door and glass and wood and iron or anything else if he needs to, anybody at all, and specially Arnold Friend. If the place got lit up with a fire, honey, you'd come runnin' out into my arms, right into my arms an' safe at home—like you knew I was your lover and'd stopped fooling around. I don't mind a nice shy girl but I don't like no fooling around." Part of those words were spoken with a slight rhythmic lilt, and Connie somehow recognized them—the echo of a song from last year, about a girl rushing into her boyfriend's arms and coming home again—

Connie stood barefoot on the linoleum floor, staring at him. "What do you want?" she whispered.

"I want you," he said.

"What?"

"Seen you that night and thought, that's the one, yes sir. I never needed to look anymore."

"But my father's coming back. He's coming to get me. I had to wash my hair first—" She spoke in a dry, rapid voice, hardly raising it for him to hear.

"No, your daddy is not coming and yes, you had to wash your hair and you washed it for me. It's nice and shining and all for me. I thank you sweetheart," he said with a mock bow, but again he almost lost his balance. He had to bend and adjust his boots. Evidently his feet did not go all the way down; the boots must have been stuffed with something so that he would seem taller. Connie stared out at him and behind him Ellie in the car, who seemed to be looking off toward Connie's right, into nothing. This Ellie said, pulling the words out of the air one after another as if he were just discovering them, "You want me to pull out the phone?"

"Shut your mouth and keep it shut," Arnold Friend said, his face red from bending over or maybe from embarrassment because Connie had seen his boots. "This ain't none of your business."

"What—what are you doing? What do you want?" Connie said. "If I call the police they'll get you, they'll arrest you—"

"Promise was not to come in unless you touch that phone, and I'll keep that promise," he said. He resumed his erect position and tried to force his shoulders back. He sounded like a hero in a movie, declaring something important. But he spoke too loudly and it was as if he were speaking to someone behind Connie. "I ain't made plans for coming in that house where I don't belong but just for you to come out to me, the way you should. Don't you know who I am?"

"You're crazy," she whispered. She backed away from the door but did not want to go into another part of the house, as if this would give him permission to come through the door. "What do you . . . you're crazy, you . . ."

"Huh? What're you saying, honey?"

Her eyes darted everywhere in the kitchen. She could not remember what it was, this room.

"This is how it is, honey: you come out and we'll drive away, have a nice ride. But if you don't come out we're gonna wait till your people come home and then they're all going to get it."

"You want that telephone pulled out?" Ellie said. He held the radio away from his ear and grimaced, as if without the radio the air was too much for him.

"I toldja shut up, Ellie," Arnold Friend said, "you're deaf, get a hearing aid, right? Fix yourself up. This little girl's no trouble and's gonna be nice to me, so Ellie keep to yourself, this ain't your date— right? Don't hem in on me, don't hog, don't crush, don't bird-dog, don't trail me," he said in a rapid, meaningless voice, as if he were running through all the expressions he'd learned but was no longer sure which of them was in style, then rushing on to new ones, making them up with his eyes closed. "Don't crawl under my fence, don't squeeze in my chipmunk hole, don't sniff my glue, suck my popsicle, keep your own greasy fingers on yourself!" He shaded his eyes and peered in at Connie, who was backed against the kitchen table. "Don't mind him, honey, he's just a creep. He's a dope. Right? I'm the boy for you and like I said, you come out here nice like a lady and give me your hand, and nobody else gets hurt, I mean, your nice old bald-headed daddy and your mummy and your sister in her high heels. Because listen: why bring them in this?"

"Leave me alone," Connie whispered.

"Hey, you know that old woman down the road, the one with the chickens and stuff—you know her?"

"She's dead."

"Dead? What? You know her?" Arnold Friend said.

"She's dead—"

"Don't you like her?"

"She's dead—she's—she isn't here anymore—"

"But don't you like her, I mean, you got something against her? Some grudge or something?" Then his voice dipped as if he were conscious of a rudeness. He touched the sunglasses perched up on top of his head as if to make sure they were still there. "Now, you be a good girl."

"What are you going to do?"

"Just two things, or maybe three," Arnold Friend said. "But I promise it won't last long and you'll like me the way you get to like people you're close to. You will. It's all over for you here, so come on out. You don't want your people in any trouble, do you?"

She turned and bumped against a chair or something, hurting her leg, but she ran into the back room and picked up the telephone. Something roared in her ear, a tiny roaring, and she was so sick with fear that she could do nothing but listen to it—the telephone was clammy and very heavy and her fingers groped down to the dial but were too weak to touch it. She began to scream into the phone, into the roaring. She cried out, she cried for her mother, she felt her breath start jerking back and forth in her lungs as if it were something Arnold Friend was stabbing her with again and again with no tenderness. A noisy sorrowful wailing rose all about her and she was locked inside it the way she was locked inside this house.

After a while she could hear again. She was sitting on the floor with her wet back against the wall.

Arnold Friend was saying from the door, "That's a good girl. Put the phone back."

She kicked the phone away from her.

"No, honey. Pick it up. Put it back right."

She picked it up and put it back. The dial tone stopped.

"That's a good girl. Now, you come outside."

She was hollow with what had been fear but what was now just an emptiness. All that screaming had blasted it out of her. She sat, one leg cramped under her, and deep inside her brain was something like a pinpoint of light that kept going and would not let her relax. She thought, I'm not going to see my mother again. She thought, I'm not going to sleep in my bed again. Her bright green blouse was all wet.

Arnold Friend said, in a gentle-loud voice that was like a stage voice, "The place where you came from ain't there anymore, and where you had in mind to go is canceled out. This place you are now—inside your daddy's house—is nothing but a cardboard box I can knock down any time. You know that and always did know it. You hear me?"

She thought, I have got to think. I have got to know what to do.

"We'll go out to a nice field, out in the country here where it smells so nice and it's sunny," Arnold Friend said. "I'll have my arms tight around you so you won't need to try to get away and I'll show you what love is like, what it does. The hell with this house! It looks solid all right," he said. He ran a fingernail down the screen and the noise did not make Connie shiver, as it would have the day before. "Now, put your hand on your heart, honey. Feel that? That feels solid too but we know better. Be nice to me, be sweet like you can because what else is there for a girl like you but to be sweet and pretty and give in?—and get away before her people come back?"

She felt her pounding heart. Her hand seemed to enclose it. She thought for the first time in her life that it was nothing that was hers, that belonged to her, but just a pounding, living thing inside this body that wasn't really hers either.

"You don't want them to get hurt," Arnold Friend went on. "Now, get up, honey. Get up all by yourself."

She stood.

"Now, turn this way. That's right. Come over here to me—Ellie, put that away, didn't I tell you? You dope. You miserable creepy dope," Arnold Friend said. His words were not angry but only part of an incantation. The incantation was kindly. "Now, come out through the kitchen to me, honey, and let's see a smile, try it, you're a brave, sweet little girl and now they're eating corn and hot dogs cooked to bursting over an outdoor fire, and they don't know one thing about you and never did and honey, you're better than them because not a one of them would have done this for you."

Connie felt the linoleum under her feet; it was cool. She brushed her hair back out of her eyes. Arnold Friend let go of the post tentatively and opened his arms for her, his elbows pointing in toward each other and his wrists limp, to show that this was an embarrassed embrace and a little mocking, he didn't want to make her self-conscious.

She put her hand against the screen. She watched herself push the door slowly open as if she were back safe somewhere in the other doorway, watching this body and this head of long hair moving out into the sunlight where Arnold Friend waited.

"My sweet little blue-eyed girl," he said in a half-sung sigh that had nothing to do with her brown eyes but was taken up just the same by the vast sunlit reaches of the land behind him and on all sides of him—so much land that Connie had never seen before and did not recognize except to know that she was going to it.

JANE RULE

IN THE BASEMENT OF THE HOUSE

I can't go back to a women's lib meeting even if he thinks I should. When we break up into small discussion groups, rapping about kids or housework or sex, everybody else says things like, "As a mother . . ." or "As a female rake . . ." or "As a lesbian . . ." I can't start out as an anything. It's like being the only kid at camp without labels sewed in my underpants. I could say that, I guess, and nobody would mind, but it doesn't help *me* any. He's the only one I can talk to. I don't feel like it much, though, or, when I do, there isn't time. Maybe I only do when I know I can't. Like making love or thinking about it. I'd rather think about it. Not about the way it is. Nobody gets around to that. Everybody says, "Now let's really talk about sex," and pretty soon we're all talking about money or freedom or baby-sitters. Well, the girl with the deep voice did say laying girls was fun, but then someone else got off onto whether or not that was really male chauvinist stuff, and we were into politics. When Sharon said, "What's wrong with being an easy lay?" it was just like when we talked about long-term relationship: half an hour defining terms, and then somebody got into her bastard gynecologist who wanted to know how many different guys screwed her and what color they were. I did find out what a cone biopsy was that night, but the next day I read an article in *Redbook* that made it a lot clearer.

Wanting me to go to women's lib is the same as wanting me to sleep around. It's like he's got this idea in his head about freedom. He's not comfortable with it unless I'm free, too. But he doesn't screw around . . . except with me, and he doesn't go to meetings to talk about it. I don't think he talks about it with anybody, except maybe with her. I don't know about that. Funny the things you just don't know, even living in the same house. Maybe it's just me, though. Maybe almost everyone else would know.

Sometimes I think I do learn something at those meetings. That night everyone was talking about the myth of vaginal orgasm and Masters and Johnson, I wondered if that was why I only ever really come when he's licking me. But I could come the other way, or it feels like I could. I just don't want to. I don't know why I don't. There's too much going on for him then. Or I really do think coming with him would make me pregnant, pill or not. I know that's not true, even if Norman Mailer believes it. Germaine Greer says coming with a full cunt is nicer. I don't know what all that stuff has to do with being liberated. But he does like screwing better than I do. It's harder for him, but he gets more out of it, as if he'd really accomplished something. Still, I can't see that it's his fault. I didn't like any of it at first. It was like getting used to Sarah's dirty diapers. Now I don't even take a bath afterwards. I like to sleep with his smell or my smell or whatever it is.

I worry about her, more than anything. I think I really like her better, but isn't it natural that I would? I can identify with her. I can imagine how she feels. But I don't know anything about how she feels. I thought I was going to throw up or faint or scream that time I walked into the kitchen and saw her pulling her hand out of another woman's pants. It doesn't bother me at all now. Oh, I knock or whistle or somehow let her know I'm around, but for her sake, not mine. At first I thought, so that's why he wants to screw me, but now I'm not even sure he knows. And what if she does it because he screws me? She does know about that. That's what she meant when she said, "If you don't really like everything that goes along with the job, quit. Or if you do, don't get uptight about it." Maybe I like her better because she can say things like that, which make more sense than all his worry about freedom and guilt. He doesn't know how to be that kind of honest. I never hear him encouraging her to go to women's lib. If we both went, he'd have to stay home with the kids. He's nice to the kids though. He really listens to them, a lot more than she does, probably more than I do, too. And he's gentle with them. She and I do more roughhousing with David than he does. So who's making a man of David? And she doesn't even want a man, and I like him because he's so gentle. When one of the kids is sick, he's better than either of us. He doesn't get up in the night, of course, but she says, "He sleeps like a human being, not like a dog, the way you and I do." It's true, I have my head off the pillow at any sound in the night. It's not just because I sleep in the basement, all of their noises right on top of me. I slept that way at home, too, in the attic. It's being the oldest or a girl.

It really was funny when that woman said, "I dig raising kids. I really do. Only two things I miss: a good, long uninterrupted sleep and a good, long uninterrupted crap." Never had either to miss. Will I sometime? If I get through college, if I get a real job, if I move out of this house?

"The trouble with pets and husbands is that they never grow up and leave home." When she says things like that, I do feel guilty, and I'm not sure why. Am I sorry for her? She's got a good job of her own, and, in the last couple of months, she got rid of the woman who was hanging around so much and is into a new kind of thing, somebody she's really friends with. I like to see them together, but, of course, I stay out of the way as much as I can. I am getting paid to watch the *kids*.

She's attractive. I didn't use to know what that meant. It isn't good looking, though she is that, her hair particularly. It's good feeling, good vibes. I understand why people like to be around her. Sometimes I'd like to ask him straight questions, lawyer's questions, like, "Why don't you screw your wife?" Maybe he does. Maybe she doesn't want him to.

He's not attractive. One of those thin men with a watermelon pot, thin hair, thin mouth. Even his voice is thin. But that's not it. Nobody ever knows he's in the room. That his body is. His head is there all right, and people like his head. If she came into my room with a bunch of books for me, I'd know in a minute what she was there for. She wouldn't even have to smile in a certain way or touch me. Maybe women have that and men just don't. Or he's different from other people. Nobody talks about being attractive at women's lib. I couldn't talk about it.

"Speaking as a baby sitter who lives in the basement and gets screwed by the boss . . ." and I'd have to say which one, not just because of the real possibilities here, but because that sort of thing is expected. I couldn't call him "my lover." At first he was like a very gentle gynecologist, really interested in my body, only he wasn't feeling around for lumps. Then he wanted me to be interested in his, as if I were taking a course in it and might need to write up a lab report. Once I got over being afraid he'd pee in my mouth, I didn't mind sucking him, and I think he likes it that way, too, not having to think about anybody else. Just a little while ago, when he came in my mouth, I started peeing, right on the floor, and I didn't want to stop. Sometimes I wonder if sex is just learning not to be embarrassed about anything, letting it all go. So why housebreak Sarah? I'm not serious, and nobody in this house is uptight about housebreaking anything. I clean it all up, dog, kids, the lot.

I couldn't say any of that. It makes me sound like an animal. Or something worse. I haven't read enough Freud to know what people would call me, even if he is wrong. Like when I read Reich's *Sexual Revolution*. Why does he think that if you let little kids pee around and play with themselves and each other, they'll grow up to live in communes without any trouble? Serial monogamy, one hundred percent heterosexual. I don't understand what I read. If it's supposed to have something to do with me, I don't.

I'm sorry I don't think he's attractive. I don't know why I care. He's another human being. He's gentle, and he's kind. He likes to do the right thing. He talks about that a lot. But what is the good of people talking to each other if they can't tell the truth? I get scared about what will happen. Nobody at women's lib ever seems to be scared. Let it all hang out, get your head straight, be liberated.

If I ever said it like it is . . . I know my label. "Speaking as a slave . . ." that's what they'd all think. I'm a wage slave, a student slave, diddled by the lord of the manor just like some Victorian governess, and I even clean up dog shit, never mind the kids. It doesn't make me mad. Mostly I don't even mind. But it isn't safe. Sometimes, when I hear him coming down the basement steps, I pretend it's her instead, and she's got a gun, and she's going to kill me, and then I'm really relieved and glad to see him, even though I know all along it's silly. I like her better than I do him. But I'm not comfortable with her. I'm always getting out of her way.

I'd like to go some place and do something that didn't make me feel guilty. I did try to tell him that women's lib for me was just another guilt trip, but I didn't understand it well enough myself to make him understand. He started talking about good guilt. If I felt guilty about not really taking myself seriously enough, not respecting my own mind, that was good guilt and I should face it. I get really embarrassed when he tells me what a fine mind I have. He needs to think so; otherwise he's just another guy trying to forget he's going bald. It would be better for me if my psych prof thought I had a good mind. He's never raised his eyes high enough to see that I've got a head. I don't want to pass psych on the size of my tits, and I wish I could figure out whether it's wearing a bra or not wearing a bra that turns men off. Can't ask something like that at a meeting. Nobody else knows either. What's so really bad about being a guy trying to forget he's going bald? Why would he be ashamed of screwing somebody ignorant and ordinary? He loves his kids. They're ignorant and ordinary. He probably doesn't think so. Can't. Maybe that's why he can listen so well. He's hearing all sorts of amazing things.

When I was mad about getting the curse (I'm not supposed to call it that; it's unliberated) and said I wished I could give all that blood every month to the Red Cross, he told me I was an original thinker. Seriously! Would some guy figure out a way to do it and get famous? I don't even know what you'd have to major in.

Maybe part of it is that I'm younger than most of the others. I don't have their experience. Sex is still a big thing for me because I don't know much about it. If I could find out whether or not most girls pee like that, I maybe wouldn't be scared I'm abnormal. Old people go back into second childhood. They put Granddad in a home when he began to lose control of himself, "foul himself," Mother said. What if I have a senile bladder at eighteen? He liked it, but how do I know he's not some sort of pervert? Or telling me just to make me feel good? I tell him things to make him feel good, but I know when I'm doing it. Sometimes I'm not sure he does. He'd have to think I was attractive whether I am or not.

I couldn't let some kid screw me now. I wouldn't know what to do. If I don't do anything with him and just lie there, like the first time, he says it's very passive, and that's bad, but how do I know which things he's taught me are okay and which aren't? I could be really weird. If he doesn't know his own wife is queer—and I don't think he does—how would he know whether I was or not? Maybe somebody else could tell in a minute. I wouldn't show anyone else the way I showed him how I did it to myself. I didn't mind. He only wanted to see what I liked, but somebody else might know from that. She doesn't ever come on to me. Wouldn't she if I were?

"Please, could somebody tell me, if my landlady doesn't want to lay me, does that prove I'm straight or just unattractive?"

Maybe she doesn't because of him. Maybe she only likes people her own age. There's no way I'm going to find out about that at a meeting. There's no way I'm going to find out. I don't want to know.

Nobody in that room ever comes out and says they're scared to death they won't get married or will marry some guy who isn't really interested in them and is always off screwing some kid in the basement. Am I the only one who is? If I feel so sorry for her, why do I let him do it? She doesn't seem to care. I'm scared of her. I don't think she's going to shoot me. I make that up to have something I can imagine to be scared about. These last couple of months she's been so happy she has a hard time even getting irritated. What if she left him? Do women ever just go off with each other? But she couldn't take the kids. And I couldn't stay here if she wasn't here. It wouldn't look right. I wouldn't want to anyway. I think one of those women at the meeting did leave her husband and go live with another woman. When I asked him about women loving women, he laughed and said that was for flat-chested school girls. I should feel sorry for him. At least she knows. She lives in the real world. He doesn't. He wouldn't know how.

If I just didn't have to think about it, if I just didn't have to go to all those meetings, maybe I'd stop being so scared. They all talk as if there weren't any danger, as if nobody ever got really mad, as if there weren't any laws. She could divorce him because of me, take his kids and his money and the house, everything. But liberated people don't do things like that. She wouldn't. But what about him? Wouldn't he go crazy if she tried to leave him and he knew why? He's gentle, and he's kind, and he's just afraid of going bald. But if losing his hair makes him screw his baby-sitter, what would he have to do if he lost his wife?

All I want to do is get through college and then find some nice, ordinary guy to marry me. I'll do my own baby-sitting. We won't have a basement. What if it happens anyway? If somebody is afraid of losing his hair and somebody else is queer . . . are all women queer? Do they turn queer? What else could she do? The men are all after kids like me. She's not going to run after boys; she couldn't kid herself they were original thinkers, and she'd be bored. So what's left?

One thing I wish I had the guts to tell him: you send me to women's lib meetings much longer and I'm not going to be lying here making up her footsteps coming down the stairs to kill me. I'm going to be praying she's coming down the stairs to love me. And one thing I wish I had the guts to tell all of them is, if that's what women's liberation is all about, some of us may get killed for it, and I wasn't socialized like that. I'm too young to die.

It isn't funny. I shouldn't be living in this basement at all. There must be a basement somewhere else that's different, where I could just do my work and hole in until it's over. All I really need to figure out is how to use my very ordinary head and keep my tits out of my classwork and my landlord's mouth. I don't need to go to meetings for that. I just have to get out of here.

But what about her? What if he doesn't like the next one? What if the next one said something? She's not that careful. What if the next one was attractive? To her. Oh, shit! shit! Why do I have to live through all this shit and then all the marriage and baby shit before . . . before a woman like her would look at me. She can't make me up the way he does. I'm just a kid. What do my tits mean to her? She's got her own. She isn't afraid of losing her hair or her husband. I'm scared. I'm just too scared to love her. I won't be able to for years.

If he makes me go back to another one of those meetings, I'm going to tell him I won't. I'll move. I don't want to be liberated. There's got to be another way out.

BARBARA BARACKS

PLEASURE

Lily sat in a corner and stared over at us hunkered by the light of the door. We were talking in low tones and I could feel her behind me because at eleven years old you know how the light is blocked by other bodies. But right then I was just finding out after all that time that Lily was my mother. This explained the dollar bills Pauline was holding onto as if they were a tow chain. This explained why Uncle Larry, who came twice a month ever since I knew enough to avoid his licorice breath, was trying to crush me: I could hear his chest moving inside the wool vest, his best, sweaty. He was telling me he was my daddy. I whooped away from him, danced over to Lily, who raised a hand to her lips as if she were eating candy, then shoved past everyone outside. Even the hall was outside, because for Lily's sake—she screamed at sunlight—we kept the rooms dark, "like World War II," Pauline said, trying to make it a game.

The halls were filled with humming, growing louder, and my mind filled up with sweat. Only one person I knew had the resonance to make that sound and there she was on the third floor stairs: the 350-pound daughter of the super, our super the witch. Her daughter the telephone operator. She was waiting, as she did every day, for the desire to move up the next step, and while she waited she hummed, her blue eyes opening and closing like the systole and diastole of a heart. She didn't hum a tune, really, she didn't have the ear for that, she hummed a monotone, like a telephone off the hook. She hated me because she loved her mother and I surely didn't (I tortured her cats) so as I moved down the stairs she didn't move to one side, she stood, expressionless, plugging up the hole. It was the third week in August and the air stood up thick and yellow, coating everyone with grease like short-order cooks in an eggs-and-bacon joint. I held my breath and squeezed by and she let out a whinny of surprise.

Sisters in a windowless centrifuge lined with parents' portraits (they lived and died here in Manhattan too), Pauline and Lily were redeemed with the birth of Lily's bastard; the centrifuge stopped at my birth and, like the illusion-giving barbershop pole, began to whirl the other way. I, the changed center, altered all. That is, Lily declined to a rag-and-bones madness and Pauline, the elder, expanded to fill our days—no spider in the kitchen or secret hole beneath a floorboard was unaware of her command. She stopped typing in an office all day and dropped her telegraphic speech without I's and you's; her mask and robe of spinsterhood were left behind as unworthy in the presence of the screaming baby, the grubby whining child. And now me, because I know, because I grew alone like a weed in the chink of a bridge, and the kids lining the blocks mostly leave me alone, I think I will go back and kill them, with my fists, somehow.

Plunged into beauty they were, arm in arm, all affection through rows of poplars lining the walk in the Catskills. Boat rides, one-piece bathing suits, noisy brown radio. A shabby resort by Lake George, with sixteen-millimeter movies in the game room every night: *Beau Geste* with Susan Hayward and Gary Cooper, *Sing You Sinners* with

Bing Crosby and Fred MacMurray. Two weeks free from the offices which carried on without them though the shadow of their hours forced them up at seven, two hours before hotel breakfast, when they sat on the porch and shivered, not knowing what else to do.

"Lily of the Valley," said Pauline, and Lily, small and always between words, smiled. My crazy mother had got through four solid years of high school without saying a single word. Some teachers thought she was deaf but the smart ones knew she was crazy; she liked going to work a whole lot better, because there she could say a word now and then: she didn't have to say anything special. "Good girl," Pauline said when Lily started bringing home paychecks. There were plenty of odd ones like them around the hotel, taking their air, dead angel parents watching in the sky.

Every day the great silence—the one in first snows, wounds made alone, the TV cackle turned off—on the lawn drew Lily out to walk circles around the hotel, keeping to the edges of the rubbery shrubs and plants, observing the silence from all sides. It was almost as perfect as her own. Pauline rocked on the porch, chatting with the sweet old ladies in robin's-egg-blue sweaters; they forgave Pauline being thirty years younger than they because she could sit for hours. But as one blue morning swelled into lunch, Pauline began to stare: Lily, her mainspring, was no longer passing by, placing one dreaming foot before the next. Another body had intercepted her orbit. drawing her out to the lake, the woods, Edwardian pleasures and a short spasm of rapid and fertile sex.

Oh yes, that's my dad. See him in action now. A little clerk from Gristede's, dumb enough to go fishing in lakes too polluted for fish. But there she is, my mom, circling like a nice silvery trout in a clearwater pool. So he snagged her on the west side of the hotel, the blind side where Pauline, catching the sun, couldn't cast a possessive eye. And when he discovered that Lily, demure, with a perfect dimple in her cheek, was obedient to the point of idiocy, and was already worrying about her absence from her sister, he had her take her clothes off, using the same bland coaxing you use to get some kid, filled with urgency but shy around strangers, to pee. He gallantly escorted her back to the hotel as she stumbled now and then over roots, feeling everywhere the enormous pain he had introduced to her. It was, as close as humanly possible, a virgin birth, and Pauline slapped her around plenty for it. All to seal things up tight, of course, to remind Lily of the chain of succession and or relative degrees of pain.

But the remarkable thing, the really spectacular part, the one that keeps me laughing, now that I know who he is, is that he came back, he even tried to stick around. Uncle Larry bought our address from the hotel clerk and, by the time he got around to dropping in I, a great mound in Lily's belly, was making myself known. It was almost spring and Larry wanted another walk in the woods, no doubt, but he discovered that he was, after all, making a business call. And would be making them far into the future. As I grew, so did he: Uncle Larry became the manager of an A & P and sent us whole caseloads of Mott's applesauce, Dole pineapple, and Heinz beans. We'd eat pounds of the same thing for days and weeks on end, Pauline growing fat and Lily thin. For eleven years we camped out this way, Pauline working as a temp when we needed the money, but mostly staying home, inside, to keep track of us, to check up on Larry. I went to school: ate paste in the back of the room, held a boy down and stuffed dirt up his nose, wrote "Albert Shanker sucks" slanting downhill on the blackboard.

"A girl-boy," said the vice-principal.

"Is that the same as a tomboy?" I asked.

"No," he said, "it's worse."

"Good."

So I walked outdoors with two dollars pressed into my hand: my alimony. For after Larry patted his alligator-green wallet as he slipped it back to bed, he said something extra: "Your Aunt Pauline and I are going to get married." Pauline smirked from the bridge of her nose as if a bug had crawled up there. And all this time I thought I'd dropped from a hole in the sky as natural as ants in the sugarbowl; me hollering as Lily chews the end of the TV antenna, lips and noisy teeth making the picture out of whack while Pauline sleeps in the armchair, one long hair sticking out from under her armpit's wet armhole, a metronome to her snores. Larry had squatted down to my face. "You can't marry her," I whispered into his staring ear, "she's too fat." I got out so fast his arm didn't raise to hit.

Saddened animal, I left the chop suey joint carrying the fruit of two dollars: egg foo yung. But my weapons were down and, flashing from around the corner, a kid on skates thundered up and grabbed the carton from my unresisting hand. Grief died as supper skated over the curb and, laughing, through red lights' cars.

In the lack, I saw something that happened last year: a hand on the windowsill snow, winter sun freezing the blue sky into the snow, the hand frozen blue in the snow, veins rising to purple. Lily was staring out the wide open window into the world, face ribbed with light so I could see how she'd caved in to the vacuum in the cheeks, the jaw, the forehead just above and next to her eyes. She didn't feel her hand but I did. So I reached out and pulled it inside; she turned, sitting on about one inch of the chair, hair curved down to the corner of her mouth, her hand still clawed and paralyzed with cold. Her eyes were covered with targets, and empty as if large arrows had been shot into the pupil of each eye.

That power loosened me now into a run, legs dividing scissorslike over the squares of sidewalk, cutting through tides of slow bodies, my sweat breaking out again under the day's dirt. The kids monkeying around with firehydrants and hoses pointed their water at me as I ran by. I slammed my hands against the hot lids of garbage cans and heard my voice rise to a wail; the old ladies withering in their chairs did me dirt by paying no attention. I was running too fast to spit. So I caught at a pole with my hand and whirled around it, stirring the world around until I let go and fell spinning on the ground, howls broken into laughter. Larry would never stand for Lily's drool, I'd have to take her away with me before they shoved her out a window, watching her ass hit the ground.

I made it back to the apartment, where everything was still there: Pauline and Larry were snuffling around in the bedroom while Lily crouched next to the kitchen stove as if it were winter. I coaxed her downstairs with half a candy bar I stole from the refrigerator and on the street she clung to me from behind; she felt just like a kid riding piggyback who chokes the ride with a stranglehold to save herself from believing in falling. Lily held on so tight all the stoop-rats turned, thinking me her prisoner marched home for the pleasure of punishment. They called out with joy.

We duckwalked out of the neighborhood until the heaps of people grew scarce and piles of rubble and giant weeds crawling up cyclone fences surrounded us. The river was flowing grey in the evening; it probably was the first body of water bigger than a bathtub Lily had seen since Lake George. In fact I never could remember seeing her outside before, as if she were one of those deformed monsters locked in a box by parents you read about in the supermarket newspapers. A pink mist was rising above the barges and buildings on the opposite shore and the head of the first star had already pushed through. I gave Lily the other half of the candy bar and we sat on the rocks which lined the water, smelling the fish, sewage, salt, and chocolate. Lily rattled the candy bar wrapper out loud and I fell asleep, to wake in the night, her skinny bones nesting into my right side. I'd never felt so much of another's body before and I squirmed: I didn't want to be eaten up.

But maybe she had slept too, because in the light from the arc lamps and the half-open moon the stiffness knotting up her muscles had dissolved; in fact, at first I thought she was dead. For the first time she looked like she was moving into something and when she lifted her hand I knew something horrible was going to happen and it did.

For years I'd been listening to Lily talk whole books to spiders and cats, making words sounding like Russian, except they had the harshness of peeing ground glass. And sometimes, especially when I was mad at Pauline and wasn't talking to her for days, I heard Lily's words in my own head, so full of tiny changes in feeling, so much easier to spit with than the big round common words like eat and sleep and school and play everyone else is using all the time. It was easy to think up strings of Lily's words in school, using them against the teacher and everybody in the class. It was easy to crouch in the corner with Lily half the night and repeat the pieces of words and sharp sounds she made. It was like learning to be a bug; I always thought that was what Lily knew how to be and I wanted to be that too.

But now she stroked my hair, as if I were a cat, and she spoke to me in regular sentences with regular words just like everyone else. It was as if the cat came in one day and spoke in English.

"Amy," she said—that's what they called me—"be a good girl. Go home now."

I rose and hit her in the face. "You disgusting old bag," I shrieked, "is that the first thing you've got to say?" I danced out over the rocks, the bones in my toes twisting between the crevices but not bothering about it. "Go where! Go where!" I heard from far off the hoots of boys further down the river and hoped they'd follow my screams so I could fight them all until they smashed me up. But there was no more sound and Lily had turned back into herself again, staring out, her mouth hung open, its wet surfaces inside reflecting light.

TONI CADE BAMBARA

RAYMOND'S RUN

I don't have have much work to do around the house like some girls. My mother does that. And I don't have to earn my pocket money by hustling; George runs errands for the big boys and sells Christmas cards. And anything else that's got to get done, my father does. All I have to do in life is mind my brother Raymond, which is enough.

Sometimes I slip and say my little brother Raymond. But as any fool can see he's much bigger and he's older too. But a lot of people call him my little brother cause he needs looking after cause he's not quite right. And a lot of smart mouths got lots to say about that too, especially when George was minding him. But now, if anybody has anything to say to Raymond, anything to say about his big head, they have to come by me. And I don't play the dozens or believe in standing around with somebody in my face doing a lot of talking. I much rather just knock you down and take my chances even if I am a

249

little girl with skinny arms and a squeaky voice, which is how I got the name Squeaky. And if things get too rough, I run. And as anybody can tell you, I'm the fastest thing on two feet.

There is no track meet that I don't win the first place medal. I used to win the twenty-yard dash when I was a little kid in kindergarten. Nowadays, it's the fifty-yard dash. And tomorrow I'm subject to run the quarter-meter relay all by myself and come in first, second, and third. The big kids call me Mercury cause I'm the swiftest thing in the neighborhood. Everybody knows that—except two people who know better, my father and me. He can beat me to Amsterdam Avenue with me having a two-fire-hydrant head start and him running with his hands in his pockets and whistling. But that's private information. Cause can you imagine some thirty-five-year-old man stuffing himself into PAL shorts to race little kids? So as far as everyone's concerned, I'm the fastest and that goes for Gretchen, too, who has put out the tale that she is going to win the first-place medal this year. Ridiculous. In the second place, she's got short legs. In the third place, she's got freckles. In the first place, no one can beat me and that's all there is to it.

I'm standing on the corner admiring the weather and about to take a stroll down Broadway so I can practice my breathing exercises, and I've got Raymond walking on the inside close to the buildings, cause he's subject to fits of fantasy and starts thinking he's a circus performer and that the curb is a tightrope strung high in the air. And sometimes after a rain he likes to step down off his tightrope right into the gutter and slosh around getting his shoes and cuffs wet. Then I get hit when I get home. Or sometimes if you don't watch him he'll dash across traffic to the island in the middle of Broadway and give the pigeons a fit. Then I have to go behind him apologizing to all the old people sitting around trying to get some sun and getting all upset with the pigeons fluttering around them, scattering their newspapers and upsetting the wax paper lunches in their laps. So I keep Raymond on the inside of me, and he plays like he's driving a stagecoach which is O.K. by me so long as he doesn't run me over or interrupt my breathing exercises, which I have to do on account of I'm serious about my running, and I don't care who knows it.

Now some people like to act like things come easy to them, won't let on that they practice. Not me. I'll high-prance down 34th Street like a rodeo pony to keep my knees strong even if it does get my mother uptight so that she walks ahead like she's not with me, don't know me, is all by herself on a shopping trip, and I am somebody else's crazy child. Now you take Cynthia Procter for instance. She's just the opposite. If there's a test tomorrow, she'll say something like, "Oh, I guess I'll play handball this afternoon and watch television tonight," just to let you know she ain't thinking about the test. Or like last week when she won the spelling bee for the millionth time, "A good thing you got 'receive,' Squeaky, cause I would have got it wrong. I completely forgot about the spelling bee." And she'll clutch the lace on her blouse like it was a narrow escape. Oh, brother. But of course when I pass her house on my early morning trots around the block, she is practicing the scales on the piano over and over and over and over. Then in music class she always lets herself get bumped around so she falls accidently on purpose onto the piano stool and is so surprised to find herself sitting there that she decides just for fun to try out the ole keys. And what do you know—Chopin's waltzes just spring out of her fingertips and she's the most surprised thing in the world. A regular prodigy. I could kill people like that. I stay up all night studying the words for the spelling bee. And you can see me any time of day practicing running. I never walk if I can trot, and shame on Raymond if he can't keep up. But of course he does, cause if he hangs back someone's liable to walk up to him and get smart, or take his allowance from him, or ask him where he got that great big pumpkin head. People are so stupid sometimes.

So I'm strolling down Broadway breathing out and breathing in on counts of seven, which is my lucky number, and here comes Gretchen and her sidekicks: Mary Louise, who used to be a friend of mine when she first moved to Harlem from Baltimore and got beat up by everybody till I took up for her on account of her mother and my mother used to sing in the same choir when they were young girls, but people ain't grateful, so now she hangs out with the new girl Gretchen and talks about me like a dog; and Rosie, who is as fat as I am skinny and has a big mouth where Raymond is concerned and is too stupid to know that there is not a big deal of difference between herself and Raymond and that she can't afford to throw stones. So they are steady coming up Broadway and I see right away that it's going to be one of those Dodge City scenes cause the street ain't that big and they're close to the buildings just as we are. First I think I'll step into the candy store and look over the new comics and let them pass. But that's chicken and I've got a reputation to consider. So then I think I'll just walk straight on through them or even over them if necessary. But as they get to me, they slow down. I'm ready to fight, cause like I said I don't feature a whole lot of chitchat, I much prefer to just knock you down right from the jump and save everybody a lotta precious time.

"You signing up for the May Day races?" smiles Mary Louise, only it's not a smile at all. A dumb question like that doesn't deserve an answer. Besides, there's just me and Gretchen standing there really, so no use wasting my breath talking to shadows.

"I don't think you're going to win this time," says Rosie, trying to signify with her hands on her hips all salty, completely forgetting that I have whupped her behind many times for less salt than that.

"I always win cause I'm the best," I say straight at Gretchen who is, as far as I'm concerned, the only one talking in this ventriloquist-dummy routine. Gretchen smiles, but it's not a smile, and I'm thinking that girls never really smile at each other because they don't know how and don't want to know how and there's probably no one to teach us how, cause grownup girls don't know either. Then they all look at Raymond who has just brought his mule team to a standstill. And they're about to see what trouble they can get into through him.

"What grade you in now, Raymond?"

"You got anything to say to my brother, you say it to me, Mary Louise Williams of Raggedy Town, Baltimore."

"What are you, his mother?" sasses Rosie.

"That's right, Fatso. And the next word out of anybody and I'll be *their* mother too." So they just stand there and Gretchen shifts from one leg to the other and so do they. Then Gretchen puts her hands on her hips and is about to say something with her freckle-face self but doesn't. Then she walks around me looking me up and down but keeps walking up Broadway, and her sidekicks follow her. So me and Raymond smile at each other and he says, "Giddyap" to his team and I continue with my breathing exercises, strolling down Broadway toward the ice man on 145th with not a care in the world cause I am Miss Quicksilver herself.

I take my time getting to the park on May Day because the track meet is the last thing on the program. The biggest thing on the program is the Maypole dancing, which I can do without, thank you, even if my mother thinks it's a shame I don't take part and act like a girl for a change. You'd think my mother'd be grateful not to have to make me a white organdy dress with a big satin sash and buy me new white baby-doll shoes that can't be taken out of the box till the big day. You'd think she'd be glad her daughter ain't out there prancing around a Maypole getting the new clothes all dirty and sweaty and trying to act like a fairy or a flower or whatever you're supposed to be when you should be trying to be yourself, whatever that is, which is, as far as I am concerned, a poor black girl who really can't afford to buy shoes and a new dress you only wear once a lifetime cause it won't fit next year.

I was once a strawberry in a Hansel and Gretel pageant when I was in nursery school and didn't have no better sense than to dance on tiptoe with my arms in a circle over my head doing umbrella steps and being a perfect fool just so my mother and father could come dressed up and clap. You'd think they'd know better than to encourage that kind of nonsense. I am not a strawberry. I do not dance on my toes. I run. That is what I am all about. So I always come late to the May Day program, just in time to get my number pinned on and lay in the grass till they announce the fifty-yard dash.

I put Raymond in the little swings, which is a tight squeeze this year and will be impossible next year. Then I look around for Mr.

Pearson, who pins the numbers on. I'm really looking for Gretchen if you want to know the truth, but she's not around. The park is jam-packed. Parents in hats and corsages and breast-pocket hand-kerchiefs peeking up. Kids in white dresses and light blue suits. The parkees unfolding chairs and chasing the rowdy kids from Lenox as if they had no right to be there. The big guys with their caps on backwards, leaning against the fence swirling the basketballs on the tips of their fingers, waiting for all these crazy people to clear out the park so they can play. Most of the kids in my class are carrying bass drums and glockenspiels and flutes. You'd think they'd put in a few bongos or something for real like that.

Then here comes Mr. Pearson with his clipboard and his cards and pencils and whistles and safety pins and fifty million other things he's always dropping all over the place with his clumsy self. He sticks out in a crowd because he's on stilts. We used to call him Jack and the Beanstalk to get him mad. But I'm the only one that can outrun him and get away, and I'm too grown for that silliness now.

"Well, Squeaky," he says, checking my name off the list and handing me number seven and two pins. And I'm thinking he's got no right to call me Squeaky, if I can't call him Beanstalk.

"Hazel Elizabeth Deborah Parker," I correct him and tell him to write it down on his board.

"Well, Hazel Elizabeth Deborah Parker, going to give someone else a break this year?" I squint at him real hard to see if he is seriously thinking I should lose the race on purpose just to give someone else a break. "Only six girls running this time," he con-tinues, shaking his head sadly like it's my fault all of New York didn't turn out in sneakers. "That new girl should give you a run for your money." He looks around the park for Gretchen like a periscope in a submarine movie. "Wouldn't it be a nice gesture if you were . . . to ahhh . . ."

I give him such a look he couldn't finish putting that idea into words. Grownups got a lot of nerve sometimes. I pin number seven to myself and stomp away, I'm so burnt. And I go straight for the track and stretch out on the grass while the band winds up with "Oh, the Monkey Wrapped His Tail Around the Flagpole," which my teacher calls by some other name. The man on the loudspeaker is calling everyone over to the track and I'm on my back looking at the sky, trying to pretend I'm in the country, but I can't, because even grass in the city feels hard as sidewalk, and there's just no pretending you are anywhere but in a "concrete jungle" as my grandfather says.

The twenty-yard dash takes all of two minutes cause most of the little kids don't know no better than to run off the track or run the wrong way or run smack into the fence and fall down and cry. One little kid, though, has got the good sense to run straight for the white ribbon up ahead so he wins. Then the second-graders line up for the thirty-yard dash and I don't even bother to turn my head to watch cause Raphael Perez always wins. He wins before he even begins by psyching the runners, telling them they're going to trip on their shoelaces and fall on their faces or lose their shorts or something, which he doesn't really have to do since he is very fast, almost as fast as I am. After that is the forty-yard dash which I use to run when I was in first grade. Raymond is hollering from the swings cause he knows I'm about to do my thing cause the man on the loudspeaker has just announced the fifty-yard dash, although he might just as well be giving a recipe for angel food cake cause you can hardly make out what he's saying for the static. I get up and slip off my sweat pants and then I see Gretchen standing at the starting line, kicking her legs out like a pro. Then as I get into place I see that ole Raymond is on line on the other side of the fence, bending down with his fingers on the ground just like he knew what he was doing. I was going to yell at him but then I didn't. It burns up your energy to holler.

Every time, just before I take off in a race, I always feel like I'm in a dream, the kind of dream you have when you're sick with fever and feel all hot and weightless. I dream I'm flying over a sandy beach in the early morning sun, kissing the leaves of the trees as I fly by. And there's always the smell of apples, just like in the country when I was little and used to think I was a choo-choo train, running through the fields of corn and chugging up the hill to the orchard. And all the time I'm dreaming this, I get lighter and lighter until I'm flying over the beach again, getting blown through the sky like a feather that weighs nothing at all. But once I spread my fingers in the dirt and crouch over the Get on Your Mark, the dream goes and I am solid again and am telling myself, Squeaky you must win, you must win, you are the fastest thing in the world, you can even beat your father up Amsterdam if you really try. And then I feel my weight coming back just behind my knees then down to my feet then into the earth and the pistol shot explodes in my blood and I am off and weightless again, flying past the other runners, my arms pumping up and down and the whole world is quiet except for the crunch as I zoom over the gravel in the track. I glance to my left and there is no one. To the right, a blurred Gretchen, who's got her chin jutting out as if it would win the race all by itself. And on the other side of the fence is Raymond with his arms down to his side and the palms tucked up behind him, running in his very own style, and it's the first time I ever saw that and I almost stop to watch my brother Raymond on his first run. But the white ribbon is bouncing toward me and I tear past it, racing into the distance till my feet with a mind of their own start digging up footfuls of dirt and brake me short. Then all the kids standing on the side pile on me, banging me on the back and slapping my head with their May Day programs, for I have won again and everybody on 151st Street can walk tall for another year.

"In first place . . ." the man on the loudspeaker is clear as a bell now. But then he pauses and the loudspeaker starts to whine. Then static. And I lean down to catch my breath and here comes Gretchen walking back, for she's overshot the finish line too, huffing and puffing with her hands on her hips taking it slow, breathing in steady time like a real pro and I sort of like her a little for the first time. "In first place . . ." and then three or four voices get all mixed up on the loudspeaker and I dig my sneaker into the grass and stare at Gretchen who's staring back, we both wondering just who did win. I can hear old Beanstalk arguing with the man on the loudspeaker and then a few others running their mouths about what the stop-watches say. Then I hear Raymond yanking at the fence to call me and I wave to shush him, but he keeps rattling the fence like a gorilla in a cage like in them gorilla movies, but then like a dancer or something he starts climbing up nice and easy but very fast. And it occurs to me, watching how smoothly he climbs hand over hand and remembering how he looked running with his arms down to his side and with the wind pulling his mouth back and his teeth showing and all, it occurred to me that Raymond would make a very fine runner. Doesn't he always keep up with me on my trots? And he surely knows how to breathe in counts of seven cause he's always doing it at the dinner table, which drives my brother George up the wall. And I'm smiling to beat the band cause if I've lost this race, or if me and Gretchen tied, or even if I've won, I can always retire as a runner and begin a whole new career as a coach with Raymond as my champion. After all, with a little more study I can beat Cynthia and her phony self at the spelling bee. And if I bugged my mother, I could get piano lessons and become a star. And I have a big rep as the baddest thing around. And I've got a roomful of ribbons and medals and awards. But what has Raymond got to call his own?

So I stand there with my new plans, laughing out loud by this time as Raymond jumps down from the fence and runs over with his teeth showing and his arms down to the side, which no one before him has quite mastered as a running style. And by the time he comes over I'm jumping up and down so glad to see him—my brother Raymond, a great runner in the family tradition. But of course everyone thinks I'm jumping up and down because the men on the loudspeaker have finally gotten themselves together and compared notes and are announcing "In first place—Miss Hazel Elizabeth Deborah Parker." (Dig that.) "In second place—Miss Gretchen P. Lewis." And I look at Gretchen wondering what the "P" stands for. And I smile. Cause she's good, no doubt about it. Maybe she'd like to help me coach Raymond; she obviously is serious about running, as any fool can see. And she nods to congratulate me and then she smiles. And I smile. We stand there with this big smile of respect between us. It's about as real a smile as girls can do for each other, considering we don't practice real smiling every day, you know, cause maybe we too busy being flowers or fairies or strawberries instead of something honest and worthy of respect . . . you know . . . like being people.

BIOGRAPHICAL NOTES

Glenda Adams was born in Sydney, Australia, in 1939. Her collection of stories *Lies and Stories* was published in 1976. She is currently working on a novel and is associate director of the Teachers & Writers Collaborative in New York City.

Toni Cade Bambara is the editor and a contributor to *The Black Woman* (1970) and *Tales and Short Stories for Black Folk* (1971). She has published two collections of short stories, *Gorilla, My Love* (1972) and *The Organizer's Wife and Other Stories* (1977).

Barbara Baracks was born in Rockland County, New York, in 1951. She publishes a literature/arts magazine called *Big Deal*, reviews gallery shows for *Artforum*, and is an editor for the New Wilderness Foundation. An anthology of her work, *None of the Above*, is to be published by Crossing Press.

Ann Beattie, born in 1947 in Washington, D.C., has published short stories in *The New Yorker* and *Atlantic Monthly*. She teaches at the University of Virginia. *Distortions*, a collection of her short stories, and *Chilly Scenes of Winter*, a novel, were both published in 1976.

Sandy Boucher was born in 1936. She has published in literary journals such as *Antioch Review* and *Michigan Quarterly Review*. Her feminist writings have appeared in *Ms.* magazine, *Amazon Quarterly*, *This Is Women's Work* (a poetry collection, 1974), *Lesbian Speak Out* (1974), and *The Lesbian Reader* (1975). She is now at work on a novel.

Margery Finn Brown's stories have appeared in *Redbook* and *McCall's*, her articles in *The Writer*. "In the Forests of Riga" won the Mystery Writers of America Edgar Allan Poe Award. Her book *Over a Bamboo Fence* describes life in postwar Japan.

Rosellen Brown, born in 1939, is the author of a book of poems, *Some Deaths in the Delta* (1970), a collection of short stories, *Street Games* (1974), and a novel, *The Autobiography of My Mother* (1976). She has taught at Tougaloo College, Antioch/New England, and the Bread Loaf Writers' Conference.

Margaret Drabble, born in Yorkshire, England, in 1939, now teaches in London. She is the author of *A Summer Bird Cage* (1964), *The Garrick Year* (1964), *The Millstone* (1965), *Jerusalem the Golden* (1967), *The Waterfall* (1969), *The Needle's Eye* (1972), *The Realm of Gold* (1975), and a biography of Arnold Bennett (1974).

Charlotte Perkins Gilman, born in 1860, died in 1900, was an active feminist intellectual, lecturer, and writer. "The Yellow Wallpaper" was first published in *The New England Magazine* in 1892. She wrote *Women and Economics* and *The Living of Charlotte Perkins Gilman: An Autobiography*.

Gail Godwin, born in Alabama in 1937, has published three novels, *The Perfectionists* (1970), *Glass People* (1972), and *The Odd Woman* (1974), and one collection of short stories, *Dream Children* (1976).

Diane Johnson was born in Moline, Illinois. She is now an associate professor of English at the University of California at Davis. Her work includes *Lesser Lives* (1972), a biography, and the novels *Fair Game* (1965), *Burning* (1971), *Loving Hands at Home* (1972), and *The Shadow Knows* (1975).

Doris Lessing was born of British parents in Persia in 1919 and brought up on a farm in Southern Rhodesia. In 1949 she moved to England. Her best-known novels include *Martha Quest* (1952), *A Proper Marriage* (1954), *A Ripple from the Storm* (1958), *The Golden Notebook* (1962), *Landlocked* (1965), and *The Four-Gated City* (1969). Her short story collections include *The Habit of Loving* (1957), *A Man and Two Women: Stories* (1963), and *African*

Stories (1964). She has recently published *Briefing for a Descent into Hell* (1971), *The Summer Before the Dark* (1973), and *The Memoirs of a Survivor* (1974).

Katherine Mansfield, born October, 1888, in Wellington, New Zealand, lived and published in London. She produced three collections of short stories, *In a German Pension* (1911), *Prelude* (1918), *Je ne parle pas français* (1919), before *Bliss* (1920) gained her a significant reputation, but by then she had been seriously weakened by tuberculosis. Before her death at thirty-four she published *The Garden Party* (1922) and *The Dove's Nest* (1923), two more collections of short stories. After her death her *Poems* (1923), *Journal* (1927), and *Letters to John Middleton Murry 1913-1922* (1951) were published.

Alice Munro, born in Ontario in 1931, has published two short story collections, *Dance of the Happy Shades* (1968) and *Something I've Been Meaning to Tell You* (1974), and a novel, *The Lives of Girls and Women* (1971). She teaches creative writing at York University in Toronto, Canada.

Joan Murray was born in the Bronx in 1945. She has taught at Lehman College and is the coordinator of the Bronx Poets Alliance. Her collection of poetry *Egg Tooth* was published in 1975.

Joyce Carol Oates was born in Lockport, New York, in 1938. She has been a professor of English at the University of Windsor, Ontario, since 1967. An O. Henry Prize Story winner (1967-68), she won a National Institute of Arts and Letters award for her novel *A Garden of Earthly Delights* (1970), and the National Book Award for fiction in 1970. Her novels include *With Shuddering Fall* (1964), *Expensive People* (1968), *Them* (1969), *Do with Me What You Will* (1973). Her short story collections include *The Wheel of Love* (1970), *Marriages and Infidelities* (1972), and *The Seduction and Other Stories* (1975). She has also written a play, *Sunday Dinner*, recently published.

Marge Piercy was born in Detroit in 1936. She has written four novels: *Going Down Fast* (1969), *Dance the Eagle to Sleep* (1970), *Small Changes* (1973), and *Woman on the Edge of Time* (1976). Her books of poetry include *Breaking Camp* (1968), *Hard Loving* (1969), *To Be of Use* (1973), and *Living in the Open* (1976). She is now working on a novel.

Sylvia Plath, born in 1932 in Massachusetts, ended her life on February 11, 1963, in London. She is best known for her poetry, collected in *The*

Colossus (1960), *Ariel* (1965), *Crossing the Water* (1971), and *Winter Trees* (1972), and for her novel, *The Bell Jar* (1963). Her short stories were published in British and American magazines in the late fifties and early sixties. A collection of her letters to her mother, *Letters Home*, appeared in 1975.

Jane Rule, born in 1931 in New Jersey, is a resident of British Columbia, where she teaches college. She has published four novels: *Death of the Heart* (1965), *This Is Not for You* (1970), *Against the Season* (1971), and *The Young in One Another's Arms* (1976). In addition, she has published a collection of short stories, *Theme for Diverse Instruments* (1975), and a collection of essays, *Lesbian Images* (1975).

Eudora Welty was born in Jackson, Mississippi, in 1909. Her first volume of short stories, *A Curtain of Green*, was published when she was thirty-two. She has won numerous awards, including the Brandeis Medal of Achievement, the Hollins Medal, and the Howells Medal for fiction. Her short story collections include *The Wide Net and Other Stories* (1943), *The Golden Apples* (1949), *Selected Stories* (1954), *The Bride of the Innisfallen and Other Stories* (1955), *Thirteen Stories* (1965). She has published four novels: *The Robber Bridegroom* (1942), *Delta Wedding* (1946), *The Ponder Heart* (1954), and *Losing Battles* (1970).

Virginia Woolf was born in London in 1882. *The Voyage Out*, written when she was twenty-four, but not published until 1915, was her first work to attract critical notice. In 1918 she and her husband, Leonard Woolf, published the work of two unknown writers, *Prelude* by Katherine Mansfield and *Poems* by T. S. Eliot. After the publication of *Jacob's Room* (1922), *Mrs. Dalloway* (1925), and *To the Lighthouse* (1927) her fiction was recognized as distinguished. Her other works include novels—*Orlando* (1928), *The Waves* (1931), *The Years* (1937), *Between the Acts* (1941)—essays—*The Common Reader* (1925, 1932), *A Room of One's Own* (1929), *Three Guineas* (1938)—biographies—*Flush* (1933), *Roger Fry* (1940), *A Writer's Diary* (1953)—and short stories *Monday or Tuesday* (1921) and *A Haunted House and Other Short Stories* (1944). In 1941 she brought about her own death.